A Crime of Secrets

A Donner & Longstreet Mystery

Ann Aptaker

Bywater
BOOKS

2023

Bywater Books

Copyright 2023 Ann Aptaker

Print ISBN: 978-1-61294-269-8

Bywater Books First Edition: July 2023

Printed in the United States of America on acid-free paper.

Cover designer: TreeHouse Studio

Bywater Books
PO Box 3671
Ann Arbor MI 48106-3671

www.bywaterbooks.com

This novel is a work of fiction.

*This book is dedicated to all who dare to love,
dare to question, and dare to seek no matter the danger.*

PROLOGUE

APRIL 1899

A brilliant afternoon in New York's Madison Square Park, a brilliant, sparkling spring afternoon. Water dances on the tiers of the fountain, droplets glitter in the sunlight. Colorful parasols gripped gracefully in the gloved hands of strolling women are suffused with sunshine, the colored light dappling the women's cheeks. The sun catches, too, the innocent glint in young girls' eyes, and the not-so-innocent glint in the eyes of roguish men who linger along the paths.

Children's giggles float like bubbles in the air, rising above the murmurs of promenading lovers and the hushed discussions of men of business.

Baby carriages shimmering with silk ruffles and silver fancywork delicate as their sleeping babies' dreams are tended by mothers whose flowered hats bob in rhythm with the women's maternal cooing.

The serenity of the park is but a grace note in the clang and boom of the powerful city that surrounds it, a city growing ever taller ever faster! All around, new buildings rise higher. Horse-drawn carriages are thrust aside by the latest mechanical contraption, the automobile, and by hulking cable cars, their steel wheels grinding noisily along their tracks, thrilling the cars' passengers but terrifying the remaining equine beasts who still

1

pull hansom cabs and tradesmen's wagons and the broughams of the leisurely rich. The city is shaking off its old century while it makes a mad grab for the new. The populace is lured by all that's coming and all that's promised of new inventions and wild ideas. Indeed, what was scorned as scandal just a few years ago is enjoyed on this radiant afternoon as a blaze of artistic glory: the golden, naked Diana the Huntress perched atop the tall campanile of Mr. Stanford White's vast Madison Square Garden entertainment emporium overlooking the northeast corner of the park. How the righteous howled when White and his sculptor, the renowned Mr. Augustus St. Gaudens, placed the voluptuous Diana atop the tower! And how now, on this bright day, the patrons of the park bask happily in the aura of Diana's glowing body, her archer's bow pulled taut, her arrow aimed across the restless metropolis. Oh yes, Mr. Stanford White, New York's boldest, busiest architect, has his way with the city, muscling its towers and its dubious morality into the future.

A breeze blows through Madison Square now, tossing the hems of the women's dresses above the tops of their high-button shoes, exposing a bit of skin, provoking feigned embarrassment in the women and enthusiastic delight in the men.

Ah, the allure of a woman's leg, the hint of the pleasures of the flesh. These windblown titillations add bits of drama to an otherwise pleasant afternoon in Madison Square Park, where strolling lovers, playful children, cooing mothers, and local workmen who have come by for a bit of air and sunshine have seen nothing of the vile murder nearby that moments ago took the life of a young girl whose pale blue eyes saw her own blood spew through the air in an arc of death, whose skin felt her warm blood soak her lacy blue dress. She never saw the face or hands of the monster who killed her.

Chapter One

Later That Day

F in Donner, née Finola, well-tailored androgyne of rough and iniquitous history but who now resides in contentment, was nostalgic for gaslight. True, the recently installed electric wall sconce she switched on in the parlor to counter the fading afternoon sunlight was silent and odorless, unlike gaslight which hissed and gave off an eggy aroma. Still, despite the warm tone of the amber lampshade, Fin missed the seductive flicker of the old golden light. This modern electric illumination didn't shimmer as softly along Fin's brocade waistcoat or the sleeves of her bright white shirt. It didn't slide as sinuously along the room's polished mahogany furnishings, or down the carvings on the marble fireplace, a dark red which the old flicker imbued with whimsically devilish life. It didn't enrich the deep green moiré silk-covered walls with quite the same sinewy sheen. But the electric bulb gave a steadier light, which made reading easier on the eyes. And Fin had to admit that the amber shade with its silken fringe had its own charm, its own serene radiance, creating a light companionably falling on the sticklike contours of that other newfangled object recently installed on the little table beside one of the room's pair of overstuffed leather armchairs: a home telephone. Next to the

3

telephone was its companion, the printed directory.

She sat down again in the comfort of the armchair, where she'd been reading the latest issue of the Police Gazette while she waited for her beloved Devorah to return from her afternoon at the Astor Library. With a sigh of yearning for her lover to hurry home, Fin took up the newspaper once again and continued reading the rollicking account of a bloody brawl at the Thumb In The Eye Saloon, a head-cracking brouhaha that spilled into the streets of the dockside neighborhood of Hell's Kitchen. Fin knew well the saloon and its neighborhood. Indeed, she was born in its crowded tenements, strutted its brutal sidewalks. Hell's Kitchen was even now a rough and heartless part of town where human life was chopped up as savagely as the overworked dray horses who dropped dead on the cobblestones and were carted off to the neighborhood's slaughterhouses, their body parts sold off by the piece to tanneries and glue factories. It was on Hell's Kitchen's streets, in its alleys, and along its docks where Fin learned to survive. As a child, she learned to be more cunning than the sneering so-called do-gooders who snatched the city's street urchins and put them into hellish workhouses. Eventually she, too, fell prey to the child snatchers, hauled off to an institution of cruelty where a day's punishment resulted in a broken arm or a bloodied face, but Fin refused to let it break her spirit. Later, as a young, strutting soldier of the streets, she survived by her fists and her courage. She needed both to fend off the thugs who didn't like the idea that Fin preferred men's clothes to women's and women's love to men's.

Finishing the story of the Thumb In The Eye brawl, Fin began an article recounting the latest activities of one Mr. Alistair P. Flugg, an annoying but politically well-connected prig who went around the city with a band of followers, accompanied by a detail of police, raiding brothels, smashing saloons, and terrorizing those who plied their outlaw trades in the streets and alleys. His work, he insisted, was done in the name of God and the purity of American womanhood, by which he meant white Protestant womanhood.

Fin barely skimmed the article. Her distaste for Flugg and his ilk cancelled any interest in the man's doings.

Her attention was further distracted by her eagerness for the arrival of her treasured Devorah. Fin's beautiful and cherished companion had lately been spending time reading the latest studies on patterns of crime. This pursuit of Dev's amused Fin—in Fin's hard experience, any pattern of crime was quite simple: someone possessed something; someone stronger, or needier, or greedier wanted it; hence, crime—but she would never belittle any of Devorah's endeavors. She loved Devorah from the depths of her soul and the heat of her flesh, and considered these past six years together an earthly paradise.

Frankly, it still amazed Fin that society belle Devorah Longstreet, daughter of the Fifth Avenue Longstreets, a woman of refined manners and elegant speech, would even look at rough trade like Fin Donner. Though Fin took pride in her grooming—she kept her wavy black hair oiled and combed neat; her trousers, jackets and waistcoats custom tailored to her female physique and of the finest quality—she was nevertheless thickly built, sturdy as a brickbat, and spoke with the remains of a dockside accent through a craggy, broken voice, the result of a teenage street brawl that bloodied her face and smashed her throat.

But Devorah had indeed looked at Fin with a curiosity that soon roused passion and deepened into love, an outlaw love that exacted a terrible price. It cost Dev her family's affection and protection. She was snubbed and disinherited, never allowed through the door of the Longstreets' Fifth Avenue mansion again.

That blow, especially the loss of her mother's affection, was as painful to Devorah as a physical attack, as if she had been knifed in the heart, draining her spirit. But Fin's patience and ardent attentions helped heal Dev's injured soul. Dev's natural vigor eventually revived, and she assured Fin that she did not regret her choice to follow her heart and pursue with her lover a life of crime; or rather the pursuit of criminals. Their Donner & Longstreet Inquiries enterprise gave outlet to Dev's lifelong curiosity—her family had considered it unacceptable nosiness— about people and their habits, and it netted Fin and Devorah sufficient income to maintain these cozy rooms on Irving Place near Gramercy Park. Their successful detective business further provided the funds which enabled them to attend the operas, ballets, and other theatricals that Dev so enjoyed, and for Fin's occasional nights at the prize fights and other sporting houses she still patronized, though she'd sworn off many of the vices which had filled her life before she met Devorah, lest the sordidness of her old ways soil the ecstasy she'd found with her beloved.

Around five o'clock, unable to maintain interest in the newspaper, and yawning from a slight boredom with the quietness of the approaching evening, Fin rose from the chair to pour a glass of brandy from the cabinet opposite the fireplace. As she poured the liquor, its woody fragrance floated up to her nostrils, affording her the pleasure of anticipating that first, warming sip. And it was warming indeed, a slowly expanding heat that rolled through her. Even more pleasurable, though, was the heat that rose like a caress along Fin's loins when she heard the front door open and Devorah's cheerful, "Lovey? I'm home."

When Devorah walked into the parlor—in truth, whenever Dev walked into any room—Fin took a moment to savor her extraordinary good luck at winning the love of such a superb woman. She was captivated by Dev's large, warm brown eyes set in a face whose sculpted elegance reminded Fin of the expressive beauty of Lady Liberty in the harbor.

Dev, for her part, took pleasure in her lover's gaze. She played to it now as she pertly tucked a few out-of-place strands into her crown of chestnut hair, then dexterously removed her light cloak of brown wool and opened the top button of her suit of pale green serge, the jacket and skirt fitted charmingly at the waist. Fin delighted in Devorah's easy grace, how her body moved as if the slide of every muscle and bone luxuriated in their functions.

Fin took Dev's cloak and hung it in the armoire in the hall. Walking back into the parlor, she said, "Y'had a good day at the library?"

With a mildly exasperated sigh, Devorah sat down in the big leather armchair Fin had lately vacated. "Oh Lovey, I'm not sure any of the learned gentlemen whose treatises I've slogged through have any idea what they are talking about. I mean, they all speak of patterns of crime, but no two gentlemen see the *same* pattern. Where one sees patterns based on criminals' cultures of origin, another swears that crime is the result of the measurements of the head. And then there's the fellow who says that his experiments prove *conclusively* that whatever food a criminal has eaten at dinner will determine which crime he will commit that night. The eating of overly salted cabbage, for example, evidently leads to the crime of murder! Utter nonsense. Pour me a brandy, would you? My mind is positively in tangles. I need a brandy to smooth it out."

Accepting a snifter of the spirits, Devorah settled herself more deeply into the chair. "Ahh, Lovey, thank you." She took a sip of brandy and held it in her mouth for a few moments to savor its warmth before swallowing. Restored by the heat and potency of the liquor, Dev reached for Fin's hand and smiled in anticipation of a cozy dinner, followed by an evening of absorbing conversation with her dear companion, and then to bed where Fin, her adored rogue, would once again take Devorah on a journey to rapture.

The last of the day finally faded outside the windowpanes. Shadows, like ink flowing from the brush in an artist's hand, settled into the room, defining its textures but permeated here and there by the amber glow of the electric lamp, hinting at the room's colors. The glow rested on Dev's cheek, making Fin a bit less nostalgic for the flicker of gaslight, since, it was clear, Dev's beauty gave any light a luster. Fin bent to kiss her.

Dev's lips, full and warm and with the tang of brandy, craved the taste of her beloved Fin. The lovers reached for each other. Dev's hand slid through Fin's hair. Fin stroked Dev's cheek, her neck, her breasts. The lovers moved into each other's touch, every inch of their skin alive, every nerve reaching for the caress of the other. The couple's breathing joined, rising as one single life force so powerful it caused Fin to lift Devorah from the chair. They were engulfed in this ever-building reverie when a sharp rap at the door broke the spell.

Stunned, they muttered, "Damn," in unison.

Fin lowered Dev back into the chair. The passion which a moment ago had flowed through Fin's body now flailed within her like a caged creature. Her loins hurt as she walked along the hall to the door, desirous only to send the intruder away and salvage an evening of ecstasy.

Not one but two intruders faced her when she opened the door: a middle-aged man and woman. The man, who was of average height and whose flushed, jowly face gave him the appearance of a russet pear in a derby hat, was respectably dressed in the manner of a businessman whose success was built on long hours of tireless work and scrupulous thrift. The woman, who was of wiry build and nearly as tall as her companion, was dressed in a black cloak open to a yellow-and-black plaid dress with fussy lace at the collar and cuffs. A stiff black hat with showy red and white flowers adorning the crown sat atop coils of graying brown hair framing a tight, bird-like face that had pinched traces of past beauty. Her small green eyes were rimmed red from tears which she barely kept under control.

The man looked like he wanted to cry, too, but being a man

he wouldn't give in to it.

Fin's heartbeat slowed. The lust which had heated her blood now choked in her veins. She knew her evening of love was done. These suffering people could not be sent away.

She said, as gently as her gruff voice and dockside inflection would allow, "What can I do for you folks?"

The man's pale brown eyes and the woman's small reddened ones snapped open wide at Fin's disconcertingly androgynous appearance and brusque, guttural speech. The man mumbled, "S . . . sir?" as if the word was not quite right but came closest to describing the person his eyes beheld.

Fin didn't bother to correct him, choosing instead to let the man's confusion about her hang in the air, which was how Fin always handled people for whom an explanation would be wasted.

"Are we at the address of . . . um . . . Donner & Longstreet Inquiries?" the man said.

Affecting a courtesy she didn't entirely feel but which she understood her visitors were nonetheless due, Fin said, "Sure, I'm Fin Donner," which in her dockside accent was pronounced *Donnuh*.

"I see," the man said. "Well"—he cleared his throat to cover his discomfort—"my name is William R. Godfrey, and this is Mrs. Godfrey. May we come in? Our . . . our . . ." The man's shoulders suddenly contracted and shrugged in a quick, sharp, up-and-down motion that accompanied a choked sob: *"Our daughter's been murdered."*

Mr. and Mrs. Godfrey each clutched their hands to their breasts as they wept. It was a pitiful sight which Fin had seen many times before back in Hell's Kitchen in the dives of her rogue's life where violence and death were plentiful and life was often snuffed out on the cheap. She saw it when wretched families learned that their young'uns had died in the streets. She saw it at the city morgue, where Donner & Longstreet's distraught clients identified their dead. Part of Fin was hardened to it, the part that had thrived in her once brutal life. But a deeper part of her would never get used to it, the part which allowed her to love as intensely as she loved Devorah. The Godfreys' misery tore at that deep part. "You'd better come in," Fin said. "Miss Longstreet"—which in Fin's mangled throat and speech was always Miz Lawnk*strit*—"is in the parlor. I think you folks could use a brandy."

"A brandy, yes, perhaps so," Godfrey agreed and led his sobbing wife along the hall and into the parlor. "You too, my dear," he said to his wife. "A little brandy will restore you."

Devorah, with some effort, revived herself from her disrupted passion. She rose from the armchair to help Mrs. Godfrey off with her cloak, and led the despairing couple to the sofa.

Fin poured two brandies. "Dev, this here is Mr. an' Mrs. William R. Godfrey. They got knocked by a terrible blow."

Addressing the Godfreys, Dev said, "Yes, I heard you at the door," her heart breaking for these grieving parents. "Here, take some brandy for your nerves, and then tell us what happened and how we can help."

Mr. Godfrey swallowed the brandy in one gulp. The still sobbing Mrs. Godfrey sipped the liquor, letting its warmth quiet her bit by bit. She clutched the glass so tightly Dev was afraid the nervous woman would break it and cut herself.

Devorah resumed her seat in the armchair. Fin sat in the matching chair. They rested their brandy glasses on the little Chinese table between them. Their fingertips brushed, imperceptibly to the Godfreys but electrically to Fin and Devorah, while they waited for the Godfreys to recover their wits sufficiently enough to tell their story.

Mr. Godfrey at last said, "Our daughter's name is—was—Pauline, and a more beautiful, more sweet-natured girl you could never know." He took his wife's hand. "Not an enemy in the world, right, dear?"

A handkerchief to her eyes and a sob that shook her whole body was Mrs. Godfrey's answer. Struggling to gain control of herself, she held tight to her husband's hand and took another sip of the brandy.

With paternal enthusiasm, Mr. Godfrey said, "Here, see?" as he released his hand from his wife's and reached into his pocket to pull out his silver watch fob. He unhooked the chain from a button on his waistcoat, opened the watchcase and passed it to Devorah. "That's Pauline between me and Mrs. Godfrey. The photograph was taken eight months ago, on the occasion of Pauline's eighteenth birthday."

The sweet face in the small sepia photo touched Devorah's heart and made her smile. Pauline Godfrey had been a lovely young woman indeed. She appeared not very tall, shorter even than her mother, but a dark-haired beauty with robust life in her high cheeks and whose eyes were large and pale like her father's. Standing between her proud father and her stern mother, and wearing a crisply fashionable white shirtwaist blouse above a trim dark-colored skirt, Pauline Godfrey was the embodiment of the "New Woman," the modern ideal whose eyes looked out with vigor into the limitless future that only youth can see. The smile faded from Dev's lips as she absorbed the horrible knowledge that the hopeful eyes looking at her in the photograph would never see anything again.

Devorah passed the watch to Fin, who drank deeply of the brandy as she looked at the beautiful girl in the photograph.

Dev said, "Your pride in your daughter is evident in the photo, Mr. Godfrey. Her happiness seems evident as well."

"Yes, she was happy," Godfrey said with a nostalgic smile, though it came through a heavy sigh. "Until the trouble came."

Dev shifted her gaze from Mr. Godfrey to Mrs. Godfrey, whose lips pursed tight at her husband's mention of trouble.

Mr. Godfrey continued with difficulty, "You see, she'd met a man, a most disreputable man—"

Fin broke in, "Disreputable? How?" She distrusted the word disreputable, coming as it usually did from a point of view that too often disparaged her background and her kind.

It was Mrs. Godfrey who answered, her manner of speech as fussy and affected as her plaid and lace dress. "Well," Mrs. Godfrey said, dabbing her eyes with her handkerchief, "the man was an *actor*, a *theatrical* person. How can such people *ever* be believed? They are never really what they appear to be. Illusion is their stock in trade, after all."

Dev, with the merest touch of sarcasm she was unable to fully restrain, said, "I see." Though honesty was a virtue she lived by, her intimacy with Fin made her appreciate the allure of illusion. She glanced at her lover, amused to see a tiny trace of a snicker at the corner of Fin's mouth. Fin hid the snicker from the Godfreys by lifting her glass and sipping the brandy.

Nevertheless, Dev spoke to Mrs. Godfrey with kindness, bearing in mind that the woman had just lost her daughter to a hideous crime. "My dear Mrs. Godfrey, Pauline was your only child?"

"We had no other."

"And prior to meeting this man, she had never been in any trouble?"

"She was the soul of obedience! The very soul of obedience!"

Mr. Godfrey added, "And she was a wonderful help to me. I tell you, she even increased my business."

Dev said, "You are in trade, sir?" already concluding as much from Godfrey's brown serge suit and waistcoat of sufficient quality but uninteresting cut, and by the way he fingered his derby in his lap, holding it as if its loss or damage would mean the loss of cold cash rather than the loss of an enjoyed possession.

"Why, yes, I am in trade," Godfrey said. "I own a successful mercantile establishment. Fabrics and notions and the like. The shop has done well enough for me to contemplate opening a second location. The better trade is moving further uptown, you know. Why, there's even talk it may go as far up as 34th Street. Business interests are moving fast these days, I tell you. Got to keep up!"

Devorah continued her inquiry. "Your daughter worked in your shop?"

"Yes," Godfrey said. "She was wonderful with the customers. She listened to them with great patience, tried to satisfy even their more difficult requests. And she could keep a sharp eye on the profit, too!" Godfrey's pride in his daughter nearly burst through the buttons of his waistcoat, giving the nondescript garment more personality than it had on its own. But his joy was quickly deflated by the horror of his daughter's death. The air seemed to go out of the man. Even as his wife took his hand, Mr. William R. Godfrey appeared to shrivel inside his suit.

Fin brought the conversation back to business. "This here actor, who was he? An' what kinda trouble do you think he brought with him?"

It was Mrs. Godfrey who answered, sneering, "Says his name is John Jones, but if you ask me, that's not his name at all."

"What makes y'say so?"

"Because he said it too . . . too . . . forcefully when he introduced himself to us. Said it—*John Jones*—as if he wanted to make sure everyone in earshot heard it. Whom did he think he needed to convince, I ask you?"

Fin continued to question the Godfrey woman. "You was in a public place?"

"Yes, in a restaurant, the Lexington Grill. Mr. Godfrey had taken us out as a family. We had just ordered our dinner when this Jones, this actor, this *cad,*" Mrs. Godfrey sniffed, "approached our table and introduced himself. Butted in, was more like it. I was not happy with the way he looked at Pauline." The woman shook her head with distaste, the red and white flowers on her little black hat shaking in a similarly harsh rhythm.

"Nor was I," Mr. Godfrey said.

Taking the handkerchief to her eyes again, Mrs. Godfrey continued, "But Pauline, well, it was clear she was smitten right then and there. Young girls always like the handsome ones, you know. The goose didn't give a thought to the man's impertinence."

"Now dearest . . ." Mr. Godfrey said in hopes of tempering his wife's pique.

"Well, I'm sorry, but that is how I felt about it. You raise a child with all the best intentions only to have them toss common sense right out the window. And then—" Mrs. Godfrey's whole body trembled again, robbing her of her ability to speak. She brought the handkerchief to her eyes once more, her sob a horrible sound, a wail clawing inside her throat.

Devorah allowed Mr. Godfrey a moment to comfort his wife, then said, "I take it that your daughter and this Mr. Jones embarked on a romance?"

Mr. Godfrey, his mouth pursed tight, said, "Indeed," his tone cold and clipped. "After this Jones introduced himself at the restaurant, he said he'd seen Pauline at our shop earlier in the day, and how delighted he was that she should be at the very restaurant where he was dining."

"Did she remember him?"

"No, she was embarrassed to admit that she did not recall—"

Mrs. Godfrey interrupted, "Though she couldn't take her eyes off him at dinner. The poor thing was lovestruck. That's what she was, lovestruck."

Another quick glance passed between Fin and Devorah, each wondering if perhaps Pauline Godfrey was not quite the naive girl her parents—particularly her father—believed her to be. As Dev knew well, and approved of completely, today's modern young women, while perhaps still holding on to their virginity until marriage, nevertheless were tossing aside the old, suffocating naivete, preferring instead to let their curiosity in matters of love flourish.

Godfrey continued, "But Jones explained that he'd only been looking in our shop window, looking at a display of ribbons, when he noticed Pauline through the window glass."

Fin said, "He didn't go in?"

"No," Godfrey said. "The man's excuse was that he'd be late for an appointment otherwise, but promised himself he would stop by another day and introduce himself properly. In the meantime, to his pleasure—the scoundrel pronounced *pleasure* as though his tongue was soaked in too much fragrant oil—well, to his pleasure he saw her again unexpectedly at the restaurant. Now look here, I'd say that's a bit too pat."

Devorah said, "Are you implying that he followed your family to the restaurant?"

"Well, don't you agree that the coincidence of his being at the same restaurant is rather suspicious?"

Devorah had learned that it was wise to keep her suspicions to herself, to be discussed only with Fin and in a rational manner. To Mr. Godfrey, she only said, "When did your daughter next see Mr. Jones?"

"The following day," Mr. Godfrey said. "He came to the shop. The bounder slithered his way into conversation with Pauline, asking her about ribbons and lace, which he had no intention of purchasing. He finally got around to making his unsavory invitation to accompany him to dinner. And quite against our wishes Pauline did go with him to dinner that night. After that, well . . ." Mr. Godfrey lowered his head, his shoulders sagged as if his sorrows were a heavy yoke.

Mrs. Godfrey took up the narrative. "Pauline rebelled against us," she said through undisguised irritation, which almost but not quite obliterated the remaining traces of her once youthful beauty. "Sheer rebellion, that's what it was. It's the times, I say. There's something loose in the air, a modern cheekiness. Young girls today think they can come and go as they please. They pursue pleasure and ignore decency. There is no sense of propriety anymore, no sense of responsibility." Mrs. Godfrey took a quick sip of brandy, averting her eyes to look toward the window.

Mr. Godfrey, his decorum recovered as befitting the upstanding gentleman of business he believed himself to be, placed his hand tenderly on his wife's shoulder before he picked up the thread of the story. "Their romance roared along like an unstoppable train. Pauline went out with this Jones fellow every night. Soon she was not coming home until morning. Did he not have any regard for her reputation? And he sapped all of Pauline's energy. She'd all but abandoned her responsibilities at our shop. In barely a month, our once lively and vigorous Pauline became thin and wan. She was still beautiful, but it was a distant, weary beauty. Her eyes seemed to recede into shadows."

Devorah, sensitive to the Godfreys' grief, proceeded with care. "I am sorry to have to put this so directly, but do you believe this Mr. Jones killed your daughter?"

Godfrey's head shot up. He shouted, "Yes! Yes, and horribly!" as his wife's shoulders drooped and her head sank, her little flowered hat shielding her eyes, muffling her sobs.

Godfrey restored his calm with effort. "The police wouldn't even let my wife look at Pauline at the morgue, the sight being too shocking for the female constitution. Oh, I—I beg your—" The man was unable to complete his clumsy apology, realizing he had blundered in Dev's presence, a woman whose line of work had likely presented her with any number of dead bodies, a situation she was evidently able to handle without damage to her mind. Clearing his throat, gathering himself in that flustered way men have as if they've been caught with their trouser buttons open, he continued, "It was I alone who made the identification at the morgue. Pauline, our sweet daughter, was . . . she was . . . her throat was torn and . . ." But it was Godfrey's constitution which was not up to the task. He couldn't describe the horror he'd seen, as if his mouth and tongue had gone numb, protecting him from having to speak the unspeakable. He lowered his head again.

Devorah, speaking softly, respectful of the Godfreys' mourning but needing additional information if she and Fin were to help them, said, "Mr. and Mrs. Godfrey, what time did the police determine that the murder took place and where was the body found?"

Mr. Godfrey wiped his face with a handkerchief taken from his breast pocket. He cleared his throat several times until he'd cleared it of his choking sobs and was finally able to answer Dev's questions. "She was killed this afternoon, sometime around three o'clock according to the police surgeon's best estimate. Her body was found in the colonnade outside Madison Square Garden shortly thereafter by a passerby."

Fin said, "An' what about the police? They give you any information about John Jones or the route of their investigation into your daughter's case?"

"Now that's the problem," Godfrey said, his face deepening to crimson in anger. "The police say they do not have enough evidence to arrest Jones. Frankly, I am not at all sure they have even spoken to him. I told the police about his involvement with Pauline, his ruinous affect on her. I fail to understand why they don't arrest him straight away."

Fin took a sip of brandy before she spoke, let the warm liquor smooth the bad news she was about to give Mr. Godfrey. "Well, the coppers like an airtight case, an' you ain't got one."

"But he—!"

"No sir, you ain't got no case against this John Jones nohow. You say he wore your daughter down, an' maybe that's so, but what's his motive for killin' her? What reason is there she'd be worth more to him dead than alive? None that I can see."

Godfrey was on his feet, indignant. "Just a moment! Are you impugning our truthfulness? Are you saying this man Jones didn't kill our daughter?"

Fin remained in her chair, her demeanor calm. "No, I ain't sayin' that at all. I'm sure you believe everythin' you're tellin' us, an' you may be right about the whole business. But you ain't got any evidence, an' you ain't got a motive for the crime."

Godfrey looked as if he'd been hit on the head with an iron rod, struck dumb, while Mrs. Godfrey glared.

Mr. Godfrey finally said, "Well then, can you look into this and get the evidence necessary to have this man Jones arrested? I'm prepared to put you on retainer." Ever the businessman, he quickly added, "Provided it's a reasonable amount."

Devorah said, "We will bill you, Mr. Godfrey."

"You will take the case, then?"

"Sure," Fin said. "We'll take it. We'll find out about this Jones fella. If he's a murderer, we'll tell you. If he ain't, we'll tell you that, too, an' then we'll do what we can to find your daughter's killer. Now, there's just two points to clear up in the meantime: number one, do you know where can we find Jones?"

Mr. Godfrey said, "The police were reluctant to tell us anything, but a detective finally let slip that Jones has rooms at a Mrs. Mallory's boardinghouse on Bayard Street, just off the Bowery. As disreputable a neighborhood as ever existed. Nothing but human vermin there."

There was that word again, *disreputable*, scratching at Fin's bones. "Uh-huh," she said, keeping her delivery flat but with a slight edge she couldn't blunt. "And the second point that needs clearin' up: how did you know to engage us?"

"Oh." Godfrey reached into his inside jacket pocket. "Here. The police detective gave me this envelope and said to bring it to Donner & Longstreet Inquiries at this address."

Fin took the envelope, still sealed. She opened it and read the note it contained, a note which not only puzzled her but sent an unsettling tremor through her body. It read: *I can't help these people*, and it was signed, *Detective Charles Coyle*.

After handing the note to Devorah, who was as puzzled

and disturbed by its message as her companion, Fin retrieved a pencil and a sheet of paper from a drawer and gave them to Mr. Godfrey. "Write your address an' telephone exchange if you have one—home an' business—where we can locate you."

Mr. Godfrey wrote the information and gave the paper back to Fin, who said, "G'night, Mr. an' Mrs. Godfrey. You'll hear from us."

Devorah helped Mrs. Godfrey with her cloak. The woman's flowered hat bobbed in Devorah's face. When Mrs. Godfrey was finally attired for the street, Dev tried to reassure the woman and her husband, "We will do everything in our power to bring this matter to justice."

"Thank you," Mr. Godfrey said. "Well, let's go, my dear." They shuffled along the hall and out the door as if their spirits were as dead as their daughter.

Fin helped Dev into the hansom cab, its horse breathing steam into the chill night air. Fin, closing the door, stood on the step of the cab. "Good luck, my love," she said with a tip of her straw boater hat. "It's not yet seven-thirty in the evenin', so chances are good you can still catch Coyle at police headquarters. He's famous for his nightwork. See what you can find out what he's got up his copper's sleeve, why he's suddenly sendin' business our way. Why is he all of a sudden in our corner?"

"It is odd, yes," Dev agreed. "The police have not been inclined to favor us, so I don't like the ring of this at all. Are you sure you don't want to come along?"

"You'll do a helluva lot better without me. Me an' the coppers don't have a healthy relationship. Besides, if we split up we'll get answers faster. I'll meet you at that café down the street from police headquarters after I have a look at things at the site of Miss Godfrey's killin' outside the Garden."

"See you later, then, Lovey."

Fin bent inside the hansom, cupped Devorah's face in her hand and kissed her. The couple's long, tender kiss was accompanied by hands that reached for each other and slid to find the pleasure of reassurance. Fin's hand slid to the purse in Dev's lap, where she felt the deadly little double-barreled Derringer within. Dev's hand slid under Fin's coat, where she felt the powerful Colt thirty-two caliber revolver holstered securely under Fin's left arm. Satisfied that each of them was armed against whatever danger they might encounter this night, they reluctantly separated from their kiss.

Fin whispered, "You're becomin' a first-rate sleuth, my girl," and stepped down from the cab. She signaled the cabbie to drive off.

Fin watched the cab as it moved along Irving Place, its kerosene sidelamps flickering as it carried Devorah away and into the night. Confident in Dev's ability to ferret information from Detective Coyle, Fin was nonetheless worried—as Fin always worried, secretly—about involving her beloved in the sordidness of violent crime. It scared Fin, but thrilled her, too, that Devorah was so good with murder.

Chapter Two

A killer sits alone in a small, dimly lit room, the window shade pulled down against the false glow of the city's night, afraid that light from a streetlamp or from the windows of a tall building——there are so many new towers!——will penetrate the darkness of the killer's soul. Best to hide here until duty calls. Duty, inescapable duty.

Chapter Three

hildren were everywhere, their faces flushed under the glow of street lamps on 26th Street; children giggling, running, while their parents, just as excited as their offspring if truth be told, tried to keep pace with their little ones as the crowd pressed into Madison Square Garden for that night's 8 p.m. performance of the Ringling Brothers' gargantuan three-ring fantasia of thrills.

The musky odors of circus animals and the sweet aroma of caramel-covered popcorn commingled into a voluptuous fragrance that drifted through the Garden's open doors and gathered under the colonnade sheltering the street-level facade of the enormous building. The earthy bouquet sharpened the crowd's excitement, heightening everyone's anticipation of the exotic wonders awaiting them inside.

Fin made her way through the throng. She kept the brim of her straw boater low on her brow to hide her interest in the area from the curiosity of the pressing crowd.

All around her was innocence, a vivacious multitude of innocence trampling unknowingly on the site of a brutal murder. The shifting, shoving, energy-filled crowd of children and their families made it difficult to spot whatever evidence of the murder may have stained the area. Fin had to find that evidence if she was to discover what had befallen Pauline Godfrey.

She proceeded carefully through the knots of laughing children and restless parents. She glanced around women's feathered and flowered hats, past men's rakish derbies and children's perspiring faces for glimpses of the billboard-lined yellow brick walls of Madison Square Garden, a building she knew well, in whose arena she'd spent many thrilling evenings placing bets on men who pummel each other for sport, their sweat and blood spraying the well-dressed swells in expensive ringside seats.

Tonight, though, the excitement of children was the Garden's bill of fare, and the children were eager for their measure of thrills as they held their parents' hands, pulling the grownups along toward the entrances. Fin shifted her attention down to the sidewalk, studying pavement glimpsed between tiny feet in patent leather shoes or scuffed laced boots.

And there it was, on the pavement near the corner of East 26th Street and Madison Avenue, a gruesome presence among the innocence swirling around it: a large stain of red, hideously long in places, grotesquely wide in others, a dense, dark red in its center. The horrid blotch was smudged at the edges, smudged from movement creating the angled and blurred lines of blood that Fin knew were made by the motions of a body in desperation and panic during the final frantic moments of life.

All around Fin, children and their protective mothers and shepherding fathers, unseeing, unconcerned with the remnant of horror under their feet, ran roughshod over the bloodstain, frustrating Fin that their unthinking carelessness might scrape away bits of evidence of Pauline's killing and clues to her killer. Fin had to restrain herself from pushing the crowd away from the bloodstain. She would only frighten the children, draw angry responses from their parents, and likely alert the unwanted attention of the policeman patrolling at the corner of Madison

Square Park across the street. She could only wait for the crowd to thin, wait for the circus inside to beckon the last of the excited throng into the Garden.

It felt like an eternity, a wrenching, frustrating, unmoving eternity until the laughter and admonishments of "Let's go, children!" and "Hurry now!" grew slowly quieter. Fewer and fewer feet scuffed along the ugly stain of blood, until at last Fin was alone under the colonnade, alone with the nasty business she had come to confront.

She knelt down for a closer look at Pauline Godfrey's last spill of blood and touched the thickest, darkest area of red with the tips of her fingers. The blood was dry, but freshly dry, not flaky. When Fin pressed her fingers hard against the bloodstain, she could feel a remaining trace of dampness in the pavement. It had been hours since Pauline Godfrey was killed here. The hidden dampness deep in the bloodstain meant that Pauline bled copiously, her life poured out fast and painfully.

Remembering Mr. Godfrey's choked inability to describe the mutilated state of his daughter's throat in the morgue, Fin recoiled from the bloodstain. She stood up and stepped away from it, repelled by the image it conjured of what the girl must have suffered, the viciousness of the attack. Fin could see it in her mind: the terror in the girl's widening eyes, the blood that spurted as Pauline crumpled to the ground, her body in pain, her eyes disbelieving as they watched the world darken until the darkness engulfed her in death. The only part of the crime Fin couldn't see was the murderer, the mysterious villain who finished the life of a young girl.

Fin had known plenty of killers. They were part of the bloody scenery of her youth and the violent characters in her adult adventures. The killers she'd known were all cold inside, even the ones who killed from passion, and especially the ones who killed for power or profit. Though she accepted and even understood the violence that erupts among human animals, Fin was disgusted by violence against the untainted and innocent, like Pauline Godfrey. That disgust and anger attacked Fin now, grabbing her muscles and tightening them.

The anger was also tightening her thoughts, constricting her mind. She let her eyes drift in order to allow her mind to regain the calculating calm she needed to think through the details of Pauline's murder. Her eyes wandered to the park across the street where the copper was still on patrol, walking back and forth and through the park. Fin thought, *Nice beat, that Badge Buck's got. Sweet duty in the park.* Her mind slipped into delightful recollections of walks through Madison Square Park with her beloved Devorah on sunny afternoons like the one today, when lovers, as always, wandered the paths. Fin imagined it all, and wondered, *Not a soul saw the crime or heard the girl struggle? Nobody heard her scream? Hard as the girl fought, she must've screamed.*

Unless—unless the killin' happened fast, sudden-like, no time for the victim to scream. A rage killin'. Yeah, I seen rage like that. Rage that's been boilin' inside an' just bursts out in murder.

Fin was drawn again to the bloodstain on the pavement: *So much blood an' no noise? The bastard must've come up from behind an' cut Pauline's throat. No one woulda heard anythin', not even Pauline's body hittin' the pavement, not with the noise of all the traffic 'round here durin' the day. All them noisy cable cars an' carriage wheels rattlin' on the cobblestones. All them newfangled automobiles, their motors chuggin', their side-horns honkin'. All them brayin' horses an' the streetcorner coppers blowin' whistles an' tryin' to sort it all out. A helluva public place to do a killin'. Maybe the killer just didn't care, or didn't think, just acted. Rage, sure. I seen it plenty.*

Standing up from the bloodstain, and with nothing more to learn from the scene, Fin's mind twisted around the miserable question: what was Pauline's killer so damned angry about?

Chapter Four

Police headquarters at 300 Mulberry Street, which when new nearly forty years earlier was a tidy building of civilized architecture, had aged into a battered, soot-stained fortress, oppressive in its mood. The large, arched first floor windows which were meant to boast—too hopefully even when new—that here was the open light of the law, now exuded a damaged temperament, secretive behind its dirty panes. The jagged cracks and chips in the building's granite face gave it a personality as brutish and wild as the noisy slum of desperate, mysterious immigrants which surrounded it.

The stairs to the main entrance, unswept since earlier in the day, were grimy with tobacco spittle and other refuse, sticky beneath the soles of Devorah's high-button shoes of soft kid. The disfigured building and filthy staircase were in keeping with Dev's general opinion of the police as a necessary but brutish force further soiled by the dirt of corruption. Six years of detective work with Fin, of involving herself in the dark adventures of thieves and thugs, pimps, murderers, and—most criminal of all—greedy politicians, had convinced Dev that from the bell-helmeted patrolmen on the street right up to the brass-buttoned precinct captains, crime was not something the police always fought. It was just as often something they colluded in and profited from, regardless of who got hurt.

And people did indeed get hurt, people who were unfortunate enough to be standing in the way of men whose ambition was not just powerful but vicious: people who knew too much about bad business or didn't know enough to recognize bad business when they saw it, people like the young and once vital Pauline Godfrey.

This, to Dev's mind, could be the crux of the matter. Who might benefit from sweeping this brutal crime under the rug? And it puzzled Dev how the death of a lovestruck daughter of a shopkeeper, and a rather dull shopkeeper at that, could possibly profit anyone.

Her thoughts turned to Fin, who was herself a creation of the city's underworld. Fin had lived in its foul shadows, profited from its corruption and enjoyed its vices, a reality Dev long ago learned to accept. And in truth, Fin's experience in these matters had proven helpful in many of Donner & Longstreet's investigations and could prove useful again tonight. Dev was anxious to confer with her dear companion, learn what evidence Fin discovered at the scene of the crime, and if any of it might substantiate her own deliberations.

But first there was the business of ferreting out what information she could from Detective Charles Coyle.

Getting Coyle to explain himself in the matter of police inaction regarding the Godfrey murder would not be easy. Dev knew she'd lose all chance of success unless she was able to get past the contempt with which the police held private inquiry agents in general, and the firm of Donner & Longstreet in particular. She'd seen the bitter resentment on the faces of police officers who never forgave Fin for having "crossed over" from a life of crime to a life of solving crime before they had the chance to put her behind bars. And there were many police officers who would never believe that Fin had truly left her old ways despite her romance with a pillar of New York's high society, itself a relationship the men of the Police Department regarded as loathsome. All of this made Coyle's act of sending the Godfreys to the firm of Donner & Longstreet strange in the extreme.

Entering police headquarters only deepened Dev's misgivings. The long dark hall running the length of the building was noisy with chatter and shrieks in foreign tongues from ragged men and women whose flushed and contorted faces bespoke their rage. Though Dev understood not a word of the emotion-choked babble of Eastern Europe, nor the knotted consonants and vowels of the Chinese, her sense of basic kinship to fellow human beings made it clear to her that the mob was complaining of horrid crimes against them, or objecting to being pushed about roughly by policemen herding them downstairs to the infamously hellish cells in the basement. Making matters even more disagreeable were the phlegmy snores of the inebriated vagrants, male and female, in drunken slumber on the floor. Their sour odors of whiskey-sodden breath, spit, sweat, tobacco and unwashed bodies wafted around Dev as oppressively as a greasy cloak.

Only her life with Fin, especially her beloved's patience and protection during Dev's first encounters with this harsh world, had prepared her to withstand the degradation she found here. She had early on reached the conclusion that the grinding misery and sometimes gruesome criminality of these people's lives was a blot on civilization, a blot sustained by her own uncaring society which regarded these unfortunates as cheap labor at best and disposable when used up or their bodies no longer needed. Dev believed that only an open-hearted humanity coupled with respect for these unfortunates and a determined effort to reform or even dismantle the systems which kept them under the boot could bring relief to the city's slum dwellers and cleanse the blot. What's more, she further understood that danger lurked at the core of the situation. The souls of these impoverished men and women were acidic with rage, creating a population gnawing on its own meager flesh while craving the fuller, tastier flesh of the more privileged citizenry. That rage seethed tonight. Dev saw it in the eyes of these slum denizens whose stares lingered on Dev's fine garments. They looked at her brown wool cloak and supple black leather gloves in awe and envy as she walked through the crowd toward the uniformed sergeant sitting at a battered roll-top desk.

The sergeant's thick, sweet-potato-bright hair poked out from beneath his tall blue helmet. His heavy mustache and muttonchop side-whiskers framed his thin face, his skin yellowish behind the haze of stale tobacco smoke that hung in the air. But the sergeant's blue eyes twinkled when he saw the beautiful and crisply dressed woman approaching his premises. Such a refined woman was not the usual sort he dealt with in police work and he intended to enjoy every moment of their coming encounter. Tipping the brim of his helmet and standing up to greet his elegant guest, he summoned his most impressive tone and manner. "And how may I help y'now, Miss?"

His toothy smile was friendly beneath his mustache, which put Dev a little more at ease. She said, "Would you be kind enough to tell Detective Charles Coyle that Miss Devorah Longstreet is here to see him?" whereupon the sergeant's smile slowly reshaped itself into a sneer in recognition of her name.

Ice between his teeth couldn't have made the sergeant's sneer any colder. Dev felt her skin would crack from the chill of the sergeant's disdain. But skin deep was as far as Dev would allow the man's ill will to penetrate. Her deeper nature, her heart and soul, were protected by her sense of responsibility to the Godfreys, her belief in the legitimacy of her life and pursuits, and by Fin's love. No one had better armor.

Moreover, Devorah Longstreet had a particularly potent weapon at her command, one which might force the sergeant's cooperation. In truth, she'd never cared to use this weapon very much, considering it in poor taste, but she looked forward with extreme pleasure to using it on this insufferable sergeant now. It was a weapon with which she could flatten this presumptuous man in his public-issue uniform.

"Sergeant," she said, articulating the word with a carefully studied patience meant to insinuate that his rank was a mere trifle, and that she, Devorah Longstreet of the Fifth Avenue Longstreets, had the influence to allow him to keep his rank or have him stripped of it.

Her gambit worked. Dev watched with a satisfaction that bordered on girlish glee as the eyes of this small-minded policeman widened with pompous pride before slowly narrowing with troubled rumination. For though the sergeant was likely aware that Dev was in disfavor with her family and their Knickerbocker circle, he could not entirely dismiss that she was nevertheless a Longstreet, born into an elite and powerful tribe, a woman who despite her outcast status may yet have influential connections among persons who could make life difficult for the sergeant. He heard that humiliating possibility in Dev's derisive tone of voice. He saw it in the tilt of her head and subtle but intentionally arrogant smile, and in the way Dev placed her gloved hand on the desk, as if she, and her kind, owned it.

The sergeant's eyelids lowered until his eyes were slits of blue, nervous in their hiding place. Without moving his cautious gaze, he raised an arm towards a young ragamuffin of about ten years of age who was leaning against a wall. The boy wore threadbare knee-pants, a dirty white shirt of coarse material, a jacket which was too big for him and which was dotted with rips and holes. Dev observed that the child was clearly underfed.

The sergeant shouted "Boy!" his cruel tone a tool to transfer his humiliation to one even less powerful than himself. "C'mere and escort this *distinguished lady* down the hall to the Detectives' Bureau, to Coyle. And make it snappy! We don't want to keep the *lady* waitin'!"

Dev removed her hand from the desk, enjoying her triumph but projecting—for the sergeant's benefit—an attitude of aristocratic restraint. All's fair, as far as Dev was concerned, when dealing with the police.

The sergeant sat down and rearranged the papers and telephone on the desk, making a showy display of reasserting his claim to it.

Grateful to be free of the sergeant's malicious company, Dev followed the ragamuffin out of the noisy hall and through a door into a dingy, dimly lit and stuffy waiting room. The little fellow, whose dirty straw-colored hair badly needed combing and whose shoes were tied at the ankle with bits of ragged string, was of admirably good cheer despite his shabby treatment by the ill-natured sergeant.

Dev said, "What's your name, young sir?"

"Timmy, Miss. Timmy Poole."

"Well, Master Poole, I hope the other police officers aren't as rude in their orders to you as that sergeant."

"Oh, I don't work for the coppuhs, Miss. I'm jus' here t'visit my Ma. They took her a coupla hours ago an' I figure if I can be useful they'll let me see her more quickly like."

"Oh, I see. On what charge was she arrested?"

"She's a whore, Miss. She musta missed a payoff to the district cap'n, otherwise the cops wouldn't be haulin' her in. Y'know how it is. Matter a'fact, if youse the right Miss Lawnkstrit I heard yuh say yuh was, then maybe y'heard a'my Ma. They call her Black Haired Mag."

"I'm sorry, Master Poole, but that's not a name with which I'm familiar."

"Oh, well, if youse the right Miss Lawnkstrit, then just ask y'pal Fin Donnuh. Fin knows my Ma real well. Ma talks about how Fin use t'come 'round before she met—well—you."

"Indeed," was all Dev dared say.

"Yeah, Fin an' my Ma go way back. I musta been a little kid

31

last time I sees Fin, though. Maybe six, seven years ago. Sumpin' like that. Anyways, I was little. Hey, maybe you an' Fin can help get my Ma outta jail? Whaddya say?"

"Well, I can't promise I can get her out of jail, but I can certainly look into it."

Timmy's smile at Dev, gap-toothed wide and bright past his dirty teeth, as much as said, *You're okay in my book, lady.* Dev recognized the compliment. It was sweeter to her soul than all the bouquet-bearing smiles once lavished on her by well-dressed swains at fancy Fifth Avenue balls.

Timmy said, "Wait here, Miss," and with the swagger of a proud little boy, his ragged clothing flapping along his skinny body, he ambled over to a door at the other side of the room. The words DETECTIVE BUREAU were written across the door in flaking gold letters.

Dev considered sitting down on one of the benches against the wall while she waited for Coyle, but in the bleak glare of the single overhead electric bulb, the battered wooden benches along the drab walls looked as welcoming as medieval torture racks. Large splotches of grime on the benches and walls resembled grotesquely silhouetted heads. The sordid environment proffered no comfort, leaving Dev to remain standing in the center of the waiting room.

Something far worse than grime further attacked her comfort, causing her breath to catch: terrible thuds, grunts, and moans suddenly came from behind the door as Timmy approached. Dev knew what those hellish sounds meant. The savage business of a police interrogation was taking place in the next room.

"I'll tell 'tective Coyle youse here, Miss." The boy's voice was an absurdly sweet melody filtering through the dirge of brutality taking place behind that door.

Young Timmy's knock on the door was the rat-a-tat of a little boy's chivalry, a diminutive knight errant acting on behalf of the elegant lady who'd called him Master Poole. A moment passed before the door opened and the horrible sounds of fists smashing into flesh hurtled into the waiting area, assaulting Dev like vicious blows to the mind and spirit. Her first impulse was to run from the room, flee the barbarism attacking her senses. That impulse was quickly superseded by the even stronger urge to run into the interrogation room to try to stop the acts of savagery.

Miserable, Dev remained riveted where she stood, unable to either escape the horror or alleviate it. To do the first would result in the failure of her mission on behalf of her clients, the Godfreys. To attempt the second could result in being forcibly removed or even arrested for interfering in police business. All she could do, then, was stare helplessly at the large man in the doorway who looked down at Timmy Poole, the sounds of violence surging around the boy and out towards Dev.

The man's face was not visible in the dim waiting area, but his silhouette against the brightly lit room behind him nearly filled the door frame. "Yeah?" the big man said to the boy. The brutishness in his bearing and rough tone of voice made Dev worry for Timmy's safety.

Young Timmy was unbowed by the man's rude power, unafraid of the violence the man represented. The boy's pride was a tonic to Dev, a restorative that gave her strength and renewed her sense of purpose. With a simplicity and directness that won Dev's admiration, Timmy said, "The Desk Sarge sent me back t'tell 'tective Coyle that a lady is waitin'."

The man, presumably a member of the Detective Bureau, lingered in the doorway, his huge, slightly swaying shape projecting menace. He finally turned back to the room, shouting, "Coyle! You got company!" as he slammed the door behind him.

The closed door only muffled the vicious sounds coming from the interrogation room and did nothing to relieve the strangling atmosphere of terror the big detective left behind.

Dev noticed that Timmy Poole remained unaffected. The boy sat down on one of the benches, calmly retying a frayed shoestring. His unruffled acceptance of brutality, not to mention the corruption that his presently jailed mother lived by and was equally victimized by, tore at Dev's sense of justice, at her definition of childhood as a time of innocence. Timmy Poole had neither innocence nor knew justice. All he had was his pride in his ability to navigate his world, an ability, Dev noticed, he had in abundance.

The wretched sounds from behind the door stopped. The door opened. Detective Charles Coyle, in a black suit and waistcoat, walked into the waiting room.

Except for a slight flush of his pale cheeks, he appeared calm. His wavy brown hair was well groomed. His clean-shaven face and closely spaced dark eyes were expressionless until he saw that his visitor was Devorah Longstreet, whom he knew from past dealings. His eyes suddenly glistened, but only slightly, for Detective Coyle was not one to unbind his emotions. He spoke softly, which was his habit. "What do you think you're doing here, Miss Longstreet?"

Coyle's neglect to even offer an evening's greeting, his lack of basic courtesy, was distasteful to Dev, though not unexpected, and she therefore felt no need to offer any polite salutations in return. She got right to business. "Considering the irregularity of having a police detective send a murder case to my doorstep, I think you might have expected me," she said. "An explanation is certainly due, if not to satisfy me or Fin, then to satisfy Mr. and Mrs. Godfrey, whose daughter is the victim of the worst possible crime."

Stiff and emotionless as a plank of wood, Coyle said, "What I expected was that you and Fin would take the case, make your money, and that's all. And now you'd best be on your way, Miss Longstreet. Your presence here ain't advisable." He turned to go back to the interrogation room.

Dev called after him, "There are three things I insist on knowing, Detective Coyle. First, why the police do not want to look into the murder of Pauline Godfrey. Secondly, though you could have directed the Godfreys to any number of private inquiry agents, you sent them to the firm of Donner & Longstreet. Your action is peculiar, since you've made it clear in the past how much you disapprove of our firm, and of us personally. And thirdly, you know our work, Detective, so you know that Fin and I will be tireless in our pursuit of the murderer and that nothing will scare us off or buy us off. So then, am I correct in assuming that though you do not officially want this case on your desk, you nevertheless want it pursued? If that is so, then there must be some benefit to you, Detective, and you are quite possibly using Donner & Longstreet as patsies in some corrupt game."

Coyle turned back around to Dev. He smiled a little, just a minimal baring of his teeth. "Assume whatever you wish, Miss Longstreet," he said. "Only assume it outside of this police headquarters. There ain't no assistance for you here. You'll do whatever it is you plan to do alone. No police officers are available."

"That ain't so!" piped up Timmy Poole. "I heard that tall 'tective—whatsisname, O'Brien—I heard him say he finished his load an' was lookin' t'go out'n find anudder—"

"*You*, Timmy Poole, *scram*, you hear me?" Coyle was poised as if to swat the boy, his arm raised in a straight, black diagonal line of cruelty.

Dev, horrified at a threat of violence against a child, grabbed Coyle's arm. The look in her eyes defied him to dare strike young Timmy.

Coyle wrenched his arm free with such force it nearly tore Dev's glove off and pulled her arm from its socket, but it was the only emotion that escaped from him. Coyle's face, when he turned to Dev, was as calm as when he came into the room. Dev felt as if a snake was coiling around her throat.

Timmy, with puffed-up pride, said, "Don't worry 'bout me, Miss. I knows the score. I don't wanna queer t'ings f'you, so's I'll scram." The boy sauntered out with a self-importance he enjoyed immensely.

Coyle said, "And now, if you please, Miss Longstreet—"

"And now, if *you* please," Dev countered, determined to turn Coyle's unnerving calmness to her advantage by elucidating her concerns in a most rational manner, though rational was the last thing she felt about her experiences here tonight. "Detective Coyle, why did you ignore Mr. and Mrs. Godfrey's appeal to have John Jones investigated? And just who is this John Jones who clearly ensnared Pauline Godfrey into something degrading? Do you have information that might bear on his guilt or innocence of her murder? If so, I beg you share it with me so that I may be of some use and comfort to my grieving clients."

His face still blank, Coyle said, "John Jones. You want to know about John Jones."

"I do."

The way Coyle looked at Dev now, as if she was a knot he was being forced to untie, made Dev want to step back from him lest he start physically picking at her. But she held her position and stood her ground, determined not to show any weakness or discomfort in his presence.

"Come with me, Miss Longstreet," he finally said. He waved her toward the door she'd entered with Timmy, opened it, then led her across the still noisy central hallway crowded with irate and desperate unfortunates. They approached another door, which Coyle opened for Dev with showy, insincere courtesy.

She stepped through into a large room she had never been in before but at once recognized: the Detective Bureau's famous Rogues Gallery and Museum of Criminal Relics. Despite its title as a museum, the public, Dev knew, was not permitted into this room.

Unwilling to validate whatever feelings Coyle might have about women being too emotional for detective work, Dev restrained any outward show of excitement at being in what amounted to local criminal investigation's Holy of Holies, an American Scotland Yard, a testament to the modernizing practices of the first chief of the city's new Detective Bureau, Thomas Byrnes. Dev had read his encyclopedic *Professional Criminals of America*, published nearly fourteen years earlier but a masterwork she relied on in her pursuits as a private inquiry agent. It was a pity that in other respects Byrnes proved as corrupt as the rest of the police establishment and was eventually forced to resign. Subsequent chiefs maintained the Rogues Gallery as a point of the department's pride, though it was a tainted professional accomplishment, for they, too, had fallen prey to the lure of graft and corruption. Nevertheless, this room, with its more than one thousand photographs in racks that turned like pages mounted on an elegantly carved oak breakfront the width of the room, remained an intellectual treasure trove for the student of crime. Here were photographs of every criminal arrested by the city's police since Byrnes began his compilation: from pickpockets and thieves to pimps and murderers. On the back of each photo was the subject's physical description and criminal history. What she wouldn't give to study the content of those racks!

To reach them, Dev and Coyle had to cross the room and pass by two large glass cases containing the tools of the criminal trades and the instruments of punishment used on the miscreants when caught. Along with the filed keys, shanks, brass knuckles, knives and guns, were various nooses from the hangings no longer performed in the nearby Tombs jail. Dev, whose excitement was now running through her with the heat of a fever, could only hope that one day she'd be allowed to make a scholarly examination of the fascinating contents of these display cases.

"Why, Miss Longstreet," Coyle said, interrupting her reverie, "I believe the sight of all these lowlifes and their tools excites you. Why, you're becoming quite flushed!"

Dev's embarrassment was superseded by her disgust at Coyle's bad manners in embarrassing her in the first place. He had shown himself to be as uncouth as any of the lowlifes he held in such contempt.

They stepped up the two stairs onto the platform on which the Rogues Gallery of photographs rested. Detective Coyle, in the grandiose manner of a carnival barker touting his exotic collection of rarities, turned the large pages of photos, ten rows of ten pictures per row, one hundred photos on each paged rack. "I could turn these pages all night," he said, "and read off some of the most notorious names in crime. Names like Murderin' Mike McGloin, leader of the old Whyos Gang, experts in mayhem and killing; and Christine Mayer, alias Kid Glove Rosey, a shoplifter of good taste but evil temperament; and Michael Hurley, alias Pugsey, a masked burglar who stole the life savings of invalids. But *nowhere* will we find the name and likeness of one John Jones. There is nothing here for you to learn, Miss Longstreet."

"Perhaps because Jones has not yet been caught."

"Sure, that's one explanation. Which puts me in mind of another name and photograph you won't find here, of one Finola Donner, alias Fin Donner, alias Fine Fingers Donner, alias—"

"You've made your point, Detective."

"Then you'll be going now, Miss Longstreet," Coyle said, taking Dev's arm.

She took back her arm from his grip. "I have other questions yet, Detective Coyle. To begin with, were the Godfreys brought into this room to examine the photographs, perhaps recognize Mr. Jones under another name?"

"I told you, Miss Longstreet, there's no likeness of John Jones in this room under any name."

"You're sure?"

"*Quite* sure." Coyle's impatience was sharp and cutting as a straight razor.

"Then the Godfreys did not look at these pictures?"

"There was no need, Miss Longstreet."

"Pity. This gallery and the modern methods of investigation it represents might have been of some comfort to the Godfreys, let them know that our esteemed police department really does pursue criminals. They think otherwise, you understand."

The standard coolness in Coyle's demeanor chilled even further. Barely above a whisper, he said, "Do not mistake our modern methods for modern tastes, Miss Longstreet, such as the modern taste for women living outside of their place, flaunting opinions, practicing an independence of mind."

"Women such as myself, you mean," Dev said, and added, "and perhaps Pauline Godfrey?"

"You overstep, Miss Longstr—"

The door to the Rogues Gallery suddenly swung open. A shout of "Coyle!" boomed through the room. It came from a large man in shirtsleeves and suspenders. Flecks of blood spattered his sweat-stained white shirt. Heavy locks of dark hair fell untidily on either side of his large head. He had authority and meanness in his square, gray face and deep-set eyes. Though it was the first time Dev had seen his face, she was sure he was the big detective whose silhouette had earlier been so menacing. There was no mistaking his powerful build and threatening posture. Through a coarse growl, he said, "Coyle, y'needed back across the hall. The guy's about to open up. Just needs a little more coaxin'."

Coyle nodded and took Dev's arm to lead her off the platform.

She remembered Timmy Poole, his self-possession in the face of rude power. That memory gave her the strength to hold her ground. She did not move. "But Mr. Coyle and I are not yet finished," she said.

The big detective looked her up and down in a way that

made Dev's stomach churn. He wasn't so much undressing her with his eyes, as men are wont to do; he appeared to be visually deboning her.

It was a relief when he looked away from her and at Coyle again. "Let's go now, Coyle. Duty calls."

"I'll be right there," Coyle said. Dev thought she caught a servile note in his voice, an unattractive and highly unusual slip for Coyle, a man who did not usually allow any trace of emotion to permeate his speech. "Miss Longstreet was just leaving."

The big detective stepped farther into the room, holding the door open as an usher would, though there was nothing of the polite servant in his comportment. His message was clear: Coyle was to escort Dev out of the room and send her out of the building. Their meeting was over.

Coyle took Dev's arm. His grip was firm, a physical command that Dev not show any prideful independence in pulling her arm away. He led her off the platform.

As they passed the big detective, Dev controlled a gag from his body's stench of sweat and blood.

Out in the hall, Coyle's manner was curt. "Go back to the Godfreys, Miss Longstreet. Goodnight," he said and walked across the hall and into the opposite room. The big detective said nothing, but his odor, like that of a charnel house, lingered as he followed Coyle across the hall.

The entire episode was an affront to Dev's way of thinking. Coyle's deceptions regarding Jones—he *was* being deceitful, Dev was certain—and his imperious manner, followed by an unbecoming hint of servility, were as distasteful to her as the actions of that barbaric detective with his filthy gaze and foul smell. Dev was relieved to be rid of their company as she made her way through the knots of people still thronging the hallway.

She was eager to quit the place, to meet her beloved Fin at the nearby café where Dev looked forward to being refreshed by a restorative brandy while they discussed their findings thus far.

First, though, another matter lurked.

She found Timmy Poole lounging on the floor near the door. Extending her hand to help him to his feet, she said, "Master Poole, what is your mother's name?"

"I told ya. Her name's Mag."

"Is that short for Margaret? Do people sometimes call her Maggie? I need her proper name if I'm to help her."

"I . . . I t'ink maybe it's . . . well, I heard people call her Maggie."

"That will have to do. Come with me." Still holding his hand, Dev walked to the sergeant's desk. Considering the sergeant's earlier rudeness, she saw no need to address him with anything more than the most basic courtesy. "Sir, I am in need of your telephone."

The sergeant, in turn, saw no need to accommodate this uppity woman by sharing his personal arena. All he gave her was a nod toward a wall. "You can use the magneto over there."

With Timmy in tow, Dev found the magneto telephone, its wooden cabinet and the wall it was mounted on stained with tobacco and other spittle. She cranked the mechanism, and when an operator answered, Dev gave her a connection exchange.

Soon a deep, streetwise male voice said, "Hullo?"

"Mr. Calhoun? Devorah Longstreet here. My apologies for intruding on your evening at home, but I want to engage your legal services."

"Always happy to assist you and Fin, Miz Longstreet."

"Well, this isn't for the firm. I want to assist a young friend. Can you come to 300 Mulberry right away? A Miss Maggie Poole has been—"

"Black Haired Mag? You're friends with Black Haired Mag?"

"I have many friends, Mr. Calhoun. In any event, Miss Poole needs to be released from the cells. Post her bail and pay her fines if necessary and send the bill to me. Good night, Mr. Calhoun."

When Dev rang off, the smile on Timmy's face was as bright as the sparkling tears in his eyes.

Chapter Five

*A soul will survive if it is loved; but scant of love, a soul will gnaw
on itself until it bleeds to death. It is a long, slow, tortured death.
The killer would not abide such a fate, real or not.*

CHAPTER SIX

Fin was already seated when Dev entered the Mulberry Café, a smoke-filled place popular with curbside attorneys, crooks, whores, immigrants, and other denizens of street life.

A glass of brandy was waiting for Dev when she arrived at the small wooden table where Fin rose to assist her into a chair. After a bracing swallow of the liquor, Dev said, "Thank heavens I'm out of that pestilent excuse for justice. Well, Lovey, did you learn anything interesting?"

"Rage," Fin said. "The killer was full of rage. The bloodstain on the sidewalk indicated that Pauline's killer came up behind and slit her throat."

"Coward," Dev said with disgust.

"How 'bout you? Was Coyle helpful?"

"More than he suspected."

"Y'mean he wasn't his usual cold fish sorta fella?"

"Oh, he was still that, and rude, too. He kept insisting I leave. But for the near an hour I was there, he didn't strenuously *do* anything about it until he was forced to by an ape of a detective I wouldn't want to meet in a dark alley. After all, Coyle could have summoned other officers and had me removed from the building the minute he saw me, but he didn't."

"Huh, that is interestin'. Coyle's usually a no-nonsense fella about what he wants."

"Tonight he was all nonsense. Well, maybe not nonsense, but not the soul of clarity, either. He made a point of not answering my questions, so what he *didn't* say became as important as what he did say." Dev took another sip of brandy, leaned across the table and spoke more intimately to her adored companion, lest she be overheard by undesired ears. "Listen, my love, Coyle was rather roundabout in his telling, but he made it clear that John Jones—if that is truly his name—is not to be found anywhere in the police files, which hinted that Jones is under some sort of protection, either by the police or other higher-ups, criminal or otherwise. And as an actor, accustomed to playing roles, I suppose he could easily slip between milieus; you know, between the police and the underworld. That ability could prove useful equally to police and criminals."

"Does Coyle think he's our killer? Do you?"

"Perhaps, on both counts. Or maybe Coyle is off base entirely. I don't know. And I think Coyle doesn't know, either, which may be why he sent the case to us. If Jones is under corrupt protection, Coyle can't be seen to go after him. He may not even want to, since he's loyal to his police comrades. I think he hopes we'll determine if Jones is the killer, in which case Coyle would have to go along with the orders to leave him alone. Or if someone else murdered poor Pauline, and we uncover the culprit, Coyle could then make the arrest and gain the credit."

"So Coyle is usin' us."

"So it seems. In any event, we need to question this John Jones."

Fin nodded agreement, though worry permeated her to the marrow. If John Jones was a killer, a murderer of deep rage, confronting him could expose Devorah to mortal danger. True, they both carried firearms, but Fin worried nonetheless. She could not bear the thought of her precious Devorah as a target of violence.

"By the way," Dev said, "I ran into an acquaintance of yours at the police station."

Fin, hearing a mischievous lilt in Dev's voice, smiled a careful smile and merely said, "Oh?" There were probably any number of Fin's past acquaintances she'd rather Dev not run into.

"A little fellow," Dev said, enjoying her playful game with her lover.

"Oh, Mack the Midget," Fin said with relief. "Sweet little fella, a talented pocket dipper. Sorry to hear the blue-boys grabbed him."

"No, a younger little fellow. Timmy Poole. He said you know his mother, one Maggie Poole, known as Black Haired Mag."

Fin's face, usually sturdy and resolute, went as pink as cotton candy. "That was . . . that was a long time ago," she said.

The sweetness of Fin's embarrassment brought a tender smile to Dev's lips and a forgiving pleasure to her soul. After finishing her brandy, she said, "Oh, and we'll get a bill from Calhoun for Miss Poole's bail."

"You're a wonderful woman, Devorah Longstreet."

"Finish your drink, Lovey," Dev said, "and we'll go have a chat with Mr. John Jones."

The boardinghouse on Bayard Street where Jones was said to have lodgings was a sooty, sagging three-story wooden habitat of misery. It was the sort of hard luck house Fin was all too familiar with through her childhood and beyond, but an environment Dev was still struggling to get used to.

The wooden porch stairs creaked, the doorbell was broken. Fin knocked on the door, rattling the cracked, flower-etched glass pane.

The door was eventually answered by a pathetic creature whose appearance made Dev's breath catch in her throat. Dev had never seen such a woman, not even among the desperate immigrant throng at Police Headquarters. The figure greeting her in the doorway seemed to be made of nothing more than sticks and rags.

"Whaddya want, disturbin' decent people at this hour?" the woman said in a voice destroyed long ago by hard liquor and a harder life. Suspicion oozed from her as tart as her odor of whiskey.

Fin said, "The hour's not that late, sister, barely nine-thirty. Still plenty of bottle time left. So don't give us a story about disturbin' your decent nature."

The female sack of sticks sneered in umbrage. "Well—well—whaddya want?"

"We're lookin' for John Jones."

The woman examined Fin and Devorah through watery, bloodshot eyes narrowed to slits of opportunistic greed. "What's it worth to ya?" she said.

Fin pulled a fiver from her wallet, dangled it in front of the woman whose eyes opened wide at the sight of such a grand amount of cash. The woman reached a bony hand for the bill, but Fin snatched it away until the woman finally said, "Secon' floor, back." Fin released the fiver, which the woman crushed into her fist.

Walking into the boardinghouse, Fin took Dev's arm and guided her through the shadowy, fetid vestibule, the air clogged with dust and the sour odors of human poverty. Climbing the stairs in the gloom, Dev's foot caught on a ragged edge of threadbare carpet, nearly twisting her ankle. Only Fin's strong, guiding arm kept Dev from hurtling down the stairs.

Catching her breath after her near tumble, Dev joked, "I can only assume Mr. Jones is less of a danger than these stairs."

"Let's hope you're—" But Fin's reply was interrupted by a

loud crack in the air both Fin and Dev recognized as a gunshot.

There was no doubt where the shot came from: the second floor back. Jones's room.

Whines and screams in the vestibule by the wretched woman who'd let them in followed Fin and Devorah's rush up the stairs.

At Jones's locked door, they didn't bother to knock or even call out his name. Fin simply kicked down the door from its flimsy hinge. Inside, the room was nearly smothered in shadows. A single oil lamp revealed the body of John Jones slumped over a table. The lamp barely illuminated a revolver on the floor below Jones's dangling arm and hand. His head was bloody, his blood and brains leaked onto a scrawled note: *I loved her.*

There was a sudden fluttering outside in the hall. The sound of the gunshot brought other lodgers out of their rooms. But no one screamed, no one wept, no one cried out in shock. In this neighborhood where life was often savage, death was too common for anyone to worry about except when it brought trouble. John Jones blowing his brains out could bring trouble, and the Bayard Street lodgers already had more than enough trouble in their lives. Most now scurried back into their rooms, closing their doors, keeping trouble out.

Dev said, "Coyle needs to know about this, Lovey."

One of the lodgers, a big-eyed, curvy, blond-haired woman, was still in the hall near Jones's door. The revealing bodice of her tight red dress announced her profession as a merchant of her own flesh. "You talkin' about that cute Detective Coyle?" she said.

Dev and Fin both turned to the woman, but it was Dev who answered her. "You know Detective Coyle? You've seen him here?"

"Who wants to know?" the woman said. Belligerence oozed through a coyness as false as her smile.

"My name is Devorah Longstreet. And yes, we're referring to Detective Charles Coyle. How do you know him?"

The woman looked Dev up and down, examining every thread of Dev's elegant cloak, every ripple in Dev's fine leather gloves. "Nothin' I do comes free, missy." She held out her palm. "You want what I got to say? Then slide it over."

Dev opened her purse, but Fin put a hand over it and gave a hard look to the woman in the hall. "Just a minute," she said. "Why should we trust what you're tryin' to sell? How do we know you won't give us a cock'n bull story just to get your hands on cash."

"And so who are you?"

"The name's Fin Donner. Who'd you be?"

The woman's smile faded, her belligerence deflated as if she'd been pricked by a pin. "You're Fin Donner? I heard'a you. You used to be somethin', or so they say."

Dev said, "Let me assure you, Miss—?"

"Flowers. Clara Flowers."

"Let me assure you, Miss Flowers," Dev continued, "Fin Donner is still quite something." Dev didn't bother to hide the joy she felt in saying it, nor control the smile through which she spoke.

After giving her beloved a wink, Fin brought the conversation back to the suddenly more timid Clara Flowers. "What Miss Longstreet means, Miss Flowers, is that it ain't a good idea to lie to us. You won't hold on to any money we give you for long, understan'?"

Clara Flowers, a woman of the streets who knew her share of brutes, was no weakling, and her deep breath, her chin thrust high, was her attempt to hold her own against Fin. But she was no match for Fin's hard stare, a glower Fin perfected to stay alive in the tough world she'd once inhabited. Clara simply nodded, "Sure, I understan'," she said.

"Good," Fin said. "So, how do you know Coyle?"

"I seen him around."

Dev said, "Around where? Here?"

"No, not here. Just around. I gotta say, he was a little less of a brute than some other coppers when they'd yank some of the girls off the street. So that's how I know Detective Coyle. Now gimme some money."

"In a moment," Dev said. "I have another question about Mr. Jones. Did you ever see Mr. Jones with Pauline Godfrey?"

"Never heard'a her."

"A dark-haired young woman? Pretty. Favored shirtwaists and simple skirts."

"Oh her. Yeah, sure. I seen her. I think she musta gotten sick or somethin'. Last time she was here she looked kinda pale, skinny, like she was dyin'."

"When was that?"

"Last night. I was goin' downstairs and she and Johnny was comin' up. He was holding her arm like he was tryin' to keep her from keelin' over."

Fin said, "Were they talkin' about anything?"

"She could barely talk, but when I passed them on the stairs she said somethin' about needin' fresh air. Now, my money if you please. I ain't got nothin' more to say 'cause there ain't nothin' more to say."

Fin took a money clip from her pocket, peeled off a few single dollars and handed them to the outstretched hand of Clara Flowers.

"This house got a telephone?" Fin asked.

Clara's laugh made clear the absurdity of there being a newfangled contraption in this broken-down house. "Try Smitty's saloon at the corner," she said through the laugh. "He's got a magneto. Tell Smitty I sent you."

It was a little after ten p.m. when they walked into the saloon at the corner of Bayard and Mott Streets. The saloon was a grim place no bigger than a horse stall. Its flickering gaslight and jittery shadows scratched at the faces of rough men and slovenly women who sat at the few rickety tables or stood at the wooden plank laid across three barrels that served as a bar. The air stank of rotgut whiskey and sweat, mixed with the harsh perfume of a couple of local streetwalkers come in for a pick-me-up or to catch a little business. Dev was sure she also caught the sour scent of vomit and urine.

It was understood between Fin and Dev that Fin would do the talking here. They approached the bar. With Dev safely at her side, Fin said to the bartender, "You Smitty?"

The bartender, a skinny gent with greasy brown hair and feral blue eyes, looked Fin up and down, sizing up Fin's bulk outfitted in a suit and straw boater too elegant for this establishment. He then guided his glance to Dev. The look he gave her was not gentlemanly.

Looking back at Fin, he said through a high, wheezy voice, "Who's askin'?"

"Never mind that," Fin said. "All you gotta know is Clara Flowers says Smitty's okay, an' that he'd lend me the use of his magneto. It's worth a buck to ya for the magneto an' a nickel whiskey. So, assuming you're Smitty, you don't need no name from me." Fin slid a silver dollar across the bar.

Smitty snatched the coin. He gave Fin a mean smile. "Y'say yer a client of Clara's? Sure, she takes all kinds." He added a leer at Dev to press his sordid point.

Dev held her head high and proud against the bartender's slimy insult.

Fin said, "That buck buys me a drink an' the use of the magneto. Pour me the one an' direct this *lady* to the other."

With a quick, resentful tilt of his head Smitty directed Dev toward a shadowed area along the back wall. His "Over there," came through an animal-like snarl.

This was the second time tonight that Dev had to maneuver

through phlegmy stares, only this time, unlike the enraged throng at police headquarters, the handful of men and women at Smitty's saloon were too far gone to feel much of anything. Rage and envy were long dead in them. All that remained was bitterness about their brutal lives, their misery numbed by rotgut whiskey.

The shadowed area where the magneto hung on the grimy wall offered Dev a bit of relief from the unpleasant stares. After the operator connected her with police headquarters, Dev recognized the voice of the desk sergeant she'd dealt with earlier. Not wanting to give him any reason to deny her request, she altered the tone of her voice and manner of speech, disguising her identity. "There's a dead man at Mrs. Mallory's boardinghouse on Bayard Street. John Jones is dead. Inform Detective Coyle."

CHAPTER SEVEN

There were no hansom cabs to be had in this dreary neighborhood of poverty and the drunks and gangs who savaged the night. Fin held Dev's arm close during the walk to Canal Street, a major thoroughfare offering a better chance to flag a hansom. Along the way, they discussed a course of action to learn more about John Jones and his milieu.

The immediate plan suggested by Fin did not sit comfortably with Dev. Though she understood and even appreciated her companion's desire to keep Dev from harm—"an' the hour's late now, too, my girl, nearly eleven," Fin said—Dev nevertheless chafed at Fin's idea that she return home and get a good night's sleep. Fin, on the other hand, would look into the more sordid aspects of Jones's life, starting with a visit tonight to Black Haired Mag, "who knows where the feet grow, as they say. An' besides, Mag owes us a big favor for gettin' her outta jail."

Fin, searching through the horse-drawn and cable car traffic for a hansom cab on busy Canal Street, didn't see the look of displeasure on Dev's face, nor the twinge of jealousy beneath it. Though Dev felt justified in her annoyance at Fin for considering her so delicate she must be sent home to bed rather than take action in the night, the twinge of jealousy bothered her more.

She trusted her beloved down to her marrow, and yet she knew that the lure of the past was never far beneath Fin's skin. Black Haired Mag was part of that past. Dev wondered if Mag was also part of the lure.

She said none of this as she stepped into a hansom while Fin gave the driver their address on Irving Place. Instead, Dev resolved not to meekly return home and fall asleep alone in the bed she shared with Fin. After a kiss from her dearest, and as she watched Fin walk back into the dark streets of the neighborhood, Dev gave the cab driver new instructions. "Never mind Irving Place, please take me to West 38th Street and Broadway."

The Curtain Call Bar and Grill, down the street from the Knickerbocker Theater, was a popular watering hole among New York's theatrical crowd. Unlike the bare bones furnishings and sordid environment of Smitty's saloon down on Bayard Street, the Curtain Call boasted mirrored and polished mahogany-paneled walls fitted with brass sconces with etched glass globes, marble-top tables, a black-and-white mosaic tile floor, and a Ladies' Entrance on the West 38th Street side of the establishment. By the soft glow of the frosted glass globe above the door, unescorted ladies would enter after their shows to enjoy a late supper and a nightcap, and gossip among their thespian peers.

Inside the Ladies' saloon, soft light from the wall sconces highlighted feathered hats, lace collars and ruffles, and fell across colorful dresses with bodices ranging from prim to plunging. The light sparkled on glasses of amber brandy and white foam overflowing the rims of beer mugs. It glowed across young, pretty faces, and rouged faces trying to appear young. The latter made Dev grateful that she had no inclination to be a member of the theatrical profession, with its callous demand for everlasting female youthfulness. To her mind, this was yet another example of the cruelty imposed on women in professions ruled by men.

It was clear, though, that the women in this room accepted this dictate, and the luckier ones, the ones wearing satin dresses and stoles of fur draped carelessly over a shoulder, even thrived in it.

The room was lively with female chatter and laughter, with a few guffaws and wafts of cigar smoke rolling in now and then from the adjoining main bar where the men congregated.

Dev recognized a few of the patrons from her evenings with Fin at the theater: well-known stars or actresses on the rise. Most of the women, though, were unfamiliar to her, presumably lesser players in bit parts or chorus roles. It was these workaday performers who Dev came to see, actresses who spent most of a play waiting in the wings or in shared dressing rooms with time on their hands for gossip.

A group of four young women at a back table caught her eye: a curly-haired blonde whose heart-shaped face beneath her pert little flowered hat was suitable for girl-next-door type roles; another blonde sat beside her, hatless, her hair in a row of ringlets above her forehead and a chignon at the nape of her neck, her face carved into a hard expression with wary eyes; a pretty brunette, also hatless, sat across from the hard-faced blonde, her hair in a modern Gibson-Girl poufy coif; beside her was a redhead whose almond eyes beneath her jaunty straw boater appeared to be amused at everything. All of the women nursed their mugs of nickel beer and stole glances at the more famous performers at other tables. Judging by their attire—fashionable but of the less expensive variety—and the sips they took of their beers to make them last longer, the women were exactly the type Dev was looking for: performers who usually appeared only in small roles when they were lucky enough to be in a play at all, and were still struggling to make their name and earn a living on the professional stage.

Dev spotted a runner, a young boy seated by the swinging doors leading to the main room, which had the only bar. The boy's job was to take drink orders from the women, fill the orders at the bar and bring them back to the women's table. Though the lad was somewhat better dressed than Timmy Poole, he nonetheless reminded Dev of her young guide at police headquarters. This reminiscence raised the specter of Fin's visit to Black Haired Mag's, and raised, too, the twinge of jealousy Dev forced herself once again to suppress.

She gave the lad fifty cents, told him to keep twenty-five cents for himself, and instructed him to bring five mugs of nickel beer to the table of women at the back. The twenty-five-cent tip being the biggest he'd ever received, the lad smiled a near toothless smile which broke Dev's heart before he pressed through the swinging doors.

While he was gone, Dev considered what would be her most advantageous introduction to the women she wanted to talk to. With the beers as a salve, she decided that the truth would be the best option.

The lad returned with the five beers on a tray. Only his nightly mastery of balancing beer and whiskey-laden trays that were by rights too big for his small frame prevented him from dropping the five full-to-overflowing foaming mugs of beer.

As Dev followed the lad across the saloon, she was aware of several pairs of eyes following her, their owners curious as to who she might be: a new actress in town? Competition for the eyes and attention of prominent producers? Her tasteful attire and confident manner were those of a star but her unfamiliar face aroused confused curiosity and titters of gossip. It was this taste for gossip that Dev hoped would be her ticket to ferreting out information about the late John Jones.

The lad set the mugs on the table, to the surprise of the four women seated there. "Excuse me," Dev said, "I took the liberty of ordering a round of beer in hopes you'd give me a few minutes of your time to talk."

"About what?" the girl-next-door blonde said, suspicion carving an edge into her otherwise musical voice. "You don't look like you need casting notices."

"Please, I'm not a member of the theatrical profession. I have no reason to compete with you for jobs," Dev said, taking a seat between the girl-next-door blonde and the redhead wearing the straw boater. "I just hope you might tell me about one of your colleagues, one Mr. John Jones."

The reactions around the table ranged from curious stares to outright laughter.

It was the hard-faced blonde who laughed. Dev heard no humor in it. The laugh was brittle, like wood splintering. Its harshness cut through the din of chatter in the room and caused a few heads to turn. Even the other young women at the table looked on in surprise.

When the woman's laughter subsided into a few final snorts, Dev said, "Perhaps you'd like to share with the rest of us why the mention of Mr. Jones strikes you so funny, Miss—uhm—"

"LaRose. Sylvie LaRose."

"The hell it is, Siggy," the redhead in the boater said through a snicker. "That may be this week's idea of a classy stage moniker, but you were born Sigrid Rosendorff and you'll die Sigrid Rosendorff." To Dev, she said, "I'm Mary O'Connor, and that's my name on the stage and off. Miss Sweet-face in the flowered hat is Suzanne Silver, born Suzanne Sawdy, and our Gibson-Girl fashion plate is Katherine Hazelton, known to one and all as Kissable Kate." Dev was sure she saw Miss Hazelton do her best to hide a slight wince at the nickname.

"Thank you for the introductions, Miss O'Connor," Dev said.

"And who might you be?"

"My name's Devorah Longstreet. I'm delighted to make your acquaint—"

"Wait a minute." It was Suzanne Silver. "Longstreet? Devorah Longstreet? Uh ... by any chance you wouldn't happen to be the Devorah Longstreet who ... well, let's say *works with* Fin Donner?"

Dev couldn't miss the slight sneer in Miss Silver's musical voice and the subtle curl to her lip. She would not let these pierce her dignity. "I am indeed that Devorah Longstreet. And since you know—as you say—that I work with Fin, then perhaps you also know that Fin and I investigate crimes."

She was tempted to ask how Miss Silver was acquainted with Fin, but before she could, Mary O'Connor, her eyes bright with her natural humor, said, "Oh my, then you're here about a crime? How exciting!"

All four women were now staring at Dev. The hard-faced blonde calling herself Sylvie LaRose, and who was no longer laughing, was the one who finally broke the expectant silence. "If you're telling us that Johnny Jones is involved in a crime, well, that's no surprise," she said. "He has to earn his money somehow. He's a terrible actor. Wooden as a stick. Most producers laugh him right out of their offices. Unless a production needs a pretty face to stand around and water the potted plants in a drawing room meller"—which Dev quickly assumed was theater slang for melodrama—"Johnny hardly works in shows at all. The fellow's got no talent, except for talking the knickers off women." She finished by taking a long, hard swallow of her beer.

Suzanne Silver said, "So what's Johnny involved in this time? Is some irate husband hauling him into court?" She thought this funny, giggling through her words like a bratty schoolgirl.

Dev, wishing to keep the women's cooperation, hid her distaste for Suzanne's graceless behavior. Affecting a conversational, slightly gossipy tone, she said, "Actually, the irate relative isn't a husband, it's a father. And he won't be hauling Mr. Jones into court. He can't, because Mr. Jones is dead. He committed suicide less than an hour ago."

The four faces around the table, each expert in the acting trade, failed in their talent for disguise to hide their shock. Their faces remained thus frozen until Mary O'Connor, her boater hat quivering, lost her battle to contain an escaping sob.

With all eyes on now on Mary, she managed to say, "Was it over that girl?"

The eyes of the other women drifted from Mary to Dev, their curiosity strong as a force of female soldiers pinning her to a wall.

"So it seems," Dev said. "Her name was Pauline Godfrey. Mr. Jones left a note saying he loved her. Miss O'Connor, if you know anything of their affair, please tell me."

But before Mary O'Connor could answer, Sylvie LaRose, snorting another laugh, said, "Johnny Jones in love? Oh, that's ripe. He wasn't a good enough actor to pull that script off."

Mary, another sob choking her throat, started, "No, you're wrong. I think he was a very lonely fellow. I think he really wanted to be in love, but he didn't know how. Maybe that's why he was such a lousy actor. He didn't know how to love. Maybe he thought he could or maybe—"

But Suzanne Silver, she of the heart-shaped face, musical voice, inquiring mind, and acquaintance with Fin, once again interrupted. "Just a moment, Miss Longstreet. You said the girl's name *was* Pauline Godfrey. That sounds to me like she's either changed her name— something all of us here know a little something about—or she's dead. I'm guessing it's the latter, since you admit you're investigating a crime. So it's her death you and Fin are investigating, yes? And you think Johnny might have had something to do with it."

"Her parents are under that impression, yes."

"And the police?"

A sip of beer afforded Dev a moment to consider her reply, and to study Suzanne's face, try to see into the woman's perceptive mind. She saw a flicker of humor in Suzanne's eyes, a snide humor which belied her girl-next-door face.

Suzanne Silver's probing, Sylvie LaRose's caustic laughter, Mary O'Connor's sobbing over John Jones's suicide and her question about his reason for taking his life, put Dev on her guard against this group of women she'd originally believed were merely denizens of the theatrical profession who could supply some useful gossip. Instead, she'd stumbled—fortuitously, one might say—into a circle of women whose connection to Jones was decidedly more intimate than mere gossip. Then again, perhaps any number of women in the theatrical profession, even other women in this room, had fallen for John Jones's seductive charm.

It occurred to Dev that the only woman who had not spoken up, or even smiled, laughed, or sobbed for that matter, was the table's fashionable Gibson Girl, Katherine Hazelton, aka Kissable Kate. "Miss Hazelton," Dev said gently, "did you know Mr. Jones?"

"Briefly," she said, her voice flat, her eyes cast down as she took a sip of beer. Dev had the impression the drink was an escape from Dev's question, the lifted mug a shield to hide behind.

But Dev, ever the investigator, understood that this was a moment to press the point. "Or perhaps you were acquainted with Miss Godfrey?"

"No, I never knew her."

"But you knew of her? Or perhaps had seen her with Mr. Jones?"

"What if I did? So what?" Despite Miss Hazelton's testy words, Dev observed that there was a dullness to their delivery. "Whatever was going on between them," Miss Hazelton said, still with what Dev considered an unnatural calm, "was none of my business. And I think none of this is your business, either, Miss Longstreet."

Two choices quickly presented themselves in Dev's mind:

either press Miss Hazelton aggressively in hopes of piercing her protective shield, or take a milder approach, a kindliness in hopes of fostering a woman-to-woman relationship, a sisterly alliance prone to sharing gossip.

Recalling Miss Hazelton's discomfort at being introduced as Kissable Kate, a nickname possibly implying Miss Hazelton's availability to male advances, Dev decided that the sisterly approach would be less of an irritant to Miss Hazelton's thin skin.

She placed her gloved hand gently on Miss Hazelton's and spoke with the gentleness of a trusted friend. "Distasteful as it is, Miss Hazelton, I'm afraid that whatever was between Miss Godfrey and Mr. Jones is my business. Miss Godfrey's parents have hired me and Fin to solve their daughter's murder, which makes her association with Mr. Jones my business, indeed. I'm sure you can sympathize with her parents' distress. So please, Miss Hazelton, if you have anything to share, anything which could help me solve Miss Godfrey's murder, you will be doing her grieving parents a great service by telling me what you know."

Despite Dev's warm manner, Katherine Hazelton remained silent, even sliding her hand out from under Dev's gentle touch.

There was the sound of a quick, choked sob at the table, another sob from Mary O'Connor, but it was Sylvie LaRose who spoke. "Oh, for heaven's sake. What's the matter with you two? You, Miss Kissable Kate, pretending you don't know a damn thing even though you were probably jealous enough to have any of Johnny's girls in your sights. And you, Mary, sobbing like a schoolgirl. You gave up your girlish purity before you were out of your teens. As a matter of fact, there isn't a woman at this table and plenty of others around this saloon who didn't roll her stockings down for Johnny Jones." She turned a hard stare to Dev. "So telling us that Johnny was in love with this Godfrey girl, well, it just doesn't wash, Miss Longstreet, no matter what Mary thinks about him being lonely and that song and dance about him not knowing how to love. He loved someone, all right: the one person Johnny Jones ever loved was the person looking back at him in the mirror."

Dev said, "Then you don't believe the note we found? The note that said he loved her?"

Miss LaRose gave that an unattractive sneer. "Are you so sure he wrote it?" she said.

"Well, of course he wrote—" But Dev couldn't finish. The question had taken her by complete surprise. Its ramifications were unsettling.

No, she could not be sure Mr. Jones had written that note. Nobody saw him write it, and neither she nor Fin knew his handwriting.

So if John Jones did not write it, who did? And when? And why?

A larger, more troubling question loomed: if John Jones did not write the note, if he did not kill himself over his love for the murdered Pauline Godfrey, why *did* he put a bullet in his head?

Or did he?

The look on the four women's faces made it clear to Dev that they were asking themselves the same question. Their curious expressions as they looked around the table at each other also contained something else: suspicion.

Suspicion, Dev knew from previous investigations, often resulted in minds shutting down and mouths closing tight. These four women were already uneasy with Dev's questions about Mr. Jones, and that unease had now become an impenetrable resistance to Dev's probing. No amount of questioning, no matter how gentle or sisterly, would reveal secrets these women kept from each other.

There was nothing more to be learned here. But as Dev said goodnight and rose from the table, she knew she'd actually learned a great deal.

CHAPTER EIGHT

During the day, Baxter Street is crammed with pushcart peddlers selling fruits and vegetables, meats and fish, chickens and ducks hanging by their feet. Vendors hawk slightly used needles and pins, threadbare men's suits and patched women's dresses, even homemade medicines which might or might not cure you but whose alcohol, laudanum, or cocaine content would render you uncaring about your illness.

Laundry clipped to spooling clotheslines stretching all the way across the street from fire escape to fire escape would be drying in Baxter Street's sooty sunshine, clothing, underwear, and bed linens flapping over the street like banners on election day. Rugs would hang over rails for airing. And everywhere there'd be noise: shouting pushcart peddlers, braying horses pulling wagons whose iron wheels clattered on the cobblestones. Housewives would haggle with peddlers over prices, men would gossip and brawl, all of it contributing to the noisy mishmash of crowded slum life.

At night, though, and through the wee hours before dawn, when the peddlers are gone, the housewives, husbands, and children are crammed together in their cramped beds, Baxter Street is dark and menacingly quiet. There's only the meager flicker of a corner streetlamp. The pavement and cobblestones are slippery from discarded fruits, vegetables, and the innards of fowl squashed underfoot. The only sounds are the stealthy murmurings or occasional laughter from the gang of slovenly men drinking beer or whiskey beneath the streetlamp, or the hiss the men make when a mark ripe for robbing happens by.

As Fin walked along Baxter Street she kept her hand inside her coat, her fingers curled around the butt of her revolver. When she heard the hiss of the men at the corner, she pulled the weapon out, making sure it caught the light of the streetlamp.

The men ceased their hissing.

A few paces past these local thugs, Fin turned right and walked into a dark arcade. It opened into a courtyard filthy with overflowing garbage bins, empty whiskey bottles, and the discarded furniture, bric-a-brac and rags of the slum dwellers in the surrounding two-, three- and four-story tenements. Fin put a handkerchief to her nose against the stench of garbage and urine that burned her nostrils and clawed her throat.

All the windows in the courtyard's surrounding tenements were dark except one: Black Haired Mag's place at the top of the rickety wooden stairs to the second floor of a two-story tenement that sagged like an exhausted sway-backed horse. Fin understood that the murky, reddish light was a sign that Mag was open for business, no doubt making up for income lost during the hours spent in the police cells.

The stairs creaked more often and louder than when Fin was here last, over six years ago, shortly before she met Devorah. The door to the tenement was now even more splintered, the lock still broken.

Fin wasn't one for crying over the harshness of life. She knew deep in her bones how cruel life could be and she accepted it. But a sadness overcame her at the sorry state of Mag's existence. She remembered that Mag had once harbored big dreams, dreams of running a high-class brothel for high-class clientele.

She remembered Mag saying in her velvety voice, seductively frayed from drink and tobacco, how she'd cover the walls in red brocade and put silk coverlets on all the beds.

As Fin climbed the dangerously unstable stairs, her heart ached that Mag's raw and shabby life had only become shabbier, and that Mag, like so many people scratching to survive in the city's rougher precincts, never seemed to get a break. By the time Fin reached the top of the stairs, she was acutely aware of her own good luck in escaping the same fate, and her extraordinary luck, a miracle really, of being loved by Devorah Longstreet.

Inside, Fin's twin moods of sadness for Mag and joy in her own life with Dev accompanied her through the sour-smelling hall to Mag's place. As if cruelly emphasizing Mag's hard life, Fin's knuckles stung when she knocked on Mag's rough and splintered door. Seconds later, the door opened. Flickering fleshy light from within the dark and dingy apartment revealed . . . no one, until Fin looked down when she heard the childlike mention of her name: "Fin? *Fin Donnuh?*"

"Timmy Poole," Fin said with more sentiment than she'd expected. "Y'still a whippersnapper, just a bigger one."

"Aww . . . y'know I knows the score, Fin."

You'd better, Fin thought but didn't say. *It's the only way you're gonna survive in this hellhole.* What she did say was, "I guess you're the man of the house, Timmy," and gave the boy a wink. "You gotta take good care of your ma, right?"

With a grin as wide as his little boy's face could handle, Timmy gave Fin a wink back. "C'mon in," he said. "By th'way, y'ladyfriend, Miz Lawnkstrit, she's a right one. Pretty slick the way she got my ma outta the cells t'night."

Fin gave the boy a quick, light, pal-to-pal punch to Timmy's shoulder. "We like to do right by our friends. Listen, I need to talk to your ma. She—?"

But before Fin could finish, Miss Maggie Poole, known to all as Black Haired Mag, walked through the violet curtain from

64

the bedroom and into the shadowy front room.

The light of the single wall-mounted gas lamp, its glass globe a faded shade of red, pitilessly exposed the frays and washed-out colors of Mag's Japanese style floral robe. The wavering light picked at the dry tangle of Mag's wild mane of black hair. The light mocked her shopworn beauty, laying bare every line in her face, deepening the creases at the corners of her once full mouth, the red-globed light laying a false blush over her skin.

But when she stepped out of the light, the shadows were kind to her, erasing the lines that insulted her flesh. The shadows allowed Fin to see again the seductive woman whose blue eyes had once charmed her, even as Mag would take Fin's silver dollar in payment.

"Well, ain't this a surprise," Mag said, her voice grown more tobacco-and-whiskey coarse than it used to be. "Or maybe it ain't such a surprise. Maybe y'figure I owe you for the good turn y'ladyfriend did by gettin' me outta jail. Well, all right, Fin, sure, why not?" There was a lilt in Mag's voice now: part practiced enticement, part genuine pleasure. "A favor's a favor, right? And what y'ladyfriend don't know won't kill her. I s'pose she's home all tucked up in bed and respectable. So, c'mere, Fin Donnuh," Mag said with a crook of her finger as she walked slowly toward Fin. She still kept mostly to the shadows, letting the flickers of gaslight slide only along one side of her dark hair and along one floral robed shoulder. "Y'know, Fin, y'still one grand hunk of a woman but with the vigor and desires of a man. I remember."

Mag's hand between Fin's legs made Fin's body remember, too. Her loins remembered the way Mag's fingers aroused Fin's deepest needs, even as those fingers were doing now.

"Go downstairs, Timmy," Mag said, her voice thick with lust. It wrapped around Fin with the heat of a sultry night.

Timmy yawned, and said, "Okay, sure, Ma."

Timmy's little boy's voice, the lad's too easy acceptance of his amputated childhood, cut through Fin's rising desire. She found the will to pull away from Mag, found the breath to say, "No, Timmy boy, you stay here. Listen, Mag, I didn't come here for no free pleasurin'. But you're right, you do owe me an' Dev a favor. But I'll collect it in information."

With a look in her eyes cunning as an alley cat, Mag said, "What sorta information? You know I don't snitch on any of my clients. I don't snitch on nobody. You know the rules aroun' here, Fin."

"Yeah, I know the rules, Mag. Those rules mighta gotten a young girl killed. Those rules mighta made a fella who goes by the name of John Jones put a bullet in his head. C'mon, Mag, you know a lot about a lotta people. I bet you hear plenty of pillow talk, so I'm here askin'—hey, what's so funny?"

Mag's thin laugh was sly as a sneer. "Johnny Jones put a bullet in his head? Hah! Never figured him as the type to do himself in. An' anyway, not with somethin' as messy as a bullet. He loved himself too much. He loved his pretty face an' sharp style. He'd never want no blood stainin' it all up."

"Yeah, well, I heard the shot," Fin said, "an' I saw the guy's bloody head an' the gun that made it that way. So you tellin' me you know this Jones, huh, Mag? Okay then, I'm collectin' on the favor that got you outta jail. Tell me what you know about him. How'd he make his dough? I hear he was some kinda actor, but I'd bet there was somethin' else goin' on underneath."

Timmy said, "Hey ma! Wasn't that the guy who tried sellin' yuh some—"

"Shhh! Be quiet, Timmy. Remember what I says about tellin' tales outta school."

Proud little Timmy Poole gave that a *tsk*. "I don't go to no school," he said. "An' besides, Fin's Miss Lawnkstrit treated me good at the p'lice station. An' she didn't take no guff from the cops, either."

Fin said, "She spoke real highly of you, too, Timmy. So, if you want to honor her, you'll help us out. You, too, Mag. We go back a long ways, you an' me." As if by a will of its own, Fin's hand reached out and stroked Mag's cheek, traced the line of her mouth, felt the afflictions Mag had suffered. All that hardship tempered Fin's mood. She spoke softly. "You know I wouldn't be askin' just to make trouble, Mag. I'm tryin' to solve some trouble. So c'mon, help me out here. Tell me about John Jones. What was it he wanted to sell?"

This time, as Mag backed away from Fin, the light caught her face, caught the suspicion in her eyes, the sneer intensifying the damage that a rough life had done to her. But when once again enveloped in shadow, Mag said with a sigh, "Girls. He tried to sell me some girls. He knew that someday I hoped to have a joint of my own. But I want something classier than the type of flesh he was sellin'. His women were all doped up. They'd be dead in six months, maybe less. They looked dead already."

Mag's description brought to Fin's mind Mr. and Mrs. Godfrey's anguish over the deterioration of their daughter's rosy, youthful beauty. How they described Pauline becoming thin, her face wan, her eyes sinking into shadows, fit to a T the ravaged appearance of a doper. Fin wondered if one of the girls Jones tried to peddle was Pauline Godfrey. But then she remembered the note in Jones's room: *I loved her.*

None of this squared in Fin's mind. *Helluva way to love someone, turning them into a dope fiend,* she thought.

"Funny thing, though," Mag said, lighting a cigarette, her voice and the match flame bringing Fin back from her musing. "Somethin' was, y'know, off with one of them girls."

Fin said, "Yeah? Off how?"

Mag thought about it through a drag on her cigarette, followed by a long blow of smoke, and finally a shrug. "I dunno, just off," she said. "Can't put my finger on it, but like she was a fish outta water, or maybe just swimmin' in the wrong stream. The other two with her, they were the usual type; y'know, trouble claimed 'em from the minute they were born. But that other one, she had, I dunno, some class, or seemed like she used to." After another drag on her cigarette, Mag gave the idea another shrug, then said, "Well maybe I'm the one swimmin' in the wrong stream. Maybe I just couldn't figure her 'cause a'the dope. That stuff does funny things to people. Cocaine makes 'em crazy, black tar makes 'em sleepy, and laudanum makes 'em just plain dull in the head. Y'know what I mean, Fin? I bet you seen it plenty before you took up with your high society lady an' left your old pals behind. Talk about bein' a fish outta water!" Mag's laugh, sharp and prickly, scratched against Fin's skin. "You can't tell me you don't miss all the old fun, Fin Donnuh."

Now Timmy was laughing, too, his boyish cackle ricocheting around the room. "Hey Fin! Remember when we tossed that old guy's pail a'beer? The *shmegeg* of a guy who didn't wanna pay my ma? I was just a little kid, but I remember how you—"

Fin cut him off, "You're still a little kid, Timmy, a little kid who should be tucked up in bed having a little kid's midnight dreams, not playin' front man for your ma's visitors."

"Aww ... why you talkin' t'me like that, Fin? Miss Lawnkstrit talked t'me better. Treated me like a man. Called me Master Poole an' everythin'."

"An' if she was here," Fin said, "she'd want you to be tucked up in bed, too. In fact, she might even do the tuckin'."

"The hell she would," Mag said, her maternal resentment snapping every word. "I'd break her haughty neck before I'd let her lay a hand on him. How I raise my boy ain't no concern of hers, or yours neither, Fin. Y'know," she added with a hand-on-her-hip swagger, "you didn't used to be so high an' mighty. I liked you better in the old days, when you were a human bein'. Now you're just a mug all duded up in fancy clothes. So if you ain't here for my services, I already gave you the favor you came for. You can just turn around an' get out, Fin Donnuh. Come around when you wanna spend money, jus' like everybody else who knocks on my door."

There was a reason Fin always liked Mag, and that reason was now on full display. It was Mag's ferocity that Fin liked: ferocious in bed, ferocious in life. It animated the beauty Mag once had, beauty which Fin thought she glimpsed again in Mag's outrage and sassy dismissal.

Fin reached into her inside jacket pocket, pulled out her wallet. "Whaddya chargin' for your time these days, Mag?"

CHAPTER NINE

Getting into bed, slipping between the cold sheets in the dark, sad room, the killer thinks, It was her or me, *and then puts all other annoying thoughts aside.*

Sleep didn't come easy to the killer. And when sleep finally came, it was neither peaceful nor satisfying. It was dull, it was dreamless, a bottomless void.

Chapter Ten

D ev, sipping a brandy in the peace and quiet of the parlor of the Irving Place apartment, didn't like what she was feeling. She didn't approve of jealousy, didn't like that it cramped the mind and spirit. Jealousy was poisonous enough when there was reason for it, but Dev believed down to her marrow that her darling Fin had been faithful to her ever since their very first kiss six years ago.

Her jealousy was irrational, and she knew it, which only made her annoyance worse. It was not jealousy rooted in the present; it was jealousy of the past, Fin's past, and the lure Dev worried it still held for her beloved. She'd seen its hold on Fin in the pleasure Fin exhibited when she'd return home from boxing matches or gambling dens. There'd been whoring in Fin's past, too, and though Dev was one hundred percent certain that Fin no longer indulged in that sordid pursuit—and she was just as certain that her own sexual awakening and her subsequently acquired skills of the flesh completely satisfied Fin—Dev could not escape the worry that the renewed presence of Black Haired Mag in Fin's life might prove a lure too ripe to resist.

The clock on the fireplace mantel only increased Dev's unease, its ceaseless tick, tick, tick as its hands passed 12:30 a.m.

and crawled toward 12:45, and Fin still not home from her visit with Mag. Dev tried not to think about what could be keeping her, hoping it was due to Fin's insistent questioning of the woman to gain vital information about John Jones, and perhaps even about Pauline Godfrey. Dev didn't want to think about that other possibility, that other temptation, the temptation that fed her irritating jealousy.

But pushing that disturbing scenario aside, another, suddenly terrifying thought invaded Dev's mind: that Fin was in trouble, that she'd fallen victim to the neighborhood's violence.

Dev shifted uneasily in the big chair. Even the brandy didn't quell her rising worry. Only her own mind and its discipline eventually helped to dispel her possibly ill advised or premature fear. After all, she reminded herself, Fin had survived a brutal youth and a life of violence Dev could but barely imagine.

Reassuring herself that Fin could handle any trouble which might befall her, Dev relaxed a bit, but only a bit. Her emotions still threatened to get the better of her, and she relied again on her discipline of mind to drain that poison from her thoughts and turn those thoughts instead to the matter of Pauline Godfrey's murder, the case suddenly more complicated by the death of John Jones.

She sipped her brandy, and swallowed with it the secret of her jealousy.

Fin was in need of a stiff drink when she stepped out of the hansom cab on Irving Place. The night had been one agony after another, starting with the agonizing interruption of her passion for Devorah by the arrival of Mr. and Mrs. Godfrey, who then brought their own agony into Fin and Devorah's happy home. And then there was the agony of John Jones's suicide. It wasn't Jones's death itself which bothered Fin; she'd seen enough violence and death to accept its presence in human existence. No, it was the manner of Jones's death. Fin thought of suicide as a predator stalking misery. She pitied anyone who fell prey to it.

By the time Fin went upstairs and arrived at the apartment door, all she could think of was Devorah. All she could see in her mind's eye was her lover's face, the passion lurking within the brilliant intelligence in her eyes. All she wanted was Dev in her arms and in their bed.

The selfishness of those desires descended on Fin like a cloak that needed laundering. She could kick herself for putting her needs above Dev's, whose night had been as vexing as Fin's. And as exhausting. And now, at nearly one o'clock in the morning, Dev was no doubt getting a well-deserved sleep. Fin hoped her lover's rest was peaceful, an escape from the night's agonies.

Fin was surprised, then, to see the parlor light on when she entered the apartment and walked down the hall. And she was surprised, and delighted, to see Devorah rush toward her as she approached the parlor. Fin was delighted, too, by Devorah's embrace, and her exclamation, "Oh my darling, you're home, and you're safe," though this last, about her safety, puzzled Fin.

In an effort to dispel Devorah's fears, whatever they were, Fin joked, "Did you think Mag was going to stick a knife in me? She was always sweet on me, y'know," Fin added with a wink.

Sliding back from the embrace, Dev looked into her lover's eyes, looked for an answer before she even asked the question, "Is she still?"

It was now Fin who stared back at Devorah. What she saw alarmed her, distressed her. Dev's usually clear and alert brown eyes were tense with pain and confusion. Dev's distress both confounded and worried Fin. And though Fin hoped to know the cause of Dev's pain, she decided that that knowledge could wait. Right now all she wanted to do was take Dev's pain away, soothe her the only way Fin knew how: with an enveloping embrace and a long, warm kiss.

Their lovemaking was exceptionally passionate, their trust in each other expressed through a lust so vigorous they pushed past any remnant bounds of constraint. Dev honored Fin by encouraging Fin's fullest desire of what she needed to take and what she needed to give. In turn, Fin brought Dev to an ecstasy so powerful she was sure Fin raised her into the realm of the gods.

When they were done, when their shouts and moans had subsided into whispers and finally into silence, neither wanted to drift into sleep but chose instead to remain entwined in serenity.

But as they lay there in the dark, the world outside crept through their bedroom window with the occasional staccato of horse carriages rolling along the cobblestone-paved street. It brought to Fin and Devorah thoughts of the night's activities, its death, its sordid lives, its secrets. For Fin, it brought, too, concern for what she'd seen earlier in Dev's eyes. "I was surprised to see you still up when I came home, my girl. What kept you from sleep?"

"You did, Lovey."

"Aw, that's sweet a'you," Fin said, and gave Dev a tender kiss on her cheek. "But you didn't have to wait up. It's been a rough night. You probably needed the rest."

"What I needed, my darling, was to be treated like a grown woman, not a child you sent home to bed. So I didn't go home to bed. I went to the Curtain Call Bar and Grill."

Stunned, Fin quickly disentangled from her beloved and sat up in bed. "You did what?"

"You heard me. I went to the Curtain Call Bar and Grill on 38th Street."

"I know where it is, and I . . ." But Fin's shock and her concern for Dev's well-being were replaced by a quiet laugh of adoration and respect for her brilliant, headstrong lover. "Well, that was right smart of you, my girl. Sure, John Jones was in the theatrical profession—"

"Yes, he was an actor, who it turns out was a womanizer, or so I learned from my chat with four theatrical women."

"The womanizer part's no surprise. What else did they say?"

"They told me he was a terrible actor who didn't get much stage work. But they told me a good deal more, too, whether they meant to or not. They revealed quite a bit about themselves and their relationships to Jones. Listen, Lovey," Dev said, sitting up now beside Fin and enjoying the intimacy the darkened bedroom gave to their conversation. "I learned two things which put a rather different blush on the deaths of Pauline Godfrey and John Jones. First of all, at least two of the women had romantic and definitely sexual entanglements with Jones, and those two—and possibly others among the four—knew about his affair with Pauline Godfrey."

"Hunh. So a jealousy angle might figure into it," Fin said. "Jealousy can sure inflame the senses an' cause a helluva lotta rage."

Moments ago, Dev savored the intimacy of the darkened bedroom. Now the dark gave her refuge, concealing from Fin Dev's wince of humiliation for her own earlier bout of unwarranted jealousy. The dark kept her secret. "The other things these women told me," she said, finding additional solace in getting back to business, "which really twists the case around, is that none of them believe Mr. Jones was capable of love for Pauline or anyone else. And they're not convinced he'd take his own life. Which brings us to the possibility—"

"That Jones didn't put the bullet in his brain and he didn't write that note."

The lovers said nothing for a few moments while they absorbed the significance of what Fin just said, tossing its complications over and over in their minds.

75

The darkness which wrapped them in passion earlier, and which gave Dev refuge, now seemed to hinder clarity of thought. Typical of the harmony of their lives, they both reached for their respective bedside lamps and switched them on. The light of the peach-shaded lamps swept the darkness aside, exposing to Fin and Devorah the mixed expressions of bafflement and curiosity on each of their faces.

"If someone else was in Jones's room," Fin said, speaking slowly as if searching not just for words but for thought itself, "they must've gotten out by the window an' they must've done it fast like. If that's the case—"

"Yes, *if* that's the case."

"—we're talkin' about one slick operator, probably a professional; y'know, like a second story man."

"Or woman."

"Or woman," Fin said with a touch of humor and a twinkle in her eye. "Anyway, if it *was* a jealousy killin', then maybe one of them actresses you spoke to got even by killin' Jones an' his current paramour, Pauline Godfrey. Maybe one of them got in an' out of Jones's window. Actresses can be pretty athletic when the parts they play call for it."

"I won't ask how you know, Lovey," Dev said with a playful tease in her voice. "But it seems you are indeed popular among the theatrical set, especially with one Suzanne Silver. Or maybe you knew her as Suzanne Sawdy?"

"Now there's a name I ain't heard in a long while, but sure, I know Suzanne, or I did. She was one of the women you spoke to at the Curtain Call? Hunh. Small world."

To Dev's ear, attuned to every nuance of her beloved's way of speaking, there was a leeriness in Fin's voice, something unfriendly in the way she said the woman's name.

With a shrug, Fin continued, "We grew up on the same streets, but Suzanne always thought she was better'n everybody else, even though her old man worked on the docks, just like a lotta guys in the neighborhood. But Suzanne had bigger dreams than scratchin' out a dockside life. I guess she's still dreamin'.."

"I'd say she hasn't changed much," Dev said. "She was somewhat belligerent in her attitude tonight."

"Oh sure, that's Suzanne Sawdy, all right. Back in the old neighborhood we'd say she had a sweet face and a sour heart. But it's been a few years since I seen her, so why'd my name come up?"

"Because of me," Dev said. "She recognized my name. She knew of my association with you."

"I didn't know we were that famous."

"Infamous seems to be the prevailing opinion. But tell me, would you say Suzanne's the jealous type?"

"Y'mean jealous enough to commit murder? I dunno," Fin said. "I wouldn't put anything past her. Was she one of the women who'd had flings with Jones?"

"She didn't say. But Mary O'Connor and Katherine Hazelton certainly had affairs with our Mr. Jones. Both of them were pretty upset about his death," Dev said. "And Miss O'Connor even offered the idea that there was a softer side to Jones, a lonely side. None of the other women bought it, but who knows? So here is where it becomes even more interesting: it was suggested by another of the group, a woman who calls herself by the ridiculous name of Sylvie LaRose, that Jones gave the eye to all of the women at one time or another. So I'd say the jealousy angle played a starring role at that table."

"Bears lookin' into," Fin said. "Good work, my love."

"Thank you. But what about your night?" The closeness of Fin's body, the warmth of her lover's sturdy shoulder against her own, provided Dev with enough emotional armor to ask, "What about Maggie Poole? Did you learn anything useful from her? Did she know John Jones?"

Fin was no fool. She could hear Dev's effort to speak with ease. And now that the bedside lamps were lit, Fin could see

Dev's eyes. Remnants of Dev's earlier pain and confusion, though diminished and obscure, lingered. Fin didn't understand then, but she believed she understood now. "Is that really what you wanna ask me, my love?"

Jolted by the question, Dev couldn't stop herself from shrinking slightly away from Fin. "Are you really going to make me ask it?"

"Yup, I am," Fin said. "I want you to ask it so you can get rid of it, an' so I can answer you honestly, the way I've answered every question you ever asked about my life, the good an' the bad."

Without the darkness to shield her, Dev knew it was useless to hide from the issue or from Fin's challenge to face it. "All right," she finally said, the two words of preamble allowing her a moment to rally. "You said that Mag was once sweet on you. Is she still? I mean, she was part of your old life, and I know that parts of that life still have an allure for you. Is Maggie Poole part of that allure?"

The essence of love that's painful, that hurts when your beloved hurts, twisted through Fin, tangling around her soul like tentacles squeezing out all joy. She wrapped her arms around Dev, held her close, giving solace to her lover and finding solace in Dev's warmth. Fin stroked Dev's hair, kissed her cheek, and then looked directly into Dev's eyes. She spoke softly. "If Maggie Poole is sweet on me, she's sweet on the scoundrel I used to be. She really doesn't know the Fin I am now, an' wouldn't like me if she did. So rest easy, my love. You're the only woman for me. If t'night didn't prove it," Fin said with a nod to the bed, "then nothin' will. You are my paradise."

"And you are mine. Thank you, Fin Donner."

Fin moved close for a kiss, but Dev, with a light laugh of reluctance, pushed her away. "Much as I'd enjoy another rousing tumble with you, my dear sweet Fin, we have clients who've hired us to find their daughter's murderer, so it's time to get back to the business of Donner & Longstreet Inquiries."

"If we must," Fin said through a sigh of thwarted lust.

"Yes, we must. All right, now tell me: did Mag say anything useful? Did she know John Jones?"

"Yeah, she knew him. It seems the fella got around."

"He was one of her clients then?"

"Probably, now and then I'd wager. But he tried to make a business deal with her. He tried to sell her some women. Y'know, set up a stable. But Mag didn't buy."

The mere mention of Jones trading in flesh, of selling women as if they were meat off the rack for the tastes of men, nauseated Dev. She had to push the nausea back before she was able to say, "Good for her. Maybe Miss Maggie Poole is more honorable than I've given her credit for."

"She's got her own brand of it," Fin said. "But honor had nothin' to do with Mag turnin' Jones down. She was sure the women had been doped up. She said they looked like they was already on their way to the coffin. An' the way she described one of the women, she might've been talkin' about Pauline Godfrey. So if that's true, if Jones had been turning Pauline into a dope fiend—"

Dev picked up the thread, "Then the doubts expressed by the women at the Curtain Call saloon about Jones being in love have some merit."

With a nod of agreement, Fin said, "Funny thing, but Mag said as much, too. An' she was just as sure Jones wouldn't put a gun to his head. Accordin' to Mag, the guy thought too much of himself to mess up his pretty face. So what is it we got here, my girl? Did Jones kill Pauline an' then someone did him in? Or did someone kill 'em both? Are we talkin' about two different killin's or a double murder?"

"Whatever it is we're talking about, Lovey, detective Coyle is going to have a hard time kicking it aside now."

"Well, that's his problem," Fin said with a playful leer and a long, tender stroke of Dev's breasts. "I have my own problem, a problem only Miss Devorah Longstreet can solve."

"Oh, I shall do my best. Let me just turn off the light."

"No, leave it on."

CHAPTER ELEVEN

Even a murderer must see to one's needs. Daily life needs attending. Life's daily tasks allowed the killer to move through society without anyone noticing, without anyone aware of the malice at the core of the killer's soul. Life's simplest tasks mask the bitterest secrets.

On this gray, drizzly morning, after an ordinary breakfast, the killer went shopping.

CHAPTER TWELVE

I t wasn't easy for Fin to convince Devorah not to accompany her to Hell's Kitchen, to the sordid streets where Fin grew up. Though Dev had been to the neighborhood before— once early in her relationship with Fin as a way to introduce Dev to her lover's past, and a second time on her own for a more objective experience of the impoverished, crime-infested area where the throaty bellow of ships' horns floated like a dirge from the river—this morning Fin thought it better to return to Hell's Kitchen alone. In the end, after a discussion of the logic of Fin's decision and its benefits to Donner & Longstreet's investigation into the death of Pauline Godfrey, Dev reluctantly agreed. Fin would afterward return home and they'd continue the investigation together.

Thus, a little after ten o'clock on a wet, gray morning, which only made the rundown neighborhood of soot-stained brownstones, sagging wooden hovels, and smoke-belching factories drearier, Fin knocked on the door of the Sawdy family's tenement apartment on West 50th Street, two blocks from the West Side docks.

The sour smell of boiled cabbage and vinegar wafted around Fin when Mrs. Maeve Sawdy opened the door. In the gloom of the tenement hallway, everything about Maeve Sawdy was gray: her shabby dress hanging limp to her ankles on her thin body, the stained apron over her dress, her lined, papery skin, her mood. Her gray hair, pulled back in a loose bun, framed a face slightly reminiscent of her daughter's girl-next-door prettiness, but was devoid of the latter's vivacity. Mrs. Maeve Sawdy was too tired for vivacity—tired of endless toil, of endless poverty, tired of the endless savagery of life in Hell's Kitchen. But there was a sudden glint in her watery brown eyes when she saw who stood in her doorway.

"Hello, Maeve," Fin said.

"Well, if it ain't Fin Donner. I see y'voice still sounds like y'swallowed rocks," Maeve said in a dockside accent even thicker than Fin's. "I heard you escaped th'Kitchen, you lucky so-'n-so. An' by the look 'a you, I'd say y'done right well f'yourself. So why y'crazy enough t'come back here?"

"I'm lookin' for Suzanne," Fin said. "I need to talk to her. She still livin' here?"

"Talk t'her 'bout what?" Maeve Sawdy's eyes narrowed, the glint gone. "She in trouble? Wouldn't surprise me. She always was one t'push things too far, remember, Fin? But I ain't gonna make her trouble worse. She's still my daughter. An' ever since my Bill passed on, I need the few dollars Suzanne sometimes gives me. I don't ask how she earns it."

"Sorry t'hear about Bill. My condolences, Maeve. I hope he went peaceful like."

Maeve's *tsk* was bitter enough to curdle the already sour air. "He bought it in a bad way," she said. "Got in th'middle of a dockside brawl. Someone clubbed him over th'head bad enough t'crack his skull but not bad enough t'kill him quick. Took the poor bastard three days t'die. But you ain't here 'bout my troubles, Fin, so what's y'business with Suzanne?"

Maeve's hard luck story weighed on Fin like a boulder pressing the air out of her lungs. It made it hard to tell Maeve one of the lousiest things a mother can hear: that her daughter might be involved in a murder, maybe two murders. Another angle was called for, one with greater kindness for the mother of Suzanne Sawdy. "I don't know if Suzanne's in trouble, Maeve, but if she is I can help her out. Y'know, for old times sake. But I can't help her if I don't talk to her. So where is she? Is she inside, or workin' somewhere?"

"She don't live here no more, Fin. She escaped th'Kitchen, too. Wants t'be a big deal actress. Well, good luck t'her, I say. Just as long as she doesn't forget her poor ol' mother. But y'mean it about helpin' her out?"

"If I can, Maeve."

"Well, okay then, Suzanne lives at a boardin' house over on the East Side. Y'want her address? It'll cost y'a fiver."

Mrs. Hilda Neumann was a stern woman. She hadn't always been stern. As a young woman she'd had a sunny disposition, but life was hard after the death of her husband twelve years ago. He'd left her with debts and a mortgage in arrears on their house on East 87th Street in the working class neighborhood of Yorkville. In order to stave off eviction and keep the roof over her head, the widow Hilda Neumann turned the narrow three-story brick-faced house into a boarding residence for women. That was when she learned to be stern. Keeping New York's young women respectable, at least on the face of it so as not to attract the sort of attention which could result in loss of rents, required a strong backbone and a stern temperament.

Thus, Mrs. Hilda Neumann, a meaty woman with straw-colored braids coiled on either side of her head, was at her most stern when her noontime lunch was interrupted with the arrival of Fin Donner and Devorah Longstreet at her front door. To her mind, the Longstreet woman, elegantly attired in a brown wool cloak and a veiled riding hat, seemed respectable at first glance. Her association with this Fin Donner, however, a person of indeterminate description in a boater hat and manly coat and trousers, lowered Mrs. Neumann's opinion of Dev. Even the calling card Dev handed her gave Mrs. Neumann pause: *Donner & Longstreet Inquiries* indeed. Mrs. Neumann held busybodies in low esteem.

"Please, may we come in?" Dev said. "The weather is damp and our business is urgent."

"And just what is the nature of your business?" Mrs. Neumann said, her words tinged with the German accent common to the neighborhood.

"We'd like to speak with one of your boarders, a Miss Suzanne Silver."

"There's no one here by that name. Now, good day to you both." She started to close the door.

Dev held it open. "Perhaps you know her as Suzanne Sawdy."

"Oh, that one," Mrs. Neumann said. Dev's request to see the Sawdy woman, the actress, a practitioner of a profession Mrs. Neumann didn't particularly approve of, only deepened Mrs. Neumann's distaste for the peculiar couple at her door. Her posture now rigid, she said, "Well, what do you want with her? I won't allow any illicit doings in my house."

"Rest assured, madam," Dev said in her most soothing tone, "we are here on an honorable errand—"

"We're here," Fin interrupted, her patience with Mrs. Neumann worn thin, "to speak with Suzanne Sawdy." With that, Fin gently took Dev's arm and walked forcefully past Mrs. Neumann and into the vestibule of the house. "If I'm not mistaken, Miss Sawdy lives on the third floor."

Unlike the Sawdy apartment in Hell's Kitchen, Mrs. Neumann's house didn't smell of boiled cabbage and vinegar. Instead, it had the heavy smell of boiled sausage and the sharp sting of hot mustard. The aroma followed Fin and Devorah up the carpeted stairs, past the second-floor landing and onto the third floor hallway, a dim and dreary passage with one small window to the street and a single flickering gas lamp wall sconce, the flame low. In the thin light, the roses on the floral wallpaper looked dead.

Of the two rooms on this floor, Suzanne's was the one at the rear, the cheaper one, a room which wouldn't face the street but would likely overlook a back courtyard used for garbage cans and laundry lines.

Fin's knock on the door brought an impatient, "I'm busy, Mrs. Neumann! Whatever you want has to wait until later."

"It ain't Mrs. Neumann," Fin said. "It's Fin Donner and Devorah—"

The door opened before Fin could finish. Suzanne Silver stood in the doorway, for that's who opened the door, a young woman dressed in a crisp white shirtwaist and deep purple gabardine skirt, not the mismatched, patched hand-me-downs which were once upon a time the attire of Suzanne Sawdy. Her blond hair, arranged in pert curls atop her head, with a few slender strands falling along either side of her heart-shaped face, attracted what little light flickered from the hallway's wall sconce, providing an aura of youthful glow. Smiling a self-satisfied smile, she said, "After last night's chat with Miss Longstreet at the Curtain Call, I figured you two would come around sooner or later. And by the way, how'd you find me? I didn't hand Miss Longstreet my address." And then suddenly understanding, she looked quickly at Fin. "Oh, sure, you must've bribed my Ma. How much she take you for, Fin?"

"A fiver. She looked like she could use it."

Suzanne's laugh was sharp and quick, crinkling her girl-next-door looks into something coarser. "You were robbed, my old friend! She would've sold me out for two. Well, I guess you two had better come in."

Even with the shade on the single window up, the room

was gloomy, made more so by its tiny space cramped by a bed, an armoire, a chest of drawers, and a large chair upholstered in threadbare green velvet.

Fin led Dev to the chair. Suzanne, annoyed that the chair she'd wanted for herself had been thus claimed, hastily cleared a place on the bed and sat down, pushing aside a hat box and two garment boxes with the Siegel-Cooper Sixth Avenue department store monogram.

Fin said, "You sure high-classed yourself since the old days, Suzanne," with a glance at the department store boxes. "You even talk different."

"A lady of the theater can't sound like a street urchin," Suzanne said, affecting an aristocratic attitude which wasn't entirely successful. "So I took elocution lessons. Might be something you should look into, Fin."

"I ain't figurin' on joinin' the theater crowd. Anyway, you're lookin' well, Suzanne. You must be in the chips. Siegel-Cooper's ain't cheap."

"And worth every penny. I have an audition this afternoon at the Garrick Theater," Suzanne said. "That's the big time. It could be my big break, and I want to look just right for the part. So I did a bit of shopping this morning, okay? Besides, what's it to you?"

"Settle down, Suzanne," Fin said. "Like I told your Ma, we ain't here to make trouble, but maybe you're worried 'cause you already got trouble."

That brought an indignant Suzanne to her feet. In the tiny room, she was close enough to Fin to poke a wagging finger in her shoulder. "Now just a damn minute, Fin Donner. Y'can't pin that business 'bout Johnny Jones on me." Suzanne's frustration frayed her newly crafted manner of speech, returning the syllables to their rougher origin. Aware that Hell's Kitchen had escaped her lips, Suzanne Sawdy took a deep breath to restore her Suzanne Silver persona before she spoke again. "After all, that's what you two are here about, right? That's what your lady friend was asking about last night."

Dev said, "Please, sit down, Miss Silver. No one is trying to pin anything on you. We're here because you might have insight into the situation leading to Mr. Jones's death, and perhaps even the murder of Miss Godfrey."

With a less than friendly though not entirely hostile look at Dev, Suzanne sat down again on the bed. "Look, I haven't seen Johnny in months," she said. "I didn't mention it last night, not in front of those two crybabies O'Connor and Hazelton, but sure, Johnny and I had a fling. But who hasn't? I knew our affair meant nothing to him. It didn't mean much to me, either. Just a few good times with a handsome beau, though to tell you the truth, he could be sweet when he wanted to. But believe me, there's been a number of other handsome beaus since Johnny. So if you think I was pining for him, you're—"

Dev interrupted, "What about Miss Hazelton? Or Miss O'Connor? They seemed considerably upset last night about Mr. Jones's death. Were either of them jealous of Miss Godfrey?"

"Jealous enough to kill, you mean?" Suzanne smiled when she said it, as if she enjoyed the question. "Well, Sylvie hinted as much, didn't she?"

Dev pressed, "And do you agree?"

"I can't say," came on a shrug.

Fin, tired of Suzanne's evasions, took over. "This ain't the Kitchen, Suzanne. The game's played different out here. Back in the Kitchen, the code is to clam up 'bout everything. But out here, there's times to clam up an' there's times to spill. This is one of the times to spill. Because if you don't, an' the coppers get wind that you knew Johnny Jones—"

Suzanne was fast off the bed again. "And who's gonna tell 'em?" she said, her speech slipping back into its old gutter habits. "You, Fin? Boy oh boy, y'really forgot where y'came from. This fancy Miss Longstreet sure turned y'inside out."

"You misunderstand, Miss Silver," Dev said, hoping to calm the woman. "We're not here to, well, snitch on you. You might say we're here to protect you. Sooner or later the police will have to deal with Mr. Jones's death, and they'll find their way to anyone who knew him. That will put you in their sights, Miss Silver. But if you cooperate with us, we can perhaps steer them in another direction. The choice is yours."

Sitting down again, lips pursed and her hands balled in fists in her lap, Suzanne said, "Well, that's . . . that's more like it. I don't owe those two harpies anything. They've been tight with their audition notices, so why not throw 'em to the wolves. So if you ask me, yeah, sure, they could kill; well, maybe not O'Connor. The woman's got no oomph, if you know what I mean, no do-or-die spunk. That's why she'll never make it big in the theater. But that phony Miss Demure, Katherine Hazelton, she's another story. She'd push another girl out of the way even for a part so small that one blink and you'd miss her entrance and exit from the stage. So, sure, if she could kill for a part I bet she could kill for a man. Good old Kissable Kate. The woman's got a temper on her that could flatten the tower atop Madison Square Garden."

"And would you say she's athletic?"

"Athletic? Like some sort of sportswoman or something?"

"Yes, like that."

"Well, she played a circus girl in a vaudeville act for a while. Had to learn to somersault and climb up ropes and things."

Fin said, "What about you, Suzanne? I remember you were pretty spry as a kid."

"I'm still spry," she said with pride. "In fact, I've been taking dancing lessons to get ready for this audition. I can twirl and leap like a regular ballerina. Now look, I can't dawdle with you two any longer." Getting up from the bed, Suzanne went to the door, opened it, looked at Fin and Devorah with the affected air of a fancy hostess, and said, "I have to get ready for that audition, so if you don't mind, get lost."

Back outside, the damp day had grown grayer, darker, the mist more chill. The street had more the appearance of a dreary, oncoming night than an early afternoon in springtime. The narrow two- and three-story houses seemed to shrink from the raw air behind their brick or brownstone skins. Gaslight, and a few electric lamps, suddenly appeared in windows to stave off the drear.

Horses shivered as much as the drivers of the carts the beasts pulled along the slick, wet cobblestones. Pedestrians lowered their heads against the damp. Men's derbies were pulled low. Women's flowered and feathered hats went limp in the moist air.

Dev pulled her cloak tighter. Fin turned up the collar of her coat. The wet weather, though, did not dampen their spirits. On the contrary, the bracing chill sharpened their thoughts.

With Dev on her arm as they walked along 87th Street, Fin said, "So, my girl, any conclusions?"

"I'm certain Miss Silver was not as forthcoming about her relationship to Mr. Jones as she could have been, and I think she was a bit *too* forthcoming about Katherine Hazelton. Still, Miss Hazelton did exhibit an overabundance of tenderness last night for Mr. Jones and a clear displeasure about his involvement with Pauline Godfrey. That she has an athletic talent makes her a prime candidate for slipping in and out of Jones's window and down the fire escape or perhaps down the drainpipe to the street."

"Sure, but Suzanne's dancin' lessons could mean that she could do that, too."

"True enough," Dev said, enjoying, as she always did, the puzzle-solving banter with Fin. "And I think it's time for another chat with Mr. and Mrs. Godfrey. Perhaps they heard

Pauline mention one of those women. Hail us a cab, Lovey, and we'll pay them a visit."

"You'll do better with the Godfreys without me. I think they don't approve of me," Fin said, her smile mischievous. "Meantime, I'll do some poking aroun' down at the Curtain Call Bar an' Grill to try to get Katherine Hazelton's address. We can meet back at home."

"Excellent. We can have a lovely dinner and discuss the day's findings."

"An' after dinner we don't have to discuss anything at all." Fin's smile was no longer mischievous. It was absolutely carnal. Dev loved it.

Chapter Thirteen

The mercantile establishment of William R. Godfrey Fabrics & Notions boasted a gold-lettered sign above a large storefront on Sixth Avenue between West 15th and 16th Streets in the heart of the Ladies Mile. The area earned its name from the preponderance of shops catering to women's fashion needs. There were shops featuring hats exclusively, stores that sold shoes, establishments which featured evening wear, emporiums which specialized in day wear or tailored shirtwaists for the modern woman who ventured outside the home to work in offices and other non-domestic venues. The Siegel-Cooper department store was nearby, the gargantuan new store where Suzanne Silver just this morning shopped for new clothes.

The Godfreys' shop, like so many along Sixth Avenue, occupied the street floor of a multistory building hosting offices or small manufacturing concerns.

Even now, on this dreary and damp day, when the ornate facades of the shops and the buildings above them looked more like melting fancy cakes than sturdy structures of iron and stone, women crowded the avenue. As the women moved from shop to shop, their cloaks and long skirts blew around them and their hands secured flowered and feathered hats against the stiff breeze that came with the passing of each clattering train on the Sixth Avenue elevated line overhead.

Before going in, Dev paused to look into the Godfrey store's two large display windows, one on each side of the entrance. She wanted to see what John Jones may have observed when he looked into the shop window and first saw Pauline Godfrey within.

Starting with the window to the left of the entry door, Dev looked past the artfully displayed swaths of fabrics and sewing supplies, the colorful and patterned fabrics adding a festive note to the gray day. The display, arranged in tiers, occupied most of the window, allowing Dev to see only slivers of the store beyond.

The window to the right of the entrance allowed a better view. Its display of ribbons and laces was smaller in scale, and Dev was able to see a sales counter and a wall of shelves on the right-hand side of the store. Perhaps that was where Pauline Godfrey had been when Mr. Jones first saw her through the window. Today, though, it was Mrs. Godfrey, in a navy blue apron over a fussy, ruffled yellow blouse and a dark brown skirt, who was behind the counter. She compared lengths of ribbon with several bolts of fabric for a woman fashionably dressed in a green cloak and a green hat with a broad brim. Dev recognized the woman's outfit as superior quality, possibly custom designed and sewn, or at least purchased from one of the city's better shops. It was clear to Dev that the Godfreys' store catered to an affluent clientele.

Nostalgia, unexpected and unwanted, overcame Dev when she wondered if perhaps her own mother, or her mother's seamstress, had selected dress fabrics or laces from this shop.

Such thoughts and feelings were not only painful but unhelpful in the present circumstance, and Dev forced them from her mind. She was here to investigate the horror of murder, and for that she'd need razor-sharp thinking. She thus shifted her observation from the fashionable woman in green to Mrs.

Godfrey. Frankly, Dev was surprised to see Mrs. Godfrey here at all. The poor woman had just yesterday lost her daughter to a vicious crime, and yet here she was, cheerfully discussing ribbons with a customer. Then again, Dev thought maybe a more charitable assessment was required. Perhaps engagement with work helped Mrs. Godfrey handle her grief lest it crush her.

Dev walked into the store.

Inside, she encountered a veritable fantasia of fabric. Along the walls, bolts of cotton, linen, satin, wool and silk rested on shelves of polished walnut reaching almost to the ceiling. The fabrics' colors and patterns glowed in the light of the store's electric lamps, though punctuated here and there, like harsh reminders of life's bleak moments, with bolts of black bombazine, an old-fashioned fabric still used for mourning. Bolts of delicate lace were also graced by the light, and spools of colorful ribbon glowed. Anchoring the spacious shop were sales counters on either side of a center aisle and a central counter at the back with an ornate brass cash register.

Besides the well-dressed woman in green attended by Mrs. Godfrey, a woman in a purple cloak and peach hat was at the cash register, purchasing floral fabric from Mr. Godfrey. He was jacketless, the sleeves of his white shirt held in place by black garters. He was neither cheerful, like Mrs. Godfrey, nor dour, just a drab cypher amid the colorful surroundings. His jowly pear-shaped face was merely businesslike as he took the woman's cash, counted it carefully, rang it up in the register, and then bid the woman good day as she left the shop. Perhaps, Dev decided, this blandness of attitude, and fastidious attention to cash, was Mr. Godfrey's way of handling his grief.

Dev's entrance brought a change of expression to Mr. and Mrs. Godfrey's countenances: Mr. Godfrey's blandness was replaced by sad interest; Mrs. Godfrey's cheerfulness gave way to tightly controlled misery.

Clearly, Dev's arrival had upset the fragile balance the couple maintained in order to get through their day.

The woman examining ribbon with Mrs. Godfrey, sensing a change in the air, abandoned her interest in ribbons and made her exit.

When she was gone, the store was suddenly quiet as a tomb, the mood tense as a stretched tendon. Mr. Godfrey broke the silence by clearing his throat before saying, "Miss Longstreet, what brings you to us? Have you something to report so soon?"

"Yes, there has been a development," Dev said. "And I have a question as well. Mrs. Godfrey, perhaps you should turn the sign on the door to *Closed* and then join me and your husband at the center counter where we three can converse more easily and away from any prying eyes through the window."

Mrs. Godfrey's "All right," was tight, her voice ragged. The traces of past beauty Dev saw on the woman's birdlike visage last evening seemed gray as dust today.

After turning the sign, Mrs. Godfrey went to join Devorah and Mr. Godfrey at the center counter. Along the way, she lifted the bolts of fabric she'd shown to the woman in green and put them on their shelves, climbing the rolling ladder to reach an upper shelf. Once down again, she took a handkerchief from a pocket of her apron and dabbed her eyes.

Dev's heart ached for the woman. Evidently the tears Mrs. Godfrey had kept under control by immersing herself in the business of the shop were now threatening to pour forth. Mrs. Godfrey's coiled stiffness as she walked through the shop led Dev to believe that the woman was exercising a supreme effort to keep from collapsing in grief.

"First of all," Dev said gently when Mrs. Godfrey joined her husband behind the center counter, "I have news which changes the nature of the investigation. The news concerns John Jones."

Upon hearing Dev speak Jones's name, Mr. Godfrey, his jowly face tense, his cheeks flushed, looked at Dev with dread, while Mrs. Godfrey looked at Dev as if she'd uttered an obscenity.

95

Mr. Godfrey said, "What about Mr. Jones?" There was challenge in his voice, daring Dev to say anything other than what he wanted to hear: that John Jones was guilty of murdering the Godfreys' precious daughter and was now or soon would be in the custody of the police.

Firmly, but kindly, Dev said, "I'm afraid Mr. Jones is dead. And it appears, though it is not certain, that he committed suicide."

Mr. Godfrey bellowed, "Suicide?! Why would he? I mean, such people don't—"

"Suicide cuts across all classes, Mr. Godfrey," Dev said, still kindly but dismissing Mr. Godfrey's attitude toward classes of people other than his own. "And suicide is often the result of a broken heart, which might be the case here. A note was found with Mr. Jones's body, a note professing his love. There is reason to believe the note referred to Pauline."

Mr. Godfrey's "No," had the sound and weight of a thud. "I refuse to believe that a man such as Mr. Jones is capable of loving anyone but himself."

"Actually, you are not alone in that assumption, Mr. Godfrey," Dev said. "I spoke to four young women last evening who expressed the same opinion. And it is that, along with the questionable manner of Mr. Jones's death, which puts the wrinkle into the investigation. If the suicide note was not written by Mr. Jones, then who wrote it? It does indeed put his suicide in question."

"Are you suggesting that Mr. Jones was murdered?" Mr. Godfrey nearly gagged on his own question.

"That is a possibility," Dev said, "though the killer would have to be a rather spry individual to get into and out of Mr. Jones's room through a second-story window unseen and unheard."

Mrs. Godfrey blurted an amused snicker to this information, a response Dev found unsettling but oddly understandable. Grief and taut nerves can skew one's response to unexpected news.

Whatever Mrs. Godfrey found amusing, Mr. Godfrey did not. His countenance, already dour, now stiffened with impatience. "You mentioned that you have a question for us, Miss Longstreet. Please, ask it now and let us get it over with. We are already mourning our daughter, and my wife and I cannot take many more shocks today. And besides, customers have gathered at our door, wondering why we are closed. I do not wish to leave money out on the street."

"Yes, we must get back to business," Mrs. Godfrey said. "We are working people, Miss Longstreet. We keep an eye on every penny, as we must. The price I paid for groceries this morning was scandalous."

"All right," Dev said. "My question concerns the young women I spoke to last evening. Perhaps Pauline mentioned any or all of them. Do the names Mary O'Connor, Sylvie LaRose, Katherine Hazelton or Suzanne Silver mean anything to you? Or maybe you know Miss Silver as Suzanne Sawdy?"

Mr. Godfrey, his head tilted to one side in thought, said, "No. I don't recall those names. How about you, my dear?" he asked his wife.

"Never heard of them," Mrs. Godfrey said. "Who are they?"

"They are . . . or rather were . . . friends of Mr. Jones's."

"You mean his hussies," Mrs. Godfrey said.

Dev let that pass. Defending the four women would be useless in the face of Mrs. Godfrey's disdain. And though Dev did not share Mrs. Godfrey's opinion of the women, she had to admit that Mrs. Godfrey had reason to consider any woman connected to John Jones unsavory.

Mr. Godfrey said, "Do you believe these women had any connection to Pauline?"

"One or two may have known her, or at least been aware of her."

"Were they aware, then, of the reason for Pauline's declining health?"

97

"No, they would not have been in any position to assess Pauline's health. Perhaps the police surgeon's autopsy will shed light on that." Dev hoped it would. She hoped not to be the bearer of the awful news that Jones might have turned their daughter into a dope fiend only to peddle her into prostitution. An autopsy confirming Pauline's drug addiction would likely satisfy the Godfreys' suspicions about their daughter's deterioration by the machinations of John Jones. They'd already assigned him guilt in that matter. But the idea of their daughter being sold like so much meat off the rack might be too much for them to bear.

"Oh, the autopsy!" Mr. Godfrey said. "We've already been told the results of the autopsy, and rather brusquely, I might add."

"Indeed? By whom?"

"The report was delivered to us at home early this morning by a uniformed officer who knew nothing of its contents. He only said he was instructed by the police surgeon's office to deliver it."

"Well, I must say that was quick work. May I see it?"

Were it not for Mr. Godfrey's jowls, Dev thought he looked like a schoolboy who hadn't done his lessons. "I'm so sorry, Miss Longstreet, we left the report at home. We didn't know you'd be coming by the shop today."

"I see. Well, can you tell me what it said? At least the general drift of the surgeon's findings?"

No longer the sheepish schoolboy but a man annoyed at the state of things, Mr. Godfrey said, "What was in the report was insignificant compared to what was not in it. It only confirmed that Pauline died from a cut to the throat which severed the carotid artery and jugular vein. It did not address her deteriorated health. There was nothing in the report about that. Nothing at all. Miss Longstreet, it seems to me that the surgeon's office was not only hasty in its examination of Pauline's body but they are being as dismissive of this case as the police department. What is going on here?"

"I don't have an answer for you, Mr. Godfrey, but I agree that something regarding Mr. Jones is being swept under the rug. And I assure you that Fin and I will do our utmost to get to the bottom of it. We don't like being given the runaround by the authorities any more than you do. In the meantime, now that the police surgeon has completed his report, has his office released Pauline's body for burial?"

Mr. Godfrey, his shoulders slumped, his head bowed in unbearable grief, said, "Yes. She was delivered to the McAuley Funeral Parlor a little while ago. Arrangements are being made for her funeral."

"I'm sure that you and Mrs. Godfrey are anxious to put your daughter to her final rest," Dev said, "but perhaps you should contact the funeral home and tell them to refrain from embalming the body just yet, and not make any other preparations for burial while you engage the services of a private physician to perform a more thorough autopsy."

With an eyebrow raised as if he'd never heard of such a thing, Mr. Godfrey said, "A private autopsy? Wouldn't that incur additional expense?"

This constant reference to money was wearing on Devorah's sensibilities, though a second thought brought to mind Mr. Godfrey's hard work in building his business and the attention to accounting for every penny the enterprise certainly required. These were lessons Dev had to learn after her banishment from her family's privileged world of inherited, unearned wealth. Thus, with kindliness, Dev said, "You and Mrs. Godfrey deserve to have all of your questions answered regarding the cause of Pauline's deteriorated health. With your permission, I can arrange for an examination by an excellent physician who is doing remarkable work in the growing science of forensics."

The pain in Mr. Godfrey's eyes, his pain at the idea of having his precious daughter's young body cut and prodded yet again, tore at Dev. She could only assume Mrs. Godfrey's reaction was just as mournful, since the woman's face was buried in her husband's shoulder.

Wiping a tear from his eye, Mr. Godfrey, his voice weak, said, "Yes, perhaps you are right, Miss Longstreet. Another autopsy couldn't hurt." He winced at these last words, their irony breaking his heart.

The daytime bartender in the men's saloon at the Curtain Call Bar and Grill, a plump fellow with a thick red handlebar mustache on his lip but thinning hair on his pate, was wiping the shine on the dark-walnut bar when Fin walked in. After a better look at Fin as she neared, the fellow stopped his wiping. He just stared at her. It was not a friendly stare.

His weren't the only eyes on Fin. She felt the stares of the men who sat at the little marble tables or leaned on the bar, one foot on the brass rail, while they quaffed their mugs of beer. Fin assumed that many of these fellows were actors and others in the theatrical profession who frequented the saloon. Their gaze, full of curiosity and derisive humor, followed her across the room.

Such stares had ceased to rattle her years ago. These days she was merely amused, though with an undertone of alertness. Attacks by drunks or even just the tipsy were never out of the question.

Today's crowd, in Fin's opinion, were less likely to engage in fisticuffs and more likely to sniff enviously at Fin's fine tailoring, a luxury these often out of work actors could rarely afford but aspired to.

The bartender, on the other hand, was another matter. A sizable fellow with meaty hands, he looked like he could easily pick up one of the brass spittoons in front of the bar and throw it at her. Fin was sure he'd done his share of tossing the unruly or the unwanted from the saloon. Fin was also sure the man assigned her to the latter category.

She understood through experience that the best preventative against getting the toss was, as always, money. She put a ten-dollar gold piece on the bar, ordered a mug of beer for herself, and announced, "an' rounds all afternoon for everyone. Buy one for yourself, too," she told the bartender. The theater crowd which had held her in contempt moments ago now cheered.

The barkeep, though, was not so easily mollified. After filling a mug, leveling the foam on top and placing it in front of Fin, he said, "I've seen all kinds," through a voice full of New York music. "Even seen the likes of you. I don't usually let 'em hang around, but that ten-dollar eagle buys you drinkin' time and the goodwill of the customers. But it don't buy you my goodwill. So drink your beer and get lost."

"You look like a smart fella," Fin said. "You really think I wandered in here for your watery beer? Guess again, though I don't think you'll be guessin' too long. Now pour that beer for yourself and let's get talkin'." She took a sip of beer.

"Have it your way," the barkeep said, and reached under the bar. When his hand came back up there was a set of brass knuckles across his fist.

The grip on Devorah's arm was sudden, hard even through her woolen cloak, but discreet, causing no one on Sixth Avenue to look askance or come to her aid. The tight grip came from behind, out of Dev's view even as she tried to twist her head around to see her attacker. All she could see was the edge of a ratty brown hat pulled low to hide his face, but its owner's body odor was as pungent as a charnel house and the voice in her ear was rough and male: "Say nothin'. Don't make noise. Don't do nothin' to attract attention. Just listen. Quit askin' about John Jones. You hear? Quit it, or a sore arm ain't all you'll get." He pressed even harder, nearly breaking bone, and then he was gone.

CHAPTER FOURTEEN

B y the time Fin arrived at Brennan's Butcher Shop on Second Avenue at the corner of East 19th Street, her pocket handkerchief was stained with blood from the wound to her chin but the bleeding had finally stopped. Though the wound stung—the bartender's brass knuckles tore a line in Fin's flesh—she was less concerned with the pain than with Devorah's inevitable worry at the sight of it.

But the brass knuckles hadn't prevented Fin from securing a useful piece of information at the Curtain Call Bar and Grill. Though the bartender got in one good smash to Fin's chin, that's all he got. Fin's years of surviving violence honed her skills to fend off attackers far deadlier than a bartender with brass knuckles. With a swift thrust of her left arm to slam the man's fist away and an equally fast jab with her own right fist to his nose, bloodying it, Fin put an end to the bartender's threat.

That earned her a round of applause from the fellas who were enjoying the beers she'd bought for the house. For the next half hour or so, the boys kept drinking and kept talking. It was useful to Fin that the theater men were a lot more tolerant than the bartender of Fin's way of life and love. Several had acquaintances of similar persuasion, performers whose songs and banter were

103

popular on the vaudeville circuit and in the more sophisticated cabarets. *And the not so sophisticated ones,* Fin, amused, reminisced silently.

This tolerance on the part of the fellas, and the loosening of their tongues with each round of beer, proved fruitful. Good cheer and gossip revealed that a few of them knew all or some of the actresses Dev had spoken to in the Ladies bar the previous night, and one fella knew where one of the women, Katherine Hazelton, worked when not employed in theater productions: Brennan's Butcher Shop.

Thus, after yet another round of beer for the theater boys and a hearty backslapping adieu, Fin left the Curtain Call Bar and Grill and headed to Brennan's.

The shop was in a hard-knocks neighborhood of sooty tenements, the streets noisy with the clattering of horse carts and the elevated train above Second Avenue, a far cry from the bright lights and cheerful crowds of Broadway, the milieu where Katherine Hazelton harbored aspirations of stardom. Here in this part of town, instead of glittering lights and ornate theaters, two giant gas storage tanks loomed over the neighborhood, giving the area its name, the Gas House District. Here, instead of the delicate perfumes on the skin of fur-clad ladies attending first-night performances, the odor of gas drifted through the district like a poisonous vapor, bringing with it the always looming threat of an exploding gas tank and a fire to rival the blasts of Hell. Here, instead of well-heeled theater producers escorting glamorous actresses to champagne suppers, the ruling lords were the toughs of the Gas House Gang, thugs who robbed the threadbare stores, beat up slow payers, and operated squalid brothels. Brennan's Butcher Shop was squeezed between a down-and-out pool hall and a brothel whose owners, Fin heard through the grapevine of the streets, made a habit of rifling through the pants pockets of their unsuspecting clientele, stealing the cash from their wallets while they were at their pleasures."

Inside the butcher shop, the lingering smell of gas tainted the aroma of fresh meat; the steaks and chops, cuts of pork and links of sausage that were laid out in the display case. Thin streaks of water from the case's blocks of ice leaked onto the wooden floor.

A man and a woman were busy cutting meat behind the display case. A row of butcher's knives and cleavers hung on the blood-spattered white tile wall behind them. The man, tall and dark haired, was well built in his sweat-stained white shirt, the sleeves rolled up to his elbows, his hands large and bony. His butcher's apron was stained with blood.

It wasn't lost on Fin that the woman was quite pretty, her brunette Gibson Girl hairstyle framing an ingenue's face and sad eyes. Her apron, too, was stained with blood.

The woman and the man looked up from their butchering, meat cleavers in hand, when Fin walked in. The expressions on their faces were as much in response to Fin's wounded chin as to her unfeminine attire.

"Good afternoon," Fin said to the woman. "Do I have the pleasure of addressin' Miss Katherine Hazelton?"

The man spoke up, "Who's askin'?" and brought his cleaver into more prominent view.

"My name's Fin Donner—"

"Fin Donner?" the woman said with some alarm, her cleaver now raised, too. "The Fin Donner who that Longstreet woman talked about last night?"

"The very one," Fin said. "So I take it I'm speakin' to Miss Hazelton?"

The man, belligerent in that way employers or possessive men can be, said to Miss Hazelton, "What's this about, Kate? Who's this Longstreet woman?"

Fin said, "It's about a friend of Miss Hazelton's. And who'd you be?"

"The name's Brennan," he said, "like it says on the sign. You ain't here to buy a cut of meat, so you ain't got no business here."

"I tell you what," Fin said, "how about you cut me a coupla nice thick steaks, the best you got, an' you scram an' let me chat with Miss Hazelton. They got a fancy name for that kinda arrangement: a quid pro quo, Miss Longstreet says they call it. But between you an' me, we can just call it a friendly trade. We know all about friendly trades, don't we, Mr. Brennan. So why don't you go into the back an' cut me up a coupla nice big tenderloins? Charge me the goin' rate, so don't skimp."

"You'll get your money's worth," Brennan snarled on his way through a swinging door behind him to the back of the shop.

The way Katherine Hazelton, meat cleaver still in hand, eyed Fin, Fin wasn't sure if she should run for her life or give the woman a shoulder to cry on. Fin saw the anger in Hazelton's eyes, but it was a brittle anger, the sort which could crack into a million pieces, the shards doomed to melt under a torrent of tears.

"Miss Hazelton," Fin said with all the ease and gentleness her rough and broken voice allowed, "Miss Longstreet an' I could really use your help. Just think: if kin of yours was brutally murdered, wouldn't you want the killer brought to justice? Well, that's all Pauline Godfrey's mother an' father want, an' they're entitled to it. So help me out here. Help me an' Miss Longstreet find Pauline's killer."

"Aren't the police supposed to do that?"

"Yeah, sure they are, you're quite right about that. But you know how it is with the police, don't you, Miss Hazelton. They don't always do what they're s'posed to do. That's why people come to me an' Miss Longstreet. So, how about it? How about helpin' us get justice for the Godfreys."

Katherine Hazelton lowered the cleaver into a joint of lamb, separating the leg from the hind shank with the skill of a morgue surgeon. This activity raised the horrible idea in Fin's mind that this lovely young woman would have the skill to quickly and precisely cut a throat, and that she'd have access to a tool sharp enough to do it.

Fin hoped to heaven that the investigative road didn't lead to Katherine Hazelton, a young woman with dreams and aspirations to live and strive for. For the moment at least, it was too soon for Fin to travel too far down that road. But it was time to take a step.

Keeping her manner friendly, even sympathetic, Fin said, "Miss Hazelton, if that John Jones fella hurt you, well, that's lousy, ain't it. From what I hear, he was a real heel. A lotta women might've wanted him dead. Maybe a lotta men, too. Who knows how many folks he did dirty, how many women he made real jealous by takin' up with Pauline Godfrey." It didn't pass Fin's notice that at this mention of the relationship between John Jones and Pauline Godfrey, Katherine Hazelton winced slightly and her grip on the cleaver tightened. "Y'know, jealousy can really get the better of a person," Fin said, alert now to Katherine's every move and tic. "You ever hear any of Mr. Jones's women complain about his philanderin'? Maybe more than complain? You figure any one of 'em might've been jealous enough to cut Pauline's throat?"

Katherine's cleaver came down with a sharp thwack, her head snapped up. "Just what is it you're asking? It sounds to me like you're working your way around to accuse me of killing that girl. Well, let me tell you something. I didn't have to kill her or anyone else. John and his women weren't worth my time of day. I'm an actress, a good one. You'll see. Some day, you'll see, I'll say goodbye to this butcher shop, goodbye to the blood and the raw meat." With each word, the meat cleaver came up and then down, up and down.

The skin at the back of Fin's neck prickled with the rise and fall of that cleaver.

"Miss Hazelton," she said, "no one is accusin' you of anything.

107

As a matter of fact, you can clear everything up for yourself right now. Just tell me, where were you yesterday afternoon, or last night around nine-thirty?"

"Can't you see I have a job during the day? And didn't your Miss Longstreet tell you about last night? I was drinking her free beer."

"That was later, Miss Hazelton," Fin said. "Miss Longstreet couldn't have gotten to the Curtain Call Bar and Grill until well past eleven o'clock. I know, because I was with her before then. Is there somethin' you're keepin' from me, Miss Hazelton?"

Katherine put down the cleaver, stared at Fin with the defiance of someone holding tight to a secret. "What I do with my evenings is my business," she said just as butcher Brennan came back into the shop. He carried a bloody bundle wrapped in brown butcher paper.

He said, "An' what she does with her days is *my* business. Here's your two cuts of prime tenderloin. Five pounds total, at twelve cents a pound. That'll be sixty cents, if you don't mind."

Fin took the bundle, gave Brennan the coins.

Brennan said, "Now get on your way."

Katherine Hazelton cleaved another shank of meat.

Fin walked out to the street, into the smell of gas and the shadows of the enormous gas tanks that loomed over the neighborhood.

A couple of toughs, two derby-hatted members of the Gas House Gang, leaned against a lamppost at the corner smoking cigarettes. The toughs blew smoke and stared at Fin. She lit her own cigarette and stared back. Everyone understood each other.

The elevated train rumbled overhead, throwing sparks from its steel wheels, the sparks flying around the gas tanks, an explosion waiting to happen.

Chapter Fifteen

The late afternoon sun sparkled through the windows and glowed on the mahogany furnishings in Fin and Devorah's parlor. The sunlight touched the fine details of the deep green moiré silk wall coverings and highlighted the carvings on the travertine fireplace. The light lay softly on Dev's creamy shirtwaist blouse and along her navy blue skirt. But most of all, the lowering sun revealed the shock on Dev's face when Fin walked in shortly after four-thirty with a gash of dried blood on her chin and a blood-stained package in her hands.

"Don't fret, my girl," Fin said. She put the package of tenderloins on a side table before taking Devorah in her arms. "I brought home two prime steaks for our dinner, an' you needn't bother about my chin. It's just a flesh wound. You'll be pleased to know that I got the better of the bum of a bartender who bloodied me. He's gonna have a tough time breathin' through his nose for a while."

Dev gently pulled out of Fin's embrace to examine the wound to her chin more closely. Satisfied that it looked worse than it actually was, she said, "Are you speaking of the bartender at the Curtain Call Bar and Grill?"

"That's the fella. He didn't like the cut of my jib an' decided to refashion it. But it didn't do him any good. A gold eagle on the bar an' a half hour of beer an' chatter with the fellas drinkin' away their actin' careers got me some information, namely, where I could find one of them actresses you spoke to last night. I was directed to the humble establishment of Brennan the Butcher, where Katherine Hazelton is pretty good at hackin' meat when she ain't employed on the stage."

"Ah, hence the tenderloins," Dev said.

"Listen, my girl, Miss Hazelton is really handy with a meat cleaver. The way she separated a shank of lamb was as neat a slice job as I ever seen. Now, I ain't sayin' she's the one who cut Pauline Godfrey, but she surely could do it."

"That is indeed interesting," Dev said, though she considered another analysis. "Being able to kill but having the temperament to kill are very different things. Miss Hazelton was quite the teary-eyed spurned lover last night, not the type I'd immediately associate with grotesque violence. But after all we've seen as inquiry agents, you never know, do you. The most unlikely people turn out to do the most horrid things. And of course, jealousy can be . . . well . . ." Dev let the rest of that thought just float away. Taking it further would only bring back the pain of her own irrational lapse of trust, a lapse she'd come to despise. "Pour me a brandy, would you, Lovey?"

Fin poured a stiff brandy for Dev and for herself. They each took a swallow, the liquor smoothing the unexpectedly violent creases in their day. For Dev it soothed the pain in her arm somewhat, bruised from the unknown assailant's grip.

The brandy also blunted the stab to Dev's soul when Fin repeated the word, "Jealousy. Sure. Fits right in with what I figured when I examined the site where Pauline's throat was cut: a rage killin'. An' from what I saw of Miss Hazelton today, she's got plenty of rage inside her."

"But what about John Jones's death if it wasn't a suicide?" Dev said. "Are we pursuing the angle of a double murder by the same killer? Do you really think Katherine Hazelton is capable of such a thing?"

"Maybe," Fin said. "Remember what Suzanne told us about Miss Hazelton, that she could perform athletic stuff. So yeah, she could've killed Pauline Godfrey an' later that night slipped into Jones's room, killed him, left a phony note, an' slipped out again down the fire escape before meetin' her friends at the Curtain Call Bar and Grill. But there's somethin' else, Dev. Somethin' she said that's been scratchin' at me all the way home. I mean, sure, she denied killin' Pauline Godfrey, but it was the way she denied it, like a slip of the tongue."

"Yes, the tongue can sometimes betray the mind."

"I'm thinkin' the same thing," Fin said. "So here's what slipped outta Miss Hazelton's lips, an' I quote: *I didn't have to kill her or anyone else.* It's that *anyone else* bit that's scratchin' at me. I mean, she caught on that I mighta been workin' my way to maybe pointin' a finger at her for Pauline's killin' but I wasn't pointin' at her for *anyone else's* killin', meanin' the Jones killin', at least not yet."

Dev took another sip of brandy, let its warmth slide through her body while she turned over Fin's revelation in her mind. Soon, with a nod and her eyes narrowed in thought, she said, "I see what you mean. Perhaps the lady doth indeed protest too much, her tongue too soon defending its owner from accusations yet unsaid. Well, we'll certainly take that into consideration." Dev accepted Fin's hand as she led her to one of the big leather armchairs.

Seating herself in the other armchair, Fin said, "What about your day, my girl? Was your conversation with the Godfreys fruitful?"

"In its way. They were, of course, surprised to hear of Jones's death, but they did not accept the idea of suicide."

"It seems nobody who knew him buys that story."

"Indeed. What's more," Dev said, warming to the pleasure

111

of a stimulating investigative discussion with her lover, "the Godfreys have already received the autopsy report. It was delivered to them by a uniformed police officer on behalf of the police surgeon's office. And they were not pleased with its contents."

Fin gave that a sympathetic nod. "Sure, it must've been real painful for them to read."

"Actually, it's what *wasn't* in the report which pained them more," Dev said. "The police surgeon simply stated the obvious, that Pauline Godfrey died as a result of a deep cut to the throat, severing the carotid artery and jugular vein. The report made no mention of her deteriorating health, which most certainly would have been evident in a thorough examination of the body, especially if narcotics were involved. From what I've read in the latest scientific and criminology journals, forensic examination can now detect traces of narcotics in the blood. The Godfreys are therefore convinced, and so am I, that the surgeon's office is as guilty as the rest of the police department in shoving Pauline Godfrey's death under the rug. The question is why?"

"An' on whose orders?" Fin said. "What secret are they all tryin' to keep? An' by the way, what secret are you tryin' to keep, my girl?"

A chill twisted through Dev, the chill of being found out. She'd hoped to spare Fin—and herself—of admitting to the embarrassing bout of last night's irrational jealousy, but her lover knew her too well. Fin's love enabled her to read Dev's face, her eyes, her moods. Dev would normally treasure this deep knowledge of her heart and soul. Now though, that same knowledge seemed to pin her to a wall.

Fin said, "I ain't never seen you hold your brandy glass in your left hand. Looks to me like you're favorin' your right arm. If you're in pain, Dev, don't keep it a secret. What can I do to help?"

Relief flowed through Dev like an infusion of warm blood in her veins. Her secret jealousy was safe. But a new concern arose:

Fin's inevitable worry for her safety when she'd tell her beloved of the attack and threat by an unknown man after leaving the Godfreys' shop. Dev knew that if the man's identity ever became known, Fin wouldn't hesitate to tear him limb from limb.

"It's nothing," Dev said with as much nonchalance as she could summon. "Just a bruise. But yes, it was in connection with our investigation. When I left the Godfreys' shop, a man came up behind me, gripped my arm, and warned me to quit the Jones case. No doubt I was followed to the shop."

Anger and worry clawed at Fin. Dev saw it in her lover's eyes. She saw Fin's jaw tighten, saw the struggle in Fin to check her anger and keep her worry from overcoming her judgment.

Fin reached across the little Chinese table that separated the two armchairs. She took Dev's hand. Assuring herself that Dev was not seriously hurt, and realizing that Dev would certainly want the incident viewed as just another element in their investigation, Fin finally pushed aside her urge to vengeance and tried to put the attack in a less threatening light. "Or maybe the fella had been spyin' on the shop and you walked into his surveillance."

"Could be," Dev said with some reluctance. "But all he mentioned was the Jones case, not the killing of Pauline Godfrey, though I suppose they are possibly one and the same issue. The Godfreys seem to think so, and I'm inclined to agree. Which is why I suggested the Godfreys postpone their daughter's funeral and have a private autopsy conducted in order to get a fuller picture of Pauline's health at the time of her death. Perhaps a more complete report will contain evidence of Pauline's relationship to Jones. The Godfreys agreed, at least Mr. Godfrey did. His wife was evidently too distraught to deal with it. She just buried her head in her husband's shoulder. Anyway, I told them we'd make the arrangements with a physician we trust. Dr. Nettinger comes to mind. Perhaps I'll telephone her now and have her send the report directly to the Godfreys. They'll be anxious to receive it, and we can then discuss it with them."

"Good idea," Fin said. "And while you're telephoning, how about I cook up these here tenderloins?"

"Isn't it a little early for dinner?"

"The sooner we finish dinner," Fin said, getting up from the chair and bending to Devorah, "the sooner we can get to dessert." Her passionate kiss on Devorah's lips indicated the dessert Fin had in mind.

Chapter Sixteen

The killer was annoyed, annoyed at all the snooping. There wasn't supposed to be this much snooping. Snoops ask questions. The killer was sure that if those two snoops, that Longstreet woman and her peculiar companion, didn't get the answers they want they'll just keep asking questions. They're nothing but busybodies, *the killer decided,* digging around in people's lives but with no sympathy for those lives. They certainly have no sympathy for mine.

CHAPTER SEVENTEEN

The pleasure of the silky slide in the throat of the fine Bordeaux which accompanied Fin and Devorah's dinner was interrupted by a harsh knocking at their door.

With the reluctance of someone whose enjoyment has been unforgivably disrupted, Fin left the dining table.

The knocking continued, harsh and impatient, as Fin walked through the hall. "Just cool your knuckles," she said under her breath.

When she opened the door, Detective Charles Coyle, his dark eyes stern under the brim of his derby, stood rigid in his plain gray coat, the collar turned up. He held a black walking stick and black gloves, both of which he gripped tightly.

He did not wait for an invitation to enter, but just walked past Fin and along the hall. "Is Miss Longstreet here with you?" he said. Though he spoke in his usual soft-voiced manner, it carried a tense undertone. "It's time the three of us had a talk, Donner. And what's that nasty business on your chin?"

"It ran into a bartender," Fin said, striding to Coyle's side. "You've interrupted our dinner, Detective. Didn't your Ma raise you any better?"

"Your dinner ain't my concern. Your activities are."

They arrived at the dining area, a large alcove off the parlor. With the descent of evening through the windows, the polished walnut table was lit by an arrangement of candles in silver holders, illuminating the dinner fare and the alcove with a gentle, flickering glow. On this evening, as on most of their evenings at dinner, Fin and Devorah preferred candlelight to the light of the electric wall sconces.

Without bothering to give Dev even the merest of greetings, Coyle said, "According to the residents at Mrs. Mallory's boardinghouse on Bayard Street, you and Fin were present at the time of Mr. Jones's death." He put his walking stick and gloves on the table, which roused a raised eyebrow from Dev. He ignored it.

"I would not say we were present at his death, Detective," Dev said. "That implies that we were in the room at the moment of the shot. We were not. We were merely on our way to speak with him when we heard the gunshot."

"Look, Coyle," Fin said, taking her seat again at one end of the dining table while Coyle stood at the other, "it was you who sent those Godfrey folks to us in the first place so we could look into their daughter's death. They brought us the story of their daughter takin' up with Jones. So we went to see the fella. What did y'think we'd do?"

Coyle sat down in a dining chair. He opened his coat, took off his derby and put it on the table, drawing another raised eyebrow from Dev. He took a deep breath and blew it out as if it was the last dregs of air in his lungs. At length, he said, "I didn't expect you to bump into a hornet's nest." The contrasting timbres of Coyle's soft voice and Fin's rough one were, to Dev's mind, like their contrasting personalities: Coyle, sly and slithering; Fin, tough and forthright.

Dev said, "And it's you who are in danger of being stung by those hornets, am I right, Detective Coyle?"

"Hornets sting whoever gets in their way, Miss Longstreet." Coyle's words carried an unmistakably acidic tone of warning. Still looking at Dev, who sat to his left, and then shifting his gaze to Fin, who sat opposite him, he said, "It seems that I miscalculated in sending the Godfreys to you. I now realize that I was mistaken in my assessment of their case. So there is no further need for your services. I advise you to walk away from this investigation."

This time, both of Devorah's eyebrows went up. "I'm shocked you'd even suggest such a thing. You know very well it's not our habit to abandon our clients. And for that matter, Detective," she added, leaning toward Coyle, her voice and manner now more sympathetic, "we don't abandon people who assist us, or people who need our help."

Coyle rose so fast from his chair the thrust nearly toppled it over. "You assume too much, Miss Longstreet. I didn't come here looking for help. Nor would I."

Fin said, "Then why did you darken our door, Coyle?"

"I came here to caution you. There are people who are not pleased with your activities. You'd best leave off of this investigation, stop pokin' the hornets' nest, or I won't be the only one who's stung."

Coyle grabbed his walking stick, his derby and his gloves, and quickly left the dining alcove. Moments later, Fin and Devorah heard the apartment door slam.

Fin said, "I ain't never seen a fella so terrified."

"Indeed," Dev said. "Something very sinister has infiltrated dear Detective Coyle's cozy fraternal world of the police. Whatever it is, it has been disturbed by the murder of Pauline Godfrey and the subsequent death of John Jones."

"We need a spy inside police headquarters," Fin said. "An' I know just the person who can get us in there."

"Five Cent" Frankie Swann, so named due to his habit of asking everyone to "loan" him five cents for a nickel beer, was, among other things, a promoter of the manly art of prizefighting. Frankie's "other things" included the occasional robbery, the offhand picking of a pocket, even a bit of extortion now and then if a mark was ripe for it. But it was Frankie's involvement with the fight game that made him useful to the denizens of the underworld. He'd been a master at evading the laws which made prizefighting illegal in New York prior to 1896; organized fights had to be held in hastily created "athletic clubs" hosting secret bouts in empty warehouses, the halls of slaughterhouses, or the back rooms of saloons. The police had to be handsomely paid off to look the other way. Five Cent Frankie was highly skilled at organizing the clandestine bouts and equally skilled in cultivating palm-greasing relationships with the police, relationships which endured even after the anti-prizefighting ordinances were abolished. Frankie's goodwill with the police department continued to enable him to escape serious consequences, even jail, when engaged in his "other" activities.

As a serious member of the prizefighting fraternity, Five Cent Frankie would often spend his days and evenings at Silkie's gymnasium on Gansevoort Street in the Meatpacking District. With the gym's supply of dumbbells, its row of punching bags, and a roped-off ring for fights and sparring, Silkie's was a favorite training spot among the city's boxers and their handlers.

By day, Silkie's, its whitewashed brick walls stained with smears of sweat and spatters of blood, was well lit through its big windows and an arched skylight. By night, the place was shadowy, illuminated by the few recently installed electric lights, with most of the light trained on the boxing ring in the center of the room.

Two beefy men in blood-spattered tan leggings and blood-and spit-smeared leather gloves were slugging it out when Fin walked in shortly before eight o'clock. A half dozen other fighters stood outside the ring, studying the combatants' moves while other groups of men in derbies or straw hats and assorted styles of suits and shirtsleeves shouted encouragement. Their shouts nearly drowned out the *thwacks* of thinly gloved fists against flesh or the thud of feet pounding the ring's canvas-covered wooden floor. The very air in the room was bloated with primitive maleness, redolent with the odors of cigar smoke, tobacco spit, sweaty bodies, and blood.

Fin spotted Frankie on a bench next to the ring. Always a flashy dresser, Frankie's soft felt purple hat and tan-and-purple plaid suit made him easy to see in the crowd, even in the shadows alongside the boxing ring.

She sat down next to Frankie. "Which one's yours?" she said.

Without missing a beat, without even a turn of his head or a hello, Frankie said, "The blond fella. The boy's got big hands and fast feet. See? He would've been great in the bare-knuckle days. Ah, that's when fights were fights. Skin to skin and bone to bone. Puttin' gloves on the boys takes some of the sport away." He finally turned to Fin, giving her a glad-hander's grin in his hollow-cheeked face, his blue eyes crinkling with good cheer. "Well hello there, Fin Donner. What brings you around? I know you're not eyeing the beefcake to admire it," Frankie said with a friendly if somewhat smarmy chuckle, "but maybe you're here to pick up some inside tidbits for future bets? Word is you cleaned up at last month's fights at the Garden."

"I came away with heavy pockets, yeah. But no, I ain't here about the muscle. Listen, Frankie, I need a favor," Fin said, and took two nickels from her pocket. "I'll spot you two beers, even bet big on your boy when he's on a Garden card an' you can keep my winnin's. Here's what I'd like you to do. Oh, an' you'll need this, too." She slipped a ten-dollar gold piece into Frankie's hand.

The desk sergeant on duty, a portly fellow whose mousey brown hair was as greasy as his face, was rendered near speechless when Five Cent Frankie Swann walked into police headquarters on Mulberry Street, his hand gripped tightly around Fin's arm, and with Fin's wrists bound with rope. "I've been robbed," Frankie said, "and I want you to arrest the perpetrator, Fin Donner."

Two other police officers and a clutch of jailhouse lawyers nearby were also rendered near mute by this unlikely scenario. About the only occupants of the room who either didn't notice or couldn't care less were the usual crowd of enraged immigrants or inebriated down-and-outs who clogged the floor.

With a show of impatience, Frankie said, "Well, sergeant?"

The desk sergeant, at first flustered, but soon finding satisfaction in this odd but welcome turn of events, retrieved the appropriate paperwork from a drawer in his desk and took his watch from his pocket. After noting the date and hour— 9:05 p.m.—and jotting it on the paperwork, he said, "State your complaint."

"I told you. I was robbed, and Fin Donner did it."

Fin said, "I am completely innocent of this here trumped-up charge."

The sergeant, smiling an excessively satisfied smile, said, "Save your objections for the judge. Now, mister—?"

"Swann, Franklin M. Swann. You know who I am."

"You're Five Cent Frankie Swann?"

"Friend of the police department, at your service."

The sergeant's attitude improved even further, from mere satisfaction to near schoolboy respect. "Yes, well, Mr. Swann, exactly what is it Fin Donner is purported to have stolen from you?"

"Money, of course. What the hell else is worth stealin'?" This drew chuckles and guffaws from those nearby.

"How much money?"

"Fifty dollars. Yes, fifty dollars, an exorbitant sum, you'll agree, taken from my tin box at my lodgings. Now, as you know, sergeant, I am a busy fella. I can't stand here all night jabberin' with you, pleasant as this experience is. Kindly have this thief, this . . . this *criminal* taken into custody so that you and I can then continue to go about our business."

"Indeed, Mister Swann, indeed," the sergeant said. "But first we have to satisfy the law, you understand. The District Attorney likes his *T*'s crossed and his *I*'s dotted. We don't want this hardened criminal, who the proud New York City Police Department has been trying to apprehend for years, to slip through some loophole now, do we."

"Certainly not," Frankie said. "Do your duty, sergeant."

The sergeant cleared his throat, an announcement of the start of his official proceedings. He smoothed the paperwork on his desk. "Well then, when was your tin box of money last seen, Mr. Swann?"

"Earlier this evening, say, oh, seven o'clock."

"And all was in order? Your money was in the box?"

"It was. There was forty-five dollars in that box, and I put in five to make it an even fifty. But when I went to the box later, the fifty was gone."

"And why do you say this here Fin Donner took it?"

"Because she came by to jabber a bit, and we tossed back a few drinks. She must've done it when my back was turned, pourin' us another round. You know her reputation as a lightfinger."

"Indeed I do, Mr. Swann," the sergeant said with an obsequious nod and a smug smile. "Indeed I do. Well, well, Fin Donner, alias Fine Fingers Donner, looks like we finally got you. It's time you paid for your crimes, even if it's a little late."

Fin said, "Some pal you turned out to be, Swann."

Frankie shared a grin with the sergeant, who was thrilled to be so honored.

With a wave of his arm, the sergeant summoned one of the nearby officers. "Take Donner down to the cells."

"Where do I put the prisoner?" the officer said, eyeing Fin as if she was some sort of unidentifiable or exotic animal. "In a cell with the men or the women?" This brought guffaws from the nearby clutch of coppers and jailhouse lawyers.

Fin gave the officer what was known in her Hell's Kitchen neighborhood as Hell's Grin: part smile, part sneer. "With the women, if y'don't mind."

The officer shrugged. The desk sergeant smirked.

Devorah was not altogether happy with Fin's plan to have herself arrested and thus gain access to the whisperings of police headquarters, but Dev had to admit that the logic of the plan was undeniable.

Still, the idea of her beloved in the clutches of the very group who hated her to the point of endangering her life and freedom worried Dev down to her marrow.

There was nothing for it, though, but to wait. And wait.

CHAPTER EIGHTEEN

The killer's day, a busy day, dragged into the night; another night of nervous chatter, of anger disguised, hidden, a secret festering in the killer's soul.

CHAPTER NINETEEN

adger Game Betty, a pretty young woman with sly eyes, laughed in friendly greeting when the officer cut the rope from Fin's wrists and pushed her into a cell where half a dozen other women were crowded into the grimy, dark, and odorous space. Betty's laugh clanged against the cell's stone walls and joined the other boisterous voices crammed into the basement cells of the Mulberry Street police headquarters.

Sadie Grebenstein, called Sadie the Slick because of her slick way with a knife, gave Fin a nod.

Louise O'Sullivan, a faded beauty still seductively plump in her ruffled pink satin gown, greeted Fin with, "Well, hello Fin Donner. This ain't our usual place to meet, though it's been a while. A few years or more, if mem'ry serves," her pearly voice rolling through the jailhouse din.

"Good evenin', Madame Lou," Fin said. "Surprised to see you here. I thought your place was protected by the Hudson Stompers gang an' coppers on the take. What happened? You miss a payoff?"

"Nah. I'm still in good with the Stompers. They're good boys. I'm in here because that hypocrite Alistair Flugg"—Madame Lou spit after saying his name—"and his prissy crowd of church dames showed up at my joint for one of his smash-'em-ups. He had his usual handful of newshounds and coppers with him, too. You'll probably read about it in t'morra's paper. For a fella who fancies himself a gentleman, Flugg sure plays a lowlife game, the way he pushes my girls around. Even gives some a swat with the back of his hand." This thought, and the memory which came with it, caused Madame Lou to spit again. "But don't you fret about me, Fin Donner. I'll be outta here in the morning. My girls are already bailed."

"You always did know how to take care of business, Lou."

"Sure, gotta stay ahead of the game or you're sunk. But what about you, Fin? You here because the boys in blue finally nailed you? Last I heard, you'd left the pavement and joined the hoity-toits; though with that battlefield voice of yours," she added with a chuckle, "do they understand a word you say?"

"Don't believe everything y'hear about the hoity-toits," Fin said with a chuckle of her own, a chuckle born of her private knowledge of one past member in particular of the town's hoity-toits, one Miss Devorah Longstreet. "An' the coppers ain't nailed me yet, Lou, though they're still tryin'."

"So whaddya in for? You kill somebody? Wouldn't surprise me, what with your rough days around the docks."

Sadie the Slick's sharp, "Hah," sliced through the jailhouse noise. "Takes more than a thick skin to be a croaker. What about it, Fin? You got it in you to croak someone?"

"I never went lookin' for it like you do, Sadie, if that's what you mean. But the coppers wouldn't mind pinnin' me—or any of us," Fin said, addressing all the women in the cell—"for any spare murders they've got lyin' around. Listen, everybody, we've all been aroun' the block more than once, sometimes even together."

"Sure," Badger Game Betty said, throwing an arm around Fin's shoulder. "We've surely had our fun. I'm always ready for more after I get out, Fin, if you're willin'." Betty's practiced smile always carried the unspoken suggestion that its recipients should take off their trousers.

Fin gently slid Betty's arm from her shoulder and brushed a kiss on her hand. "First I gotta get out from under the coppers," she said with a wink, then looked around at the other women. "If any of you got information that can help me out, well, y'know how it is: one hand washes the other. I'll owe you, an' you know me well enough to be sure you'll collect."

"What sorta information?" Sadie said. "You know better than to ask us to snitch on anyone, Fin."

"An' you know I wouldn't ask it. Look, you all have your ears to the street, an' some of you even have mutually beneficial relationships with a copper or two. So I'm figurin' a lotta you know about the death of a fella went by the name of John Jones. Anybody hear why the coppers are sweepin' his death under the rug? An' why they ain't botherin' to find out who really killed his latest lady friend?"

Sharp gasps, quickly silenced, escaped from some of the women at the mention of Jones. Badger Game Betty chuckled. Madame Lou offered an annoyed *tsk*. But then there was silence, a silence so complete Fin could hear the scuttering of mice and the scratching of rats in the holes and crevices of the cell's stone walls.

She said, "I'm getting' the feelin' that Jones was a scary fella."

"You have it all wrong, Fin Donner," a new voice spoke up, a tired voice from someone in a shadowed corner of the cell. "There was nothin' scary about Johnny Jones. He could even be real nice. The fella always gave me a few coins when he seen me in the street, asked if I had what to eat that day. No, what was scary about Johnny Jones was maybe who he associated with. They're scary as hell."

Fin followed the sound of the voice, finally saw who it belonged to: someone much too young to be so tired, her eyes too wise for her age. She was pretty as a schoolgirl, but her blond ringlets hung limp at either side of her head. Her shoulders were slumped. Her blue dress was blotched with grease. Fin didn't know the young woman but her exhausted shoulders announced the life she led. She was a Hot Corn Girl, barely a teenager who'd been carrying a heavy pot of hot corn suspended from her shoulders since she was a child, selling the corn on the streets for pennies, and herself for not much more.

"Scary how?" Fin said.

"You don't wanna know," the girl said.

"If I didn't wanna know, I wouldn't be askin'."

Madame Lou said, "Leave her alone, Fin. As a matter of fact, leave all of us alone. We ain't squealin'. Some secrets are better left secret."

"Even if those secrets give the big boys more power to scare you to death? Look, I ain't askin' anyone to squeal on one of our own. I'm lookin' to get out from under—maybe get us all out from under—the big boys whose deep pockets hire dangerous pals to squeeze every penny from everyone who makes their livin' in the streets. Maybe it's time to take some of 'em down so you can go about y'business an' not be scared of anybody."

A meek, "You still got it all wrong," came from the Hot Corn Girl.

Fin said, "Okay, then straighten me out. An' by the way, what's your name?"

"Lily. My name's Lily Bohan. We ain't scared of what those big boys might do to us. We're scared of what they'll take away from us. Now that's all you'll get from me, Fin Donner, whoever you are. If the coppers want to pin you for somethin', it ain't no concern of mine."

"Or mine," Betty the Badger said. "Not this time, Fin. If you was lookin' to get even with some street cheat or even some dirty copper, sure, any one of us would help you out. But you're pokin' the wrong bear this time, Fin, a bear that's got big paws."

There was nodding and "Mmm-hmms" of general agreement

among the women in the cell. Even Madame Lou turned her satin-clad bulk away.

"So none of you are willin' to gimme a name then?"

"I already told you," Madam Lou said. "We don't squeal. Go back to your hoity-toits, Fin Donner."

The cell was quiet again, the women turning their backs on Fin. Instead of the warmth of a life once shared with these underworld sisters, their shunning wrapped around Fin like an ice-encrusted cloak.

There was nothing for her to do but bear it, use her time in the cell to think, and warm her bones with thoughts of getting back to her cherished Devorah.

The jailhouse noise quieted over the course of the three hours since Fin was pushed into the cell. The midnight chatter was low, just murmurings of gossip spoken under the snores of sleeping prisoners. Everyone in the cells knew the score. Some knew they'd be out by morning, their bail money or bribes paid, their cases dropped. Others settled into the routine knowledge that the cells were their first stop before a stint in the House of Detention—the dreaded Tombs jail—before a trial which would inevitably end in a stretch in prison or, for some, a death sentence. Such was the cycle of their lives.

For Fin Donner, though, these three hours in the cell would be the extent of her incarceration, because upstairs in an office of police headquarters, the plan she'd put into place was playing out: Five Cent Frankie—whose longstanding and cozy arrangements with the police made his word unquestioned—was rescinding his accusation of theft against Fin. "It was a grievous mistake on my part," Frankie told the officer in charge. "You see, I'd misplaced my tin box, which I found moments ago. My fifty dollars is quite in my possession. You can surely imagine my relief, and my regret for the trouble I've caused my good friend Fin Donner. You must release Fin at once and with my deepest apologies." Frankie gave the officer his sincerest smile and a handshake with Fin's ten-dollar gold coin pressed in his palm.

A hansom cab stood at the curb outside the Mulberry Street police headquarters. Its flickering kerosene sidelamps and the two recently electrified lamps at the entrance to the police building were the only light in the middle-of-the-night darkness, giving the street an atmosphere of mystery and menace. Dev, wrapped in her woolen cloak against the midnight chill and the gloomy ambiance, waited in the cab, her eyes trained on the entrance to the grim building. She'd only been there mere minutes, arriving in the cab with Five Cent Frankie Swann, but in her impatience to reunite with her lover and make sure she was unharmed, the minutes felt like hours.

When Fin at last emerged, with Swann at her side, Devorah finally let out the breath she hadn't even been aware she was holding.

Their embrace was warm and strong when Fin stepped into the cab. Fin buried her head in Dev's neck. Dev, looking over Fin's shoulder to Frankie, who stood outside the cab, whispered, "Thank you, Mr. Swann."

"At your service, ma'am," he said with a sweep of his soft felt hat. Frankie then tapped the side of the hansom for the cabbie to drive on.

"Thank goodness you're safe and unharmed, my love," Dev said, as the cab drove through the dark streets of Lower Manhattan.

"I told you not to worry, my girl. I was never in any real danger. The coppers never doubt the word of Five Cent Frankie."

"Maybe so. But after Coyle's outburst tonight, I had no

faith in the police treating you fairly. In any event, was your scheme successful? Did you learn anything which will help our investigation?"

"I'm not sure," Fin said with an exhausted sigh. "But I did learn this: it ain't just the police who are closing ranks about John Jones. The whole underworld is buttoning their lips, too. Coyle said we've stirred up a hornet's nest? I think it's worse than that, love. It takes a lot t'scare the tough ladies of the streets, an' the ladies I talked to tonight are shakin' in their skin."

Chapter Twenty

"**R**evoltin' fella, that Alistair Flugg," Fin said in response to the morning newspaper's account of the raid on Madame Lou's establishment. "The man makes me choke on my breakfast. He oughta stop puttin' his nose up other people's arse."

Dev continued to butter her scone, though she slowed the knife while her mind examined Fin's remark. "Oh, I don't know, Lovey," she finally said. "Yes, I admit he is a bit of a prude, but I find him rather courageous. He does go into some of the most dangerous places in the city: thieves' quarters, opium dens. Let's face it, the police certainly aren't doing all they should to keep crime at bay. Pass me the coffee urn, would you?"

"Depends on what y'call crime, I guess," Fin said. "If the fella was goin' after murderers or corrupt coppers, well, sure, I'd back him. But raidin' a bawdy house, well, it just ain't right. A bawdy house is a business like any other, even like upright Mr. Godfrey's fabric shop. Both places provide somethin' people want."

Dev couldn't disagree with the fact of that, though she wanted to debate it. She wanted to point out that maybe the women in the bawdy houses weren't always there by choice, that their lives perhaps left them few other opportunities. She wanted to remind Fin that the women often had to perform acts which either turned their stomachs or even put them in danger just to satisfy the twisted lusts of paying customers. But Dev didn't say any of those things because, while true, something else kept her silent: her acceptance of Fin's reprobate past and its ongoing allure in Fin's present. It was a conversation for another time, if at all.

Thus, all Dev said was, "Well, I take your point, Lovey, but I still consider Alistair a fine man who believes in what he's doing. Not many people are willing to risk their own safety for their beliefs nowadays."

"'*Alistair*'? You say his name like you know the fella."

"I've met him a number of times when he came to our house. He and my father were good friends. I assume they still are," she added almost under her breath. The pain of losing her family's affection threatened to break her heart once again.

But something else came over Dev, an awareness which lifted her spirits. She saw an opportunity which reinforced her sense of usefulness, a course of action which only she could provide. "I will talk to Alistair," she said in a voice firm with purpose. "After all, he has contacts in City Hall and other offices of city government, officials who evidently support him."

Fin put down her coffee cup and with a smile of recognition picked up on Dev's line of thought. "Sure," she said, "the fella may have the story on why the coppers are sweepin' the Godfrey killin' under the rug, an' why they're warnin' us off any questions about John Jones."

"Indeed," Dev said, gratified, as always, at how in tune she and her lover were with each other. It was almost like a shared mind, a shared heartbeat. "All right, I'll visit him this morning. What will you do in the meantime, Lovey?"

Fin picked up the newspaper again, looked briefly at the story about the raid on Madame Lou's brothel. It reminded her of something Madame Lou said in jail last night. "Well, my girl, while you're pumpin' an arm of the upper class, I'll pump an arm of the gutter trade. I think I'll have a chat with an old pal."

The morning sun was well up over the river by the time Fin arrived at the dockside hangout of the Hudson Stompers. The sunlight picked out the sleek hulls and monumental smokestacks of the new steamships, and the tall masts and riggings of the older but still proud sailing vessels. Beyond the docks, the sunlight washed across the sooty facades of the warehouses and tenements of the city's lower West Side.

Fin stepped lively between the tangle of horse carts and wagons that crammed the dockside avenue. She worked her way around braying animals and shouting people, everyone fighting for space as the carts and wagons took on cargo hauled from the ships by brawny men of every race, their sweat-covered faces and muscular arms glistening in the midmorning light off the river.

Two hard-faced men sat on chairs on the porch of a floating shack tied up to the end of a pier. One of the men was stocky in a pair of canvas pants, a short black jacket and a derby hat. The other gent was less bulky but just as menacing in his tight black suit and soft cap. The lapels of his jacket were covered with glittering stick pins. The stocky fellow held a thick wooden club. The other fellow picked his teeth with one of the stick pins.

Fin knew both men. "Beer Barrel" Bill Riley held the club; Cecil "Goo Goo" Stokes wore the stick pins. Fin gave the men a smile and a wave as she walked along the pier and approached the shack.

The men recognized Fin, too. Goo Goo smiled and waved back. Beer Barrel Riley didn't. But then, Riley rarely smiled. He saved his smile for scaring people out of their wits. Before he'd rob you, for instance, or pummel you, or before a brawl with a rival gang. Beer Barrel Riley's smile was terrifying because his teeth were pointed with spikes of steel.

"Mornin', gents," Fin said. "How y'been?"

Goo Goo, picking his teeth, said, "Can't complain. Ain't seen you around much, Fin. Word has it you got fancy. That spiffy suit an' shiny waistcoat says that's so."

"Y'know I always liked a bit of spiffy," Fin said with a friendly lilt. She opened her jacket wide to give the boys a full view of her striped satin waistcoat, crisp white shirt and gray silk tie.

"Very nice," Goo Goo said. "Now all y'need is a banquet to go to. So what brings y'aroun', Fin?"

"I need to powwow with the boss. He inside?"

"Yeah, but he ain't in a very good mood."

"Well, maybe I can make him happy," Fin said with a wink. This brought a guffaw from Goo Goo. Fin thought she even saw Riley's lips stretch ever so slightly.

"Go ahead in," Goo Goo said with a toss of his head followed by another pick of his teeth. Beer Barrel Riley swayed his club.

Inside the shack, Fin found the Stompers' leader, Ned "The Noggin" Hennessey, seated at a table reading a newspaper. A short but powerfully built brawler with wavy black hair and keenly alert green eyes in a thick face, Hennessey was not only possessed of strong fists but of a sharp mind. His talent for out-thinking any rivals, figuring how an enemy would come at him and his Hudson Stompers, earned him his moniker. His gang brothers respected his instinct for strategy and for sniffing out profitable opportunities. Their loyalty, together with Ned's intelligence and the gang's success at street warfare, made the Hudson Stompers the most powerful, well-connected gang in New York.

Right now, Ned Hennessey's mind was engaged with a news article which appeared to annoy him, his strong fists tightly balled up in the pockets of his coarse brown jacket.

Two other gang members sat reading newspapers at the table. One was Charlie "The Gouger" Montague, a big, rough-hewn fellow in a longshoreman's getup of heavy canvas pants, loose white shirt, and a derby hat at a rakish angle. He earned his moniker as a result of his habit of gouging his enemies' eyes out. Seated next to him was Handsome Harry Blaine, whose blue-eyed, curly dark-haired good looks earned him his nickname. Harry was fussy about his appearance. There wasn't a speck of dirt or lint on his flashy, nipped-waist, belted red suit. In a fight, though, Harry's fancy clothes were no impediment to how he earned his other nickname, The Hammer, a reference to his weapon of choice. It hung from his belted jacket.

Seeing Fin, Hennessey put down his newspaper. His annoyance at the news story shifted into a mischievous smile. "Well, if it ain't Fine Fingers Fin Donner," he said, "dipper extraordinaire. Guard yer wallets, gents. We're in the company of one of the canniest pickpockets ever was. An' she has other fine talents, too. The kinda talents that kept her alive in Hell's Kitchen."

"Good to see you, too, Ned," Fin said.

"Ain't seen much of you for a while, Fin, 'cept now an' then at a dice game or a prizefight. From what I hear, you been livin' upstairs."

"Y'go where life takes you," Fin said, feeling no need to explain her life to Ned Hennessey or to anyone else. "Listen, I came by to poke around in that famous Ned Hennessey noggin."

Hennessey picked up his newspaper and gave Fin a grin so sly it could intimidate a fox. "I been readin' all about last night's raid of Madame Lou's place by that gospel grinder, Alistair Flugg. You bein' here wouldn't have somethin' to do with that, now, would it? I mean, everyone knows Lou's place is under the Hudson Stompers' protection, so maybe you wanna know why the raid happened under my nose? An' if that's what you came down here to poke my head about, I wanna know what's it got to do with you?"

"I ain't here about Lou," Fin said. "She can take care of herself, but now that y'brought it up, I do wonder why y'didn't push back against Flugg. Not like you to be slippin', Ned."

Hennessey snapped, "I ain't slippin'. That Flugg fella has connections, damn his eyes. Sometimes it's just best to step outta his way, let him make his big show, an' then get back to business when he moves on to some other operation an' takes his carnival with him. That way I can keep the damage minimal, know what I mean? So if it ain't about Flugg, why are you here, Donner?"

"I wanna know about John Jones."

"John who?"

Fin considered Hennessey's too easy posture and flippant tone about as convincing as a medicine show sales pitch. "Aw, don't gimme that *John who* spiel, Ned," Fin said. "We go back too far for me to fall for that line. An' tell your boys here to come out from behind their newspapers, because I'm bettin' that all three of you fellas knew Jones, so all three of you might have somethin' to say about him. But it's you I'm countin' on, Ned, to give me the straight story. First of all, I'm sure y'know the fella's dead."

Without taking his eyes off Fin, Hennessey pulled a pint bottle of whiskey from his pocket. He uncorked it, took a swig. "People die every day, Fin," he said with the smug air of a man to whom human life means little and their deaths even less.

Hennessey's attitude, its coldness, its dismissal of life's possibilities for hope and pleasure, was familiar to Fin but it was an attitude she no longer lived by or shared. She no longer needed to. But she understood that Ned Hennessey did, and Fin liked Ned Hennessey. She always did. She liked his courage, his intelligence, his loyalty to his gangster brothers. And she liked Ned's past respect for her and her streetwise talents. It was through this admiration for Hennessey that she said, "Look, Ned, Jones's death is the sorta thing that could bring trouble.

137

Sure, the coppers wanna bury it, but who d'you think they're gonna come after if the Jones case won't stay buried? They're gonna come after people like us, Ned. It won't matter how many coppers you do business with these days, sooner or later they'll turn their backs on you an' on everyone in the streets whose money they've gladly taken. You know it's true, Ned. You an' I have seen it happen dozens of times. You gotta get ahead of this thing."

Ned took another swig on his bottle, leaned back in his chair and gave Fin a squint-eyed look that made it clear the wheels were turning in his mind. "I'm listenin'," he said.

"It's like this," Fin said, taking a seat at the table. "It seems Jones was involved in the crummy end of the flesh trade; y'know, gettin' women doped up an' then sellin' them into the trade. It mighta led to his latest lady friend gettin' sick, even gettin' her throat cut. But the coppers, an' who knows who else in City Hall, are sweepin' the girl's killin' under the rug. Look, Ned, you an' your Hudson Stompers have your teeth in the gears of the city. You either know or can find out why the coppers are puttin' the silence around Jones an' the murder of his lady friend."

Hennessey held his bottle of whiskey out to Fin. "Join me in a taste?"

"It's a little early in the day for me, Ned."

"Oh boy, y'really have gone soft. The Fin Donner I used to know, the one who used to strut the streets, could drink any man under the table, even first thing in the mornin'."

"An' the Fin Donner you used to know also knew when not to bother. So, c'mon Ned, for old times' sake, help me out here. I mean, hey, you an' the Stompers run the whole West Side these days. All the other gangs—the Mighty Thieves, the River Boys, the Pluggers an' all the rest of 'em—they all step outta your way. You're the top dog, you ain't got nothin' to fear anymore from anybody, or so I hear." There was a hint of a taunt in Fin's last words.

Hennessey got up from his chair, kicked it back. Charlie the Gouger and Handsome Harry stood too, imitating their gang boss, as followers always do.

But these followers were dangerous killers, as Fin well knew. She also knew that cringing or showing fear was a losing strategy, one that invited smacks and kicks and gouged eyes. Sympathy for weakness was not in these boys' nature.

Hennessey said, "Take a walk with me, Fin."

"Y'know what I like about the Hudson River? No bridges," Ned said as he and Fin stepped off the Stompers' pier and into the dockside fray of horse carts and wagons. The late morning sunlight off the river shone on the blackness of Ned's hair and heightened the ruddiness in his thick cheeks. In Fin's eyes, he could pass for the Devil himself. "Now, on the East Side of this here Manhattan Island, on the East River, see," he said, warming to his commentary, "you got y'Brooklyn Bridge an' the city's already started buildin' another bridge to Brooklyn from Delancey Street. That means if y'bein' sought by the coppers or any of the East Side boys, you can run across a bridge to Brooklyn an' get good an' lost. You can keep goin' to them ash piles out in the sticks in Corona, then keep goin' all the way out to the end of Long Island an' catch a ferry to wherever the hell those ferries go. But here on my river on the West Side of town, where there ain't no bridges to run across, if my boys are after you, yer back's to the water. I got people coverin' the ferry depots, so you ain't getting' on no ferry for a trip to Jersey. An' me an' the Stompers are tight with the barge folks an' the tugboaters, so you ain't getting' no ride across the river there, either. An' you can forget about the ocean liners or the boats that take vacationers up and down the river. I got people I pay to show me the passenger lists. So y'see, Fin, if yer on my side of Manhattan Island, I got

139

you. Y'know what I'm sayin?" Hennessey's green eyes twinkled with his pleasure in his power over his extended turf, while his slow strut along the waterfront signaled his menacing readiness to use it.

Fin smiled back at him, using her smile as a shield to fend off what she knew in her bones was a warning or even a threat from gang boss Ned Hennessey. "That's why they call you The Noggin," Fin said through the smile, "always thinkin' all the angles. But tellin' me about the strategic advantages of the Hudson River ain't why you invited me to take this walk. What's on your mind, Ned?"

"The question is, what's on yours, Fin? You come aroun' talkin' about some girl's throat gettin' cut an' askin' questions about this Jones fella, a guy people don't want questions asked about. Makes me think somethin's up, somethin' that maybe I either want in on or want no part of, an' to tell the truth I'm thinkin' the latter."

"If you're tellin' me you don't know or never heard of John Jones, I don't believe you, Ned. You just told me how tied in you are, so I'm bettin' you heard all about Jones, about his business an' about his dyin'."

"That still don't mean I want any part of it."

"Since when does Ned Hennessey pass up a chance to make a buck? You may look like a longshoreman, you might even dress like one," Fin said with a poke at Ned's shabby lapel, "but like you said, your Hudson Stompers control every nickel an' dime that slides through every hand along the West Side waterfront. You got money in those ratty pockets of yours, Ned, an' I know you long enough to know you're always lookin' for more."

"Not every nickel's worth my time, Fin," Ned said, waving the uncomfortable subject away.

But Fin grabbed the moment. She would not let Ned dodge and weave. "Okay, why not?" she said, staring him down. "What is it about John Jones that makes the smart Ned Hennessey pass up those nickels an' gets the coppers an' everyone on the streets tied up in knots?"

They'd arrived across the street at the entrance to an alley between Sheffield's Maritime Warehouse and the Herbert M. Burrell & Sons rope factory. The sun lost its way in the narrow, crooked alley, throwing the brick sides of the buildings into deep, sooty red. Mere slivers of weak sun touched the men and women who leaned against the walls, hiding or doing business in the alley's gritty shadows.

Fin knew this place, this unnamed alley where she used to enjoy the paid company of its women and the whiskey of its dive saloon run by Ned and his Hudson Stompers in a basement room of the rope factory. The saloon served a fiery rotgut which banged into your senses with the first gulp, while your eyes feasted on—and your belly laughed at—the bawdy entertainment in the center of the smoky, gaslit room. Sometime in the hours before dawn, Jamie O'Hara, a washed-up prizefighter with an angel's voice, would sing the songs of old Ireland, bringing tears to everyone's eyes, even to the eyes of Julie "The Jew" Moskowitz and Bootblack Harlan Sharp, so named because of his profession and the skin color of his African ancestry. The saloon was also good for a game of cards or throws of the dice with players who'd knife you if they thought you were cheating or if they didn't like your looks or if they were just plain drunk.

Oh yes, Fin remembered this alley, remembered its pleasures and dangers. Standing here at its mouth, a terror rose in her: not terror of the dangers of the place but the terror of missing them. "Why did you bring me here, Ned?"

"Because if you want information, you have to pay, Fin. You know the game."

"If you want money for talkin', all you hadda do is ask. How much you want, Ned?"

"What's it worth to you?"

Fin wanted to say that it was worth everything. It was

worth walking away from the temptations that lingered here, temptations that threatened her paradise with Devorah.

These were not things she'd say to Ned Hennessey. These were not things Ned Hennessey, gang leader and head basher, would respect. Ned only had respect for cash and power and brute survival in New York's stone jungle. Love and its refinements to human nature had no place in his rough world. But it had found a place in Fin's.

And yet . . .

She understood Ned's world, understood its rules, its codes of honor and its wink at dishonor. Fin understood its games, like the one Ned was playing.

She said, "You're makin' the wrong deal, Ned. Y'think the only benefit to you is cash outta my pocket. But you're forgettin' that information is a currency every bit as good as cash, maybe better. So, yeah, I want information from you, but I got information to give you, the sorta information that keeps you in the know about the coppers. You gettin' the picture, Ned?"

She'd set the wheels in Ned's noggin turning again. Fin saw it in the way he leaned against the rope factory wall, the way he looked at her, as if probing behind her eyes. "Okay," he finally said, "let's parlay over the secrets we can tell each other. But let's do it the way we've always done it, Fin, with a bent elbow an' a drink." Ned took Fin by her arm. He led her through the alley and into the dive saloon in the basement of the rope factory.

Chapter Twenty-One

Another day for the killer to face. Another day to stick to business and enjoy the quiet of life without that snoot of a girl who got in the way.

Chapter Twenty-Two

Alistair Flugg's comfortable life was centered in a handsome brick three-story Greek Revival house on Washington Square, an address associated with some of New York's oldest, most distinguished families. Mrs. Flugg, *née Martha de Haas,* could trace her ancestry back to Peter Stuyvesant and the Dutch establishment of New Amsterdam. Her marriage dowry, a sizable slice of the de Haas banking fortune, was rumored to be among the largest ever recorded in the annals of the city's important marriages. Mr. Flugg, for his part, claimed ancestry dating from the English acquisition of New Amsterdam and the subsequent renaming of the colony New York. Mr. Flugg, in fact, was of the belief—expressed to many—that it was his ancestor who suggested the new name in honor of his distant relation to the English lord of the shire of York.

On this particular sunny April morning, Mr. Flugg enjoyed with his breakfast the newspaper account of his successful raid on Madame Lou's brothel. Oh, he knew that the foul woman would reopen her den of sin, but he considered the raid, and the others he'd conducted, a success nonetheless. For if nothing else, his activities called attention to the sordid practices and impertinent aspirations of the city's lower classes, a populace he considered inferior beings no better than filthy sewer rodents. In the mind of Alistair P. Flugg, these people were fit for manual labor and nothing else.

He was aware, however, that a number of his fellow citizens did not share his views, and as a result some even avoided him socially, which baffled Mr. Flugg. Was he not a kind man? Did he not treat those in his milieu with the utmost courtesy and a sunny disposition? Did he not give generously to various charities for the benefit of instilling moral values in the children of the city's gutter classes? Though he had no expectation—nor did he have the desire—that these children grow up to become equal to their betters, it was Mr. Flugg's hope that they would at least adopt a more moral view of life and would simply go about their labors and forsake the temptations of low and sordid amusements.

This sunny morning, though, was too pleasant a day to trouble himself with these irritating conundrums. He had reason enough to feel happy and serene: his raid last evening had been well publicized, the photogravure in the newspaper was flattering, his wavy locks of hair flowing; the eggs and coffee of his breakfast superbly prepared by the Fluggs' cook; and his lovely wife, Martha, modestly attired in a high-necked deep maroon silk dress devoid of fussy ornament except for a bit of ruffle at the neck, remained unobtrusive as she read her women's publication silently while breakfasting and refrained from admonishing her husband about their loss of friends.

Mr. Flugg's serenity was thus undisturbed until the doorbell rang while he and his wife were still enjoying their coffee.

"I have no recollection of appointments this morning," he said to his wife. "Are you expecting anyone?"

"No, dear, I have no engagements, either. Perhaps it's one of those door-to-door peddlers. I'm sure Rogers will see to their dismissal."

Within moments, Rogers, the Fluggs' longtime butler, arrived. "You have a guest who wishes to speak to Mr. Flugg. She says she knows you, sir. A Miss Devorah Longstreet."

It was Martha Flugg who responded, her face pale, her expression bewildered. "Devorah has come *here*?"

Alistair Flugg sniffed the air as if something foreign had seeped into his realm. "Kindly tell Miss Longstreet I will not see her, Rogers. Send her away."

Before Rogers even finished his "Yes, sir," Martha Flugg rose from the breakfast table. "I'll tell her, Alistair. After all, we do know the family, and allowing a servant to dismiss her would be disrespectful to her father."

"As you wish, my dear. But I won't have that fallen woman in our home."

The so-called fallen woman who stood on the Fluggs' doorstep when Martha Flugg opened the door was elegantly attired in her brown woolen cloak over a pale lavender suit, its simple skirt discreetly trimmed in darker violet at the ankle. A small, brown equestrian-style top hat with a delicate net veil adorned the woman's fashionable crown of thick chestnut hair.

Dev's "Hello, Martha. May I come in?" was met with surprise, which grew close to shock when Dev added, "I must speak with Alistair about his activities."

Martha had long ago learned to control her sometimes flabbergasted reaction to her husband's excessively moral crusade. After all, a wife simply didn't register disapproval of her husband, especially if he was respected by the city's leaders, was a member of a prominent family, and especially if she enjoyed the privileges which came with that prominence. Martha called upon that discipline now. Though she was flabbergasted, indeed, to see the once distinguished but now ostracized socialite Devorah Longstreet at her door, Martha gave Dev a curt if not entirely unfriendly, "Hello, Devorah. I'm afraid you've made the trip for nothing. Alistair won't see you. He made that clear when

Rogers informed us of your arrival."

"And I wouldn't be here if it wasn't important, Martha. We've known each other a long time. You know I don't impose. But I insist on an audience with Alistair." Without waiting for an invitation, Dev stepped into the vestibule. She put her gloved hand on Martha's arm as a gesture of friendly affection born of years of warm acquaintance. "How are you, Martha? You're looking well." She meant the compliment, for Martha Flugg, née Martha de Haas, retained the warm blue eyes, delicately blushed cheeks, soft blonde hair now slightly graying, and the trim figure of the once most sought-after debutante at society balls, courted by the city's handsomest swains. Her marriage to the stiff Alistair Flugg surprised everyone, though Dev understood through her own experience of life's turns that love arrives on the arm of the least expected or likely people.

Martha, unsteadied by Dev's warmth, stuttered her response. "I . . . I must say, this visit is, well, rather a surprise. You know how my husband feels about your . . . uhm, current way of life."

Dev, through the sadness of a friendship severed, was tempted to ask Martha if she shared her husband's disdain, but the woman's obvious discomfort, her none-too-well-hidden effort to control an emotion Dev could only guess at, kept her tongue in check. She said instead, "Still, it's good to see you, Martha. I've missed our tea times together, how we'd laugh at how seriously my father and Alistair took our smallest social infractions."

A small smile lit on Martha's lips and a glint flashed in her eyes. "Yes, I've missed those days, too, Devorah. In fact, I—" But Martha could not complete her thought, disappointing Dev. She wondered if Martha found the loss of their past days too painful or, in her current life and attitudes as Mrs. Alistair P. Flugg, their memory too distasteful.

In either case, it was clear to Dev that restoring a friendship with Martha Flugg was out of the question. It was time to move on to business. "I've come to see Alistair. Please take me to him."

"Devorah, I don't mean to be indelicate, but he will not see you. Perhaps it might be better if you spared yourself the insult of being turned away from his company."

"I'm willing to take that risk, Martha. It's important I speak with him."

"May I at least tell him what it's about?"

"I've come to ask his help."

The surprise Martha felt at Devorah's calling at this house in the first place was no match for her surprise at the improbable idea that Devorah Longstreet, whose current life and scandalous relationship was despised by Alistair Flugg, should seek his help. Martha Flugg was flabbergasted, indeed.

She was also a responsible hostess, knowledgeable in the habits and social requirements of her class. She owed her visitor at least the courtesy of bringing Dev's request to her husband. It was the dutiful thing to do.

"I see," Martha said. "Well, we can't have you standing around in the vestibule. Please wait in the library. It's been a while, but I believe you know the way?"

The illicit, clandestine saloon in the basement of the Herbert M. Burrell & Sons rope factory was much as Fin remembered it, though if anything it was even dingier. The tobacco smoke stains on the whitewashed walls and low ceiling seemed even dirtier, the wooden floor more splintered, the bar more scratched, the tables and benches more rickety. Devoid even of gaslight, kerosene lanterns around the room still rendered the saloon in flickering light and sooty shadows clogged with cigarette, cigar, and pipe smoke. The air still smelled of the river and unwashed men. The buzz of snoring men sleeping it off, their heads on the tables or their bodies on the floor, accompanied the sour music of sad men moaning sad songs or the drunken laughter over a card game or a throw of the dice. It was the kind of place where the passage of time had no meaning, where the city's primitive past kept residence, and the fast approaching modern century couldn't even find the door.

The clientele was as primitive as the saloon. Some of the men were rough sailors, some brawny dockworkers. The singers of sad songs were usually red-cheeked Irishmen, while olive-skinned Italians played cards with bearded Jews and even with Chinese and Negroes, as this was one of the downtown saloons where everyone of every sort was welcome. Everyone here was a member of the brotherhood of the bottle, the price of a drink the only dues.

Several of the men in the room were familiar to Fin, fellows who were somehow still alive after years of imbibing the saloon's rotgut whiskey. A few nodded at Fin in recognition. Others were beyond recognizing anyone or anything at all.

The barkeep, a boulder-sized brute named Mike Sloane, said, "How fiery you want it?" when Fin stepped to the bar with Ned.

It wasn't a mere question. It was a challenge: did Fin want her rotgut watered down or strong enough to eat the brain?

"She'll take the full fire," Ned answered before Fin had the chance.

Sloan poured a double shot from a large tin can of the golden liquid, the whiskey's pretty color a camouflage for its vicious bite.

There was challenge in Ned's eyes as Fin picked up the glass. She stared right back at him. She even smiled, enjoying the game. A few of the men in the room started knocking their knuckles in rhythm on the tables and the bar. Phlegmy voices chanted, "Drink, drink, drink, drink."

Fin drank. She knocked back the double shot in one swallow. The near poisonous concoction of grain alcohol mixed with the dregs of whiskey and beer singed her throat, watered her eyes, and tore into her head like a claw. But she stood up straight, suppressed a gag, and didn't dare cough. She just let out a long breath, licked her lips, wiped her mouth with the back of her hand, and smiled again at Ned.

The men around Fin cheered and patted her on her back. Others knocked on tables in recognition of her imbiber's courage. Barkeep Sloane slapped down a chaser of beer to soothe Fin's throat. She downed it fast.

"Okay, Ned," she said, her always rough voice made even more ragged from the lingering bite of the rotgut, "let's parlay, startin' with what you know about John Jones an' why the law's ignorin' the death of his lady friend."

"An' you'll tell me somethin' I don't already know about the coppers?"

"Didn't I say I would? You know I don't welch."

Ned rapped a knuckle on the bar for Mike Sloan's attention. He ordered a beer for himself and another for Fin. When the foamy beers arrived, Ned picked up his mug, toasted Fin with a "Salud," and he and Fin both drank. The thick foam further soothed Fin's throat and her rotgut-clawed brain.

Ned wiped the foam from his mouth with the sleeve of his jacket, then said, "Yeah, I know a thing or two about Jones. But he was just small p'taydez. Handsome fella, fancied himself an actor, which made him useful to certain people. But word has it he got too big for his britches. From what I hear, he was just supposed to romance young women, get 'em doped up an' keep 'em on the dope. What happened to them after that was none of his business. Other people took over."

"What other people? An' took over what?"

"That's where things get fuzzy," Ned said. "Tell you the truth, Fin, I dunno. There's some real shadowy people in this town, y'know? People y'don't see but who control the strings an' pull 'em." A trace of bitterness creased the corners of Ned's mouth, a barely suppressed expression of the suspicion that he, Ned The Noggin Hennessey, leader of the city's most powerful gang, was himself dancing at the end of some boss's string.

Fin said, "You got pals in all the political clubs, Ned. Hell, you probably put 'em there. You tellin' me you ain't heard a thing about who controlled Jones or what they was up to? Or why the coppers are keepin' their hands off the murder of his lady friend?"

"Look, Fin, I never asked no copper or no politician about it. Never had no reason to, understan'? The big boys do what they do, an' they stay outta the way to let me an' my Stompers do what we do. Sometimes I do a favor for the big boys, sometimes they do a favor for me. The arrangement works for everybody. Puts a lot of money in everybody's pockets. You know the score, Fin, you been in the game. So no, I ain't heard a thing about Jones's lady, an' no, I ain't gonna ask. Okay, now it's your turn. C'mon, come across with what you know about the coppers."

Fin did indeed know the game, and she also knew how to play it. Even better, she knew how to survive it, which is why she understood that Ned knew how to survive it, too. One of the ways to survive the game was not to ask questions.

But Fin lived by different rules now, and she wasn't finished with questions for Ned Hennessey. "You said word got aroun' that Jones got too big for his britches. Too big how? Finish tellin' me about Jones, an' then we'll talk about the coppers."

Ned finished his beer, wiped his mouth with his sleeve again, then gave Fin a shrewd smile. He finished off with a shrug. "They say Jones pulled a skim on his bosses," he said. "Seems he tried to sell some of his dopers to brothels around town, but there weren't any takers. Who wants a near-dead dolly in their bed?"

Fin nodded. Ned's information dovetailed with Black Haired Mag's story about Jones. "But what about the murder of Pauline Godfrey?"

"Who?"

"Jones's lady friend. The girl who got her throat cut. You hear anything about that or why the coppers don't want any part of it?"

"Jeez, Fin, the coppers don't tell me what's on their minds. So I never heard of this Godfrey girl. But if she was one of Jones's dopers—"

"Yeah, seems she was."

"Then that's probably why the coppers are leavin' it alone. Somebody higher up don't want the coppers diggin' aroun' in any murder connected to John Jones, 'cause diggin' around in the business of John Jones might mean diggin' a path to a big boy's door."

Fin gave that a *tsk* and an annoyed wave. "I can figure that for myself, Ned. I need somethin' deeper. You got the goods on a lotta politicians. Any in particular come to mind?"

Ned met that with a testy chuckle and a dismissive wave of his hand. "Take y'pick," he said. "Could be someone in City Hall, or a buncha fellas on the Board of Aldermen, or maybe not even a pol at all. Could be someone with a lotta dough, or just a friend of a friend of a pol, someone with a lotta secrets. Now, that's all I know, Fin. I'm tellin' you the truth. I'm empty pockets on this one. So now it's your turn. Tell me about the coppers."

"You know a detective by the name of Coyle? Charles Coyle?"

"Not personally, but I heard the name."

"Well, here's all the information you need to know about what's goin' on down on Mulberry Street. Detective Charles Coyle is scared to death."

Alistair Flugg's library was a celebration of gentlemanly civilization, a bastion against the encroachment of modern tastes and their accompanying vulgar attitudes. The room's only nod to the here-and-now was the telephone on Flugg's mahogany desk. The desk was, of course, tastefully neo-Classical in style, reinforcing an ambiance of time brought to a standstill. The desk chair and two club chairs opposite, all of rich brown leather, furthered the sense of gentlemanly nostalgia. The Persian carpet of subdued colors added a colonialist touch. The floor-to-ceiling shelves were lined with books by great historians and philosophers through the ages. All of the books were by Northern European and American thinkers; Mr. Flugg was not inclined to give credence to scholars native to other locales, populated as they were by those lesser races currently flooding into New York and tainting the very air Mr. Flugg was forced to breathe.

Dev lingered over the single trace of heart-over-mind in the room: a photograph on the desk of Alistair and Martha on their wedding day. What a handsome couple they were. The hand-colored photo caught the happy sparkle in Alistair's blue eyes, the bridal blush in Martha's youthful cheeks, and the soft glow on her coils of blond hair. Dev had not seen either Alistair or Martha smile so warmly in all the years she'd known them.

The wedding photograph was the only family memento in the library. Dev thought it odd that there was no photo of the Fluggs' daughter Eliza and her husband, the handsome and strapping Charles O'Hare. Well, perhaps not so odd; Dev recalled that Alistair was dead set against his daughter's marriage to a man he considered "not our sort." And despite the enterprising young Irishman's rise from the streets to become an attorney currently practicing in Philadelphia—a move Dev now considered might have been to avoid his father-in-law's ongoing animus—Alistair further sniffed at O'Hare's habit of representing that city's less fortunate, often the very same sorts of people Alistair targeted in his New York raids.

The absence of any photographs of his daughter, or with her parents, or with her husband made it clear that Alistair's attitude had not budged. Dev's heart went out to Martha, who surely must miss her daughter. But Dev's sympathy for Martha Flugg was cut short: hadn't her own mother turned her out, and for a similarly rigid attitude of disapproval?

The old pain once again threatened Dev's equilibrium, but now it was not only Dev that harbored such pain; she felt the room itself radiated it.

It was then that Flugg walked into the library. Dev noted that except for a bit of gray in his hair and a slight hollowing of his smooth-shaven face, he'd changed little since she last saw him six years ago. In his dark gray suit and black waistcoat it was clear he still favored excessively conservative attire. Though Dev always knew him to be a serious man, it now appeared to her that his facial expression had hardened from merely serious to stern.

"Devorah," he said with a distinct chill. "Were it not out of respect for your family and my friendship with your father, I would not have agreed to see you. But my wife said you are here to ask for my help. Perhaps you are here to ask me to help you renounce your foolish and obscene romantic choice, in which case I will gladly—"

"I am here to ask about John Jones."

"I beg your pardon?"

"Alistair, I've always admired you. In fact, I said so even this morning. Though I may disagree with you and your tactics, I respect the sincerity of your beliefs and admire your willingness to stand firm for them. So please, afford me the same courtesy so that we may have a frank discussion. Yes, I am here for your help, but I am not here to change my life. Is that clear?"

Though Flugg was indeed flattered by Dev's admiration, he would not allow that prideful emotion to interfere with his integrity. "Your impertinence is unseemly in a woman, Devorah, but, yes, your point is clear. Now, what is this about John Jones?"

"Alistair, may I sit down?"

"Yes, of course, forgive me." Flugg nodded to a club chair while he took a seat behind his desk. He sat stiffly, leaned forward with his hands folded on his desk, and gave Dev a humorless smile. His eyes, which once had the warmth of happiness in his wedding photo, were today a wintery blue. "May I have Martha bring you some refreshment?" he said. "Coffee, perhaps, or tea?"

"No thank you. If you don't mind I'd like to get right to my purpose in coming to see you."

"This Mr. Jones."

"Quite. Alistair, according to the news accounts of your activities, you have friendships—or at least contacts—in the police department and in city government."

"I do indeed," he said, his pride in his relationship to the city's powerful forces evident in the crispness of his words. "Many of those fine gentlemen are in complete agreement with my crusade to rid the city of filth."

The way he said it, a near hiss in his pronunciation of the word filth, felt to Dev like a thinly disguised personal attack; if not precisely against her then certainly against her romantic relationship with the dockside-born Fin Donner. She suppressed a cringe at Flugg's remark, determined to maintain her dignity not just on her own behalf but on Fin's behalf as well.

She continued with purpose. "I need you to inquire among those gentlemen about the business of John Jones, late of a Mrs. Mallory's boardinghouse on Bayard Street. I need to know why the police, and perhaps persons higher up in city government, are covering up Mr. Jones's demise and not pursuing the case of a murder of a young woman who was associated with him, Miss Pauline Godfrey."

"And why do you wish to know about these presumably sordid people?"

"First of all, Alistair, there was nothing sordid about Miss Godfrey, except, perhaps, what befell her due to her involvement with Mr. Jones. As to my interest, Miss Godfrey's parents hired the firm of Donner & Longstreet Inquiries to find their daughter's murderer, since the police have no interest in doing so." Flugg's slight wince at her mention of association with Fin Donner merely compelled Dev to sit up straighter. "And by the way, I was accosted on the street yesterday and warned to stop any further inquiries about Mr. Jones. Now I ask you, Alistair, is it the habit of your friends in the police department or city government to employ common thugs to accost women in the street? Is that their idea—or yours—of preventing crime?"

"How dare you," Flugg said. "How dare you impugn my integrity, Devorah. I am sorry you were accosted. It is the sort of behavior I normally fight against. But this . . . this investigation business of yours," he said with a haughty wave. "This is not a suitable activity for a well-bred woman."

Among the many lessons Devorah learned through her life with Fin was that breeding meant nothing. Character is what counted, and right now the character of Alistair Flugg, a man she'd admired, was to her mind less than noble and far less admirable than the sturdy character of her beloved, slum-bred Fin.

Looking directly at Flugg, finding strength of character within herself, Dev said, "You, who crusades against the scourge of crime, cares nothing for the murder of a young girl? That is not worthy of you, Alistair. And in case it soothes your delicate senses, Miss Godfrey came from a very respectable family, solid citizens indeed. They are understandably distraught over their daughter's murder, and angered and puzzled over the lack of official concern. Alistair, I ask you to put aside your feelings about me and how I live my life and open your heart to these grieving parents."

Flugg sat back in his chair, drummed his fingers on his desk, and kept his eyes on Dev. There was a hint of concern in his eyes, perhaps a remnant of past family collegiality. But Dev thought she saw something else, too, something bitter that ate at him.

At length, he said, "Devorah, if, as you imply, this Mr. Jones was a disreputable sort who somehow brought Miss Godfrey to ruin, then I must disagree with you regarding her respectability. At the very least, she dishonored her family. That is a serious transgression. Her family is better off without her."

"Alistair! That is a horrible thing to say!"

"The truth is often horrible, Devorah, but it is the truth nonetheless. And the truth is simply this: no respectable young woman would ever involve herself with the likes of Mr. Jones. Perhaps that is why the police are ignoring her murder. It may be that as far as they are concerned, it's just another death of another fallen woman, and there are far too many of that sort for the police to waste their time about. So I cannot help you, Devorah."

"Cannot or will not?"

"As you like. Now, if there's nothing else, I am a busy man." Flugg rose from his desk, came around to Devorah and reached down in a gesture of assisting her from her chair.

She did not resist. It was pointless. When she stood and allowed herself to be escorted to the library door, she said, "I'm sorry for the breach in our friendship, Alistair. I'm particularly sorry to have lost Martha's affection. Do give her my best regards, and the same to Eliza and her husband. I was sorry when they left New York for Philadelphia. I did so much enjoy their company."

"Miss Longstreet," Flugg said, his irritation made clear in the formal use of her name, "please curb your interest in my family's affairs. Now, I bid you good day."

Dev gave him a smile. It wasn't a warm smile, or even a friendly smile, but a smile Devorah enjoyed nonetheless. "You know, Alistair, the only modern thing in this room, perhaps in your life, is the telephone. Were it not for that, time and progress would simply have passed you by."

Chapter Twenty-Three

The sting of yesterday's wound by the Curtain Call bartender's brass knuckles made the buzzing in Fin's brain from today's rotgut whiskey feel even worse. These searing assaults to the exterior and interior of her head reminded Fin, like a couple of wagging-finger scolds, that perhaps she was no longer the swaggering soldier of the streets. Much as Fin had to admit that elements of her past life were excitements and pleasures she very much missed, today's aches and pains made clear that six years of a softer life had diminished her body's tolerance for it. Her occasional nights of gambling or at the prizefights were one thing; bar fights and rotgut whiskey were quite another.

Back home now in the cozy confines of the life she shared with her treasured Devorah, Fin brewed a strong cup of coffee to help clear the buzzing in her head. Ensconced in one of the comfortable leather armchairs in the parlor, Fin sipped her coffee while she waited for Dev to return after her meeting with that prude Flugg.

In the meantime, Fin thought about her conversation with Ned Hennessey, about his hints that whoever was in back of the John Jones business might be a politician or not, might be a cop or not, or might be just a big-shot private citizen pulling everyone's strings. She remembered Ned's face going pale as paper, his eyes wide before they narrowed and looked away when she told him Detective Charles Coyle was scared. Ned and Fin both understood that a scared cop is a bad omen, a warning sign of treachery somewhere in the complex web of corruption woven equally by the police, politicians, the underworld, and the powerful high-hats who control it all.

Fin thought about all this while she sipped her coffee, its rich aroma and strong kick restoring the workings of her brain. Her thoughts were interrupted by a knock at the door.

She wasn't expecting anyone, and Devorah, possessed of her own key, would certainly have no reason to knock. Fin hoped that whoever was at the door wasn't Coyle come back with more warnings.

More knocks, impatient ones, accompanied Fin all the way to the door.

"Hold y'horses," she said as her hand turned the doorknob. She opened the door, and saw a teary-eyed Black Haired Mag, her whole being quaking under the threadbare black cloak pulled tight around her.

"They took Timmy," Mag said, her voice as ragged a sound as Fin ever heard until Mag's moaning wail smothered it.

Fin brought the near hysterical woman inside and closed the door. Mag all but collapsed against Fin, her tears dripping onto Fin's waistcoat, her wails scraping against the fabric.

Fin held her, stroked her hair, tried to soothe her. "Mag, calm yourself an' tell me what's goin' on." She lifted Mag's chin so that she could speak to her face to face. "Who took Timmy?"

Mag's sobs, though quieting, still choked her throat. "A . . . woman," she finally said, every sound a rasp of misery, "an' a . . . a copper. The woman . . . she was . . . a prissy bitch—y'know the type; like her father was a . . . a stone, an' her mother . . . was a

159

stick . . . an' the bitch came outta her mother hard an' dry. The woman gave me lip . . . she said I ain't fit t'be . . . a mother. An' then the copper . . . the copper, he grabbed Timmy. Just grabbed him real rough! Y'shoulda heard Timmy holler, Fin, like he was bein' killed or somethin'! Oh, my boy, my poor boy . . ." The spigot opened again to Mag's tears and wails. She pounded her balled fists against Fin.

Fin took Mag by the shoulders, held her tight to steady her. "Mag, calm down. I can't help you if you get all hysterical." When Mag's wails subsided to tears she worked hard to control, Fin was able to ask, "Did the woman an' the copper say who sent them or where they took Timmy?"

"No," Mag said, wiping her tears with the back of her hand. "They just said that I ain't fit an' that I had to be taught a lesson." She collapsed against Fin again, her tears bursting through their weak floodgate. Mag sobbed with such force Fin was afraid the woman's vocal cords would rip right out of her throat.

Fin held her, stroked her head, her back, tried to soothe this woman who'd once been beautiful and proud, and who'd given Fin so much pleasure. "Shh now, we'll figure this out, Mag. C'mon into the parlor. I'll pour you a brandy." Fin enveloped the distraught Mag, ready to lead her to the parlor, just as Devorah walked in and saw a crying woman in Fin's arms.

In the slow-motion eternity of mere seconds, the jealousy that had yesterday threatened her faith in Fin, her worry over the temptations of Fin's previous life, now ate at Dev again. It gnawed on her with the pitilessness of a hungry animal gnawing meat from prey.

She dared not succumb to it. She did not want to believe what she saw. She did not want to believe that Fin not only gave in to temptation but brought it home. Not only did Dev not want to believe any of it, she *refused* to believe it, or tried to. "Fin?"

At the sound of Dev's voice, Mag turned from Fin. "You must

be Miss Longstreet," she said, which from Mag's tenement-bred lips came out as *Miz Lawnkstrit*, just as her son had pronounced it. "Pleased to meet you. I'm in y'debt for gettin' me outta the cells the other night."

"Oh, you're Maggie Poole?" This first meeting with the woman known as Black Haired Mag, a woman she'd helped, whose son impressed her heart, did nothing to dissipate the unwanted jealousy plaguing Dev, for despite Maggie Poole's poverty, despite the hard life which lined her face, Maggie Poole was, in her worn out, worldly-wise way, beautiful.

Mag was accustomed to the stares of men who wanted to use her, the stares of bluenoses who wanted to reform her, and the stares of coppers who wanted to lock her up, but she was not accustomed to the examining stare coming from Devorah Longstreet. Mag cringed a bit under the stare, but she was not about to crumble before the woman who had enough power to have her sprung from jail and might again use that power to save her son. Trying to smile, Mag said, "Timmy really thought you was the cat's meow, Miss Longstreet, the way y'stood up to the coppers. He couldn't stop talkin' 'bout you. But now me an' Timmy need y'help again, yours an' Fin's." Mentioning Timmy brought the return of her tears, harsh and choking.

Fin said, "Mag's here on account of Timmy, Dev. Some woman an' a copper came to Mag's place an' snatched him."

With the realization that Fin's embrace of Maggie wasn't amorous but an act of comfort, the jealousy which had shaken Dev's faith in her beloved Fin evaporated like snow in sunshine. But the pain of jealousy was replaced by her guilt at even harboring it, and the deeper pain over the horror of Maggie Poole's child taken from her.

Fin said, "I was about to take Mag into the parlor and give her some brandy."

"I think we could all use a brandy," Dev said.

In the parlor, Fin helped Mag into one of the leather

armchairs. Dev removed her cloak and offered to take Mag's, but Mag said she'd rather keep it. "I'm a bit chilled," she said. It sounded unconvincing to Dev, since the room was quite warm in the afternoon sun. But the way Mag looked at Dev's fine suit, and the way she tried to hide the ragged hem of her own green dress peeking out below her cloak, answered Dev's doubts. Maggie Poole was experiencing something rarely felt by Devorah Longstreet: shame. Though Dev occasionally felt shame over some petty grievance or unwarranted emotion— like the jealousy she had no business indulging—she had never felt shame about her life. She somehow doubted that Maggie's shame was about her profession, but the shame of poverty, this cruel world's greatest sin.

Fin gave Mag a snifter of brandy, then poured one each for Dev and herself. By the time Fin and Dev had their brandy in hand, Mag had drunk hers down. Ladylike sipping was outside her experience.

The liquor soothed Mag's misery just enough for her to speak without the words knotting in her throat. "Like I says, Miss Longstreet, Timmy thinks you're somethin' special. I know y'must think he's special, too, the way he struts aroun' when he talks about you." Mag smiled when she said it, and Devorah smiled, too, remembering Timmy's proud strut through police headquarters. "But he's just a little boy, y'know? He's my little boy, an' now they've taken him." She balled her fist, brought a knuckle to her face to try to stop more tears. It didn't work.

Dev pulled a handkerchief from her sleeve and gave it to Mag to dry her eyes.

Fin poured Mag another brandy. "Here, drink this. Slowly. The slower the better. It'll warm you up real nice that way."

With a nod of understanding, having seen how Fin and Devorah sip their brandies instead of swallowing in one gulp, Mag took a small sip.

Fin said, "By the way, Mag, how'd y'find me? I don't recall

you ever bein' here before."

Mag tilted her head toward the telephone on the little table beside her chair. "I figured y'had a telephone, so I went over to a saloon I know that's got one, too, an' I figured they had a directory. Findin' people is easy these days, y'know?"

"Yeah, not like the old days, eh, Mag?"

"Nothin's like the old days, 'cept maybe the same old slaps in our faces by hands in fancy gloves. Oh! Sorry, Miss Longstreet. I didn't mean—"

The warmth in Dev's smile elicited a small, sheepish one from Mag. "I know you didn't," Dev said. "Now let's get back to the business of finding your little boy so he can go home to his mother. Think carefully, did this woman or the police officer give any hint regarding where they were taking Timmy?"

Mag shook her head. "They didn't tell me nothin' except that I had to be taught a lesson. What sorta lesson they talkin' about? If they was talkin' about my line of business, well, okay, I know they don't approve, an' I don't care nothin' about that. But if they was talkin' about my motherin'—Fin, you know I'm a good mother. You know I love my Timmy more than my own life. There's nothin' I wouldn't do for that kid."

Dev added, "And I daresay there's nothing he would not do for you. He proved that to me at the police station. Listen, Miss Poole—"

"Please, call me Maggie, or just Mag if that suits better."

"All right, Maggie it is. Tell me more about the woman who came with the officer. What did she look like? What was she wearing? Did she have an accent or some way of speaking that caught your attention? Tell us anything you remember."

Maggie took another sip of brandy, careful not to gulp it down, which she was tempted to do. If they wanted her to remember things, all this high-falootin' sippin' wasn't going to do the job as good as a hefty slug to wake up the head. Still, the little sips had their pleasures, like the slow, smooth warmth down her gullet instead of the fiery bite of a big swallow. "Well, the woman wasn't much to look at," she said. "Maybe she coulda helped her face a bit if she rouged it up some. But she had that dry-faced look that unhappy women have." She added, with a shrug and a lewd smile, "If y'catch my drift."

Fin returned Mag's smile with an amused one. Dev, to her embarrassment, felt her face warm, sure that her cheeks reddened. And then she blurted a small laugh because if nothing else, her blushing cheeks affirmed that Devorah Longstreet did not have the dry face of an unhappy, unsatisfied woman.

Even Maggie seemed to enjoy the joke, offering Dev a less lewd, more amused smile. Perhaps she even caught the irony—Devorah certainly did—that at one time or another each woman shared the same provider and recipient of pleasure: Fin.

The moment was not lost on Fin, who brought the conversation back to business as a means to rescue herself from the emotionally shaky precipice on which Dev and Mag had placed her. And business was where this conversation belonged anyway. "What else about the woman, Mag? How'd she talk?"

"Snooty-like. Like she'd read too many books."

"So her English was fancy?"

Dev added, "Did it sound natural?"

"Y'mean, like you talk, Miss Longstreet?"

"Thank you, Maggie. Yes, that's what I mean."

Maggie closed her eyes and took another sip of brandy. She tried to hear in her memory the way the woman spoke. The woman's awful words and voice came to her: the insistence that Mag didn't deserve to raise her own son. The memory brought renewed misery, threatening to strangle in her throat what she had to say. "No . . . not like you. You use words real . . . natural. They come outta y'mouth just normal-like. The . . . horrible woman who . . . who took Timmy . . . she used words like weapons, like knives to rip my heart out."

Devorah said, "You're doing fine, Maggie. Now, can you

think of anything else which could give us a picture of this woman, anything else which could help us find her and find where she took Timmy?"

Maggie lifted the snifter of brandy for another sip, but seeing the glass empty, she held it out to Fin for more.

Her snifter refilled, she took a sip, closed her eyes again, and plunged back into her memory. After a moment she shook her head, lowered it in despair, then looked up quickly, alert. "Yeah, there was somethin', a pin on her dress."

Dev said, "A safety pin, perhaps to keep a neckline closed, or to replace a lost button?"

"No, jewelry, sorta. Nothin' fancy, no diamonds or rubies or nothin', just a round white pin, big, about the size of a silver dollar, an' it had a picture on it. Wait, lemme think." She closed her eyes again, frowned in thought, then opened her eyes. "A house," she said. "That's what was on the pin. A picture of a house."

Fin said, "Nothin' else? Just a house?"

"Yeah, a fancy house, like a castle. But not like y'see in picture books, y'know, white or maybe made of big gray stones. This castle was brown, like some of the houses y'see here in the city."

"Brownstone," Fin and Dev said in unison.

There were a few large brownstone houses resembling castles which Dev knew of, mansions of wealthy families on Fifth Avenue or around Gramercy Park. But none of the residents of those dwellings would have any reason for snatching children, nor would they do anything as bourgeois as issue jewelry with a picture of their house.

But a charitable institution might.

A prickly sensation attacked Dev's skin, as if spiders were crawling up her spine.

Fin felt an even more stinging sensation, because the place she had in mind wasn't exactly charitable.

Chapter Twenty-Four

The Grace Home for Wayward Children, occupying a full block in a still sparsely populated area of the Upper West Side, certainly looked like a medieval castle with its turrets, spires, gables, and crenellated roofline. But there were no fairytales inside the enormous brownstone structure, no knights in shining armor, and any damsels in distress here were often as young as infants.

Standing at its imposing iron gate, Fin remembered when the place was called the Home for Children of Penury. She remembered the endless grueling work, the cold rooms and cold baths, the filth. She remembered little girls too thin and weak to complain, and little boys with new bruises every day. She did not recall anyone wearing jewelry depicting the building.

"Could be we're in the wrong place, Dev," she said, "but we'll know soon enough."

A pull-rope on the gatepost rang a loud bell on the other side of the gate, announcing the presence of visitors. While they waited for someone to respond, Dev held Fin's arm. She felt the tension in her lover's muscles, but she also felt Fin's resolve to face down the hellish memories this looming brown castle conjured.

A slender fellow, who reminded Dev of an undertaker dressed in his austere black suit and white shirt, came through the massive carved blackwood doors. He walked down the broad steps, across the small courtyard and approached the gate. "May I help you?" he said, his general manner polite, his smile in his bony face insincere.

Fin's muscles tightened even more, and Dev's own posture stiffened at the sight of the man, for his lapel pin bore the image of the Grace Home for Wayward Children.

In response to the man's chilly attitude, Devorah spoke in her most courteous but firm tone, a manner of address learned early by the city's privileged class in order to nip in the bud any resistance to their betters. "We are seeking a young boy who appears to have been brought here by mistake. His name is Timmy Poole. We are here to bring him home."

"I'm sorry, but without an appointment—"

Fin said, "I guess you didn't understan' the lady." She spoke quietly but with the full force of her rough voice. The quickly pulled pistol she now held in her hand pressed the point.

The man behind the gate raised his hands in an automatic gesture of terror.

Fin said, "Your hands in the air can't open the gate. You catch my meanin'?"

Shaking, the man lowered his hands and unlocked the gate. In his terrified state, his thin, bony face was pale as a skull. "There's . . . there's no need for violence," he said.

"This place shoulda thought of that years ago," Fin said, more mumble than statement, as she escorted Devorah through the gate.

For Fin, the walk across the courtyard felt like a death march of memories. She forced them out of her mind. She'd survived this place when she was young and vulnerable; she could survive it today when she's strong not just of body but of mind and soul.

Though she no longer pointed the pistol at the nervous man

escorting them to the building, Fin made sure the bulky outline of her hand on the gun in her jacket pocket was visible to him.

Inside, the entry hall and cavernous reception area hadn't changed much, except they appeared to Fin to be cleaner, with electric light replacing gaslight, and the cast iron spiral stairway to the second floor now carpeted. Two conservatively attired women in identical gray dresses with a fringe of lace at the neck and a pin decorated with an image of the Grace Home on the bodice, were busy behind a large reception desk. Its polished wood gleamed in the sun streaming through the enormous stained glass windows, tinting the air and the women with colored light.

The man escorting Fin and Devorah brought them to the reception desk and took refuge behind it with the women. With a nod, he said, "These people are looking for a particular boy whom they believe may be here."

One of the women, the older of the two, said, "I see. And why would you assume that?" Her tone, like the look in her alert brown eyes, was not discourteous but neither was it friendly.

Fin, unimpressed with the new cleanliness or modernizing of the place, said bluntly, "Because the woman who snatched him wore a pin just like the one all of you are wearin'. Pretty stupid, to advertise a kidnappin'. Matter of fact, his Ma described a woman just like you who snatched her son."

The older woman, her eyes narrowed, snapped, "We do not kidnap children. We remove them from unfit environments."

The way the woman spoke, every word with clipped enunciation, reminded Dev of Maggie's description of the kidnapper's sharp manner of speech. Dev said, "On whose authority do you remove them?"

At the mention of authority, the man behind the desk spoke up. "We have a Board of Trustees and a legal charter registered with the City of New York to act on its behalf in performing charitable work. As for the pin we wear, it serves as our identification as legally empowered representatives of a city-sanctioned child welfare organization."

Dev, recognizing puffed-up palaver when she heard it, rebuffed it with a confident smile. She said, "Then you admit Timmy Poole is here."

Through a facial expression which somehow combined an arrogant sniff and a resentful sneer, the man said, "The names of our charges remain secret to protect their privacy. Now, good day to you, Miss whoever-you-are—"

"Longstreet. Devorah Longstreet. Yes, those Longstreets," she said when the eyebrows of the man and both women went up at the mention of her name. "Chances are I'm acquainted with at least a few of the distinguished gentlemen on your Board of Trustees. One of them might even be my father, for all I know." She didn't mention that her father hadn't spoken to her in six years.

"No, I don't believe he's—" the man started.

Fin, fed up with all the chatter, cut him off. "I don't give a damn what you believe. We ain't leavin' until we find the boy and take him home."

The other woman behind the desk, younger and less stern in countenance, remained quiet and busied herself with what appeared to Dev to be a register. Dev placed a gloved finger firmly on an open page and said to the woman, "Perhaps you could look in your book for the name Timmy Poole, or perhaps Timothy Poole."

"As I said," the man chimed in again, "to protect the privacy of our charges, their names remain secret."

But Fin had secrets of her own to keep from the three priggish sentinels behind the reception desk. She would not tell them that she knew this place inside out, knew the location and layout of the dormitories, the work rooms, the punishment rooms. She would not tell them about her middle-of-the-night escape by climbing out a bathroom window, jumping down two stories to the street and running for her thirteen-year-old life on a sprained ankle.

With these memories in mind, Fin was sure that though the place now had electric light and a newfangled telephone on the desk, the obstinacy of these three stiff sticks guarding the reception area convinced Fin that the old brutal attitudes were still in charge.

Fin, like Devorah, had her own way of speaking that brooked no backtalk from the hearer. But unlike Dev's tone of polished confidence, Fin's confident tone was hard and rough as a stone wall. "I'll just have a look aroun'."

The man said, "No, you—!"

Fin's stare was so coldly fierce, the rest of the man's words never made it up from his throat.

Fin said to Devorah, "Is that little pistol of yours still in your handbag?"

"It is."

"Good. If any of these three try to use the telephone while I have a look aroun', well, I leave it up to you." Fin punctuated it with a wink, then headed for the spiral staircase.

Dev had never killed anyone, and she wasn't about to today. She'd never maimed or even injured anyone with a bullet either, and she wondered if she could, should the need arise to keep the man or the women from using the telephone to alert any guards or other personnel.

But the three behind the reception desk didn't know about Dev's doubts. They only knew she had a gun. Dev, sensing their fear, recognized its benefit to her. Affecting an air of mock courtesy, she said, "In the meantime, while my companion is gone, let's have a look at that register, shall we?"

Upstairs, the second-floor hallway, like the reception area

downstairs, was cleaner than Fin remembered and lit with electric fixtures instead of flickering gaslight. But the brown walls and creaking wood floors evoked the same dread they did when she was a ten-year-old pup plucked from the streets, tossed into a closed wagon with other ragamuffins and brought here.

Behind the twelve doors lining the hallway were the dormitory rooms: six on one side for girls, six on the other side for boys. Fin's stomach churned at the memory of the brown-walled, dreary, heatless rooms, each holding a dozen steel beds with paper-thin mattresses and flimsy blankets. *To instill discipline*, the wardens and matrons said, their sticks in hand. Even now, the flesh on Fin's arms and the backs of her legs felt the sting of a stick slapped against her, as if her flesh had its own memory.

New arrivals were brought to the dormitories after a harsh shower and painful delousing, the children's clothes discarded for burning, replaced by sack-like uniforms of stiffly starched muslin that scratched tender young skin. Each new little prisoner was assigned a bed and a wooden footlocker for their provided underwear, soaps, and any personal items they were allowed to keep; that is, if a warden or matron didn't snatch them.

Fin did her best to squelch the memory of this agonizing routine, on guard against being paralyzed by the pain of it. She was here to find Timmy Poole, if indeed he was here, and she wasn't about to let anything stop her, least of all any remnant of the misery she'd experienced here.

She opened a dormitory door, hoping to find Timmy at his assigned bed, arranging his footlocker under the hard eyes of a warden. The room was empty.

One by one, Fin looked into each long, narrow, dreary room on both sides of the hall. These, too, were empty.

At the door to the last room, Fin's hands balled into fists. Her breath caught in her chest, as if bony fingers had her lungs in their grip. Her jaw tightened, clamped so hard her teeth hurt.

Beyond this door was the room she'd shared with eleven other little prisoners. She remembered their faces, their eyes dulled against their daily despair, the cries of the newest little ones in their beds.

Fin opened the door and walked in. The room was empty.

As if pulled by an invisible thread, Fin walked along the long row of beds to what would have been hers, third from the end. She walked past memories of Caitlin McGuire, an eight-year-old orphan who'd carried beer pails through the streets of the Five Points slums for a penny a pail before being brought here; past Theresa Donazetti, a pretty little girl of ten with dark eyes and wavy black hair whose big smile was gone after her first night in here; past Jenny Tremaine, a Negro tot of six who was pulled shrieking in terror from her bed by a matron in the middle of the night and was never seen again; past all the other little girls who'd either survived this place or didn't.

With a lump in her throat, Fin arrived at her own bed. Despite herself, despite her revulsion at the mere sight of it, she sat down.

What she felt surprised her, disoriented her: the bed was not hard. The blanket was a good wool. The mattress was not paper thin but a normal mattress comfortable enough for a night's rest.

The clean, electric-lit hallway, the comfortable beds—still, Fin wasn't sure if she could trust what she saw. She wasn't ready to believe that the horrors of the old Home for the Children of Penury had been replaced by a more enlightened care offered by the Grace Home for Wayward Children.

The name of the place sent a chill through her, a reaction against that insulting term, "Wayward Children." Fin didn't have much of a head for the finer points of the English language, but she knew what the high-hats, the do-gooders, and the gospel grinders meant by wayward: wrong side of the tracks, wrong families, wrong names, wrong lives. Comfortable mattresses might just be balms to soothe the do-gooders' intolerant souls.

And besides, a good night's sleep might be just to make sure the little prisoners were more fit for work than the children were in Fin's day.

It was time to find out.

Using a back stairway—she wasn't about to give the threesome at the reception desk a chance for another encounter—Fin went down to the first floor. It was there, beyond the reception area, where the workrooms were. Here, the hallway was wider, the walls lined in white butcher-shop tile. Fin remembered the nauseating mixture of blood spatters, tobacco spit, and other unidentifiable substances which stained the walls. The walls today were clean.

The thick steel doors to the workrooms hadn't changed, though. The doors were always kept locked, deterrents to any of the young laborers thinking to escape their tasks as launderers, coal shovelers, cigar rollers, seamstresses, loom operators, or any of the other backbreaking jobs done in these rooms. Portholes covered with small steel doors on hinges allowed supervisors to monitor the activity in the workrooms, making sure the wardens and matrons kept the children at their work.

The portholes which were once used for instilling fear were today to Fin's advantage. She could spy into the workrooms, look to see if Timmy Poole was toiling in any of them. If he was, she could shoot the lock and open the door.

Before opening the first porthole, she steeled herself against the agonies she was about to witness, memories she was about to relive: children of all ages, bent over looms or sewing machines or shoveling coal into sacks.

She opened the first porthole, put her face close to the glass, then stood back as if her breath had been sucked out of her, stunned at what she saw: children, boys and girls ranging in age from around seven or eight to maybe thirteen or so, sitting quietly at schoolroom desks, writing in notebooks, while a teacher, a woman in the same style of gray dress as the women at the reception desk and wearing the same pin stood at a blackboard writing spelling lessons in chalk: Cat. Dog. Day. Night. The cat sleeps all day and the dog sleeps all night.

Fin took a minute to let her breath and her nerves settle before she looked through the porthole again. She wanted to make sure the peaceful scene within wasn't an illusion. It wasn't. Children in neat gray uniforms were writing lessons in their notebooks while a teacher wrote more words on the blackboard: Pencil. Book. School.

Fin didn't see Timmy Poole among the children, but an uncomfortable idea crept through her, an idea she had a hard time acknowledging but could not dismiss: if the old, cruel Home for Children of Penury had become the enlightened and humane Grace Home for Wayward Children, then maybe Timmy Poole really was better off here? Maybe a good night's sleep in a soft bed, maybe clean clothes and learning his ABCs gave him a chance at a future off the streets.

She looked through the porthole again, one more chance to convince herself it was all real. The same scene was before her eyes: a teacher instructing the children; the children quietly at work on their lessons, their heads bent over their notebooks, their faces serious.

She closed the porthole and went quickly to the other steel doors and opened their portholes. There was no sign of Timmy Poole, but the scene of a quiet classroom was repeated in each room: well-behaved street urchins bent quietly over their books.

None of the girls were giggling.

None of the boys were fidgety.

These were previously children of the streets, children like Fin, children who'd never submit to high-and-mighty authority without a fight or at least disobedience, unless those misbehaviors had been beaten out of them.

Propelled by a nightmare hunch, she hurried to the back stairs again, taking them two at a time down to the cellar, down to those chambers of horror where Fin knew too well the cruel punishments administered there years ago for the tiniest infractions: if a child laughed while working, or whispered to another child in the hallway, or couldn't work fast enough, or fainted in the workroom, or talked back, or cried, or simply didn't obey. The workrooms may be gone, but the methods of taking the natural fidget out of those children she saw in the classrooms might still be as cruel as ever.

Her heart squeezed tight in her chest as she descended the stairs. Her head filled with nightmare memories, memories so awful a scream rose in her throat. Only Fin's awareness that the sound would alert the wardens or matrons or whoever was supplying the Grace Home for Wayward Children with cruelty and muscle these days kept the scream from exploding.

Reaching the cellar, Fin kicked the door open, the same wooden door which had been here when she'd been tortured in this cellar. Unlike the workrooms, there was no need for a heavy steel door. Any children confined here were locked in windowless cells; no escape to the freedom of the street was possible.

The sound of the busted door echoed through the dimly lit cellar. As the echo died away, another sound wove through it, a whimper, a delicate if ragged voice trying to form words: "No . . . please . . . no . . . I'm . . . sorry."

"Timmy? Timmy, it's Fin!"

"F . . . Fin? Fin Donnuh?"

The old kerosene lanterns had been replaced by a single electric ceiling fixture which barely made its way inside the cell where Fin found Timmy Poole. She could just make out his ragged clothes, his blood-streaked legs and bare feet, the soles crisscrossed with dark, bloody lines.

The cell was locked.

"Timmy, get back! Get as far back as you can an' against the side wall."

Through whimpers of pain and hope, the boy managed,

175

"O . . . kay," and dragged himself away from the front of the cell.

Fin said, "Cover your ears, Timmy. Put your hands on your ears."

"O . . . kay."

Fin aimed for the keyhole, keeping the nozzle of her thirty-two-caliber revolver several inches back from the lock plate to avoid back-blast and minimize any flying shrapnel. The roar from the gun echoed through the cellar, banged around the walls, and sounded like a battlefield. It terrified an already frightened Timmy, who screamed. But the bullet broke the lock, and Fin was able to open the cell door.

Inside, she lifted Timmy Poole in her arms.

Upstairs in the reception hall, though Dev held her Derringer for all to see, in truth it was a weak defense against the man and two women behind the desk and the four muscular gentlemen in black suits who'd gathered there as a result of hearing the gun blast in the cellar. The men held thick billy clubs which they swayed back and forth.

Seeing this state of affairs and its threat, Fin put Timmy down, "I know it'll hurt, lad, but walk, Timmy. Walk fast as you can to Miss Longstreet."

The boy's feet left bloody stains along the floor as he hobbled across the room to Dev, whose arms were outstretched as she moved toward him. The sight of Timmy's bloody legs, his filthy clothes and face, his once blond hair now gray-brown with soot, nearly brought her to tears, but she would not break down in front of the Grace Home's barbarous staff. Nor would she break down in front of the young Master Poole, the proud fellow who had so impressed her at police headquarters. Such a boy needed her strength, not her pity.

Fin, her hands now free, raised her more powerful gun

towards the menacing gentlemen. "I'd advise you not to stop us. This ain't no polite little pistol like Miss Longstreet's. It'll cut a big hole in whoever moves."

No one did. The four muscular gentlemen stopped swaying their billy clubs.

Dev picked Timmy up in her arms. The boy's limp body felt like a sack of loose bones. She nearly cried as she carried him out of the reception hall and into the entry vestibule, with Fin following behind.

On their way out the door, Dev saw something on the vestibule wall she and Fin hadn't noticed in their haste to enter the building and find Timmy: a photo of the Grace Home for Wayward Children's Board of Trustees. She did indeed know a number of the gentlemen in the photograph. One gentleman in particular grabbed her attention: Mr. Alistair P. Flugg.

CHAPTER TWENTY-FIVE

The day was actually going smoothly for the killer. There was work to be done, people to satisfy, people to smile at. It was getting easier to smile.

CHAPTER TWENTY-SIX

Timmy rested in Dev's arms in the hansom cab, his legs stretched across to Fin's lap. Grime from the boy's torn clothes soiled Dev's cloak, blood from his legs and feet stained Fin's trousers. Neither Fin nor Devorah cared about their dirtied garments.

Dev wiped Timmy's face with her handkerchief. The first thing the boy said when his tears were wiped away was, "How'd y'know where t'find me?"

Fin said, "Your ma came by an' told us about the people who took you. This place came to mind."

"Y'knows this place, Fin?"

Fin nodded at the boy, a slow, heavy nod Timmy understood at once. He lifted himself from Dev's lap and bent to Fin, throwing his battered arms around her.

Timmy rested against Fin for the remainder of the cab ride, dozing in thin but tender sleep.

The hansom stopped on Baxter Street at the arcade entrance to the courtyard leading to Maggie Poole's tenement. "This is

179

as far as I go," the cabman said. "I won't take me or my horse into that vile place."

Devorah couldn't blame him. Baxter Street was unnerving enough, with its jostling pushcart vendors, braying horses, noisy crowds of shoppers in the threadbare shawls and ill-fitting suits of the neighborhood's impoverished residents. Dev wondered if the laundry drying on clotheslines overhead absorbed the smell rising from the street of so many sweating bodies, the odors of vegetables, fruit, meat, poultry, and the dung of horses and stray dogs. The arcade leading from the street appeared to her as being even worse: a dark, threatening entry into filth.

With her gloved hand to her nose against the street's stench, Dev stepped out of the cab, followed by Fin, who carried Timmy in her arms. Dev paid the cabman, and the trio entered the arcade. Fin continued to carry Timmy, sparing the boy's injured feet from the rough, dirty cobblestones.

When they'd passed through the arcade and into the courtyard, Devorah stopped cold. The execrable conditions she saw there, the shabby, sagging dwellings, the stinking uncollected refuse of every sort, defied her most basic notion of human decency, not only regarding the cursed humanity forced to live here, but the cursed society which allows or even creates such a place. In her investigative work she'd seen immigrant neighborhoods, impoverished neighborhoods. She'd empathized with the struggling humanity in those places, people trying desperately to grab a bit of dignity, even if they had to break the law to achieve it. But nothing prepared her for the degradation of life in the decrepit tenement courtyard where Black Haired Mag did business and raised her young son. It made Dev ill to think—no, to be suddenly and bluntly aware—that there were, no doubt, too many places like this in the city, her city, a city where families like hers made the rules and consigned the less fortunate to misery.

She looked at Fin, her beloved Fin who carried in her arms

a child of this hellish place as if it was the most natural thing in the world. For the first time, Dev accepted that it was.

Dev resumed her walk through the courtyard, following Fin. She nearly slipped on a cobblestone slick with a substance she did not care to know. She forced from her face an expression of shock at the sight of a haggard young woman in a ragged wool dress of indistinguishable color exiting a communal latrine, a babe in her arms. Dev would not further degrade the woman, an exhausted mother whom the world already disdained.

The woman, though, wary of the well-dressed Devorah and her masculinely attired companion, didn't bother to hide her own suspicions. Such fancy people never did her any good; on the contrary, they only brought the law down on her, or kept the law from her when she needed it. And their bringing Maggie's boy Timmy with them only deepened the woman's distrust.

At the stairway to Mag's tenement, Dev followed Fin up the wooden steps. She feared that the splintered, sagging wood could crumble at any minute and send Fin, Timmy and herself tumbling to the cobblestones. Dev exhaled with grim relief when they all made it safely to the top.

Inside the tenement's dark hall, Dev raised her gloved hand to her nose again against the rank odor of stale bodies leading stale lives. But she drew her hand down, realizing that what she smelled was simply the odor of poverty. She would either have to ignore it, which was impossible, or accept it, as Fin so clearly did. And now, Dev understood, so must she.

Timmy, still in Fin's arms, exhausted but awake and joyfully aware that he was home, reached out and knocked on Mag's door with his weak fingers. His wispy, "Ma?" barely made it past his lips.

Dev, with a wink at Timmy, knocked, too. Her "Maggie?" was loud enough to be heard inside, and her added, "Timmy's home. We've brought him home," was infused with cheer.

A few moments passed before Maggie opened the door. She

wore the same Japanese-style floral robe—which she hurriedly closed over her naked body—that she wore the night Fin came by after Maggie had been released from the Mulberry Street cells. She was halfway smiling, halfway in grateful tears, and then fully in horror at the sight of her bloodied, near broken son in Fin's arms.

A man came rushing through the door, nudging past Maggie while he quickly tucked his shirt into his trousers. "Money's on the bed, Mag," he said before disappearing through the hallway and out the tenement door.

Maggie Poole's state of near undress was thus clear to Dev. Whatever goodwill she'd developed toward this woman was now sorely tested. The sorrowful mother she'd seen with Fin earlier today, the woman she'd expected to be pacing the floor or perhaps limp with worry over the fate of her kidnapped son, had spent the afternoon on her back—earning her living. Maggie Poole, Black Haired Mag, was busy earning the bread she needed to survive, the milk she needed to feed her son, and the money she needed to keep this dismal roof over their heads.

Even more than the wretched conditions Dev had seen in the courtyard, even more than the dangerously creaking stairs to the tenement, the raw truth of Maggie Poole's life now stood fully revealed. The struggle of that life and its stretched-to-breaking moral code were abruptly clear to Dev, as was the strength of the woman who lived it.

"My boy," Maggie said, stroking him as Fin carried him inside.

"I'm all right, Ma," Timmy said, mustering enough strength to speak. "I'm th'man of th'house, right?"

"Yes, you're my little man, Timmy Poole," Mag said, kissing his hand, every one of his fingers. Even the dirt on his bruised flesh was precious to her.

Fin said, "We've gotta clean his wounds, Mag, or they'll get infected, fill up with pus. Let's get him into the tub. Dev, we'll need to heat up some water. Bucket's here, next to the tub. The pump's outside, down the back stairs."

After Maggie carefully removed Timmy's torn and filthy clothes, Fin tenderly lowered him into the tin tub. It stood against the wall next to the coal stove that served as a source of heat and a cookstove. "Mag, toss in a heap of coal an' get a fire going."

Dev found the bucket, a tin container as battered as the tub that stood beside it. She removed her hat, cloak, her gloves, and the jacket of her lavender suit, rolled up the sleeves of her crisp shirtwaist blouse, and carried the bucket out the door.

She found the entrance to the back stairs at the end of the hall. Before descending, Dev steeled herself to whatever filthy conditions awaited her.

The stairs down to a small rear yard were as dangerously unstable as the front stairs, with the added danger of the wood steps soaking wet from water slopped from buckets carried day after day from the pump. Dev descended carefully, lifting the hem of her skirt to avoid puddles on the stairs. Once in the rear yard, a fetid place surrounded by a rotting wood fence and the backs of other decrepit tenements, Dev kept her hem raised to avoid the large, muddy puddle around the pump.

She pumped water into the bucket as quickly as she could, then carried it up the stairs, careful not to splash any.

Back inside Mag's parlor, while Mag tended the coal fire and Fin helped get Timmy settled, Dev poured the bucket of water into the large pot atop the stove. She went out again to refill the bucket.

It took ten trips to the pump and back to gather enough water to adequately fill the tub. By the last trip up the stairs, Dev's arms ached, several strands of her hair had escaped their pins and clung to her perspiring face and neck, her shirtwaist blouse was limp and stuck to her, and she'd ceased to care about getting her shoes or the hem of her dress wet.

In a day filled with experiences which stretched her tolerance, her mind, and her soul, Dev's heart now warmed in a way that stretched even her considerable understanding of love and devotion. It was brought on by the tableau of Maggie Poole on her knees, bent over the battered tin tub, tenderly washing the wounds inflicted on her son, while Dev's own beloved Fin held the boy's hand to calm him during each painful slide of the washcloth.

There was nothing for Dev to do but sit down in a nearby chair and watch in awe.

After Maggie Poole bathed her son's body and washed his hair, bandaged his wounds in strips of clean bed linens, and dressed him in clean though threadbare clothes, Timmy Poole was almost fully restored to the proud, streetwise little boy Dev met at the Mulberry Street police station. Seated in an old armchair, his mother seated on the arm of the chair while she held his hand, Timmy's skinny body was nearly devoured by the bumpy stuffing under the nubby upholstery. Through his gap-toothed smile, he said to Dev, "I know'd you was a right one. The way y'faced them fellas with the billy clubs, why it was even better than the way y'stood up t'the coppers down at Mulberry Street. Y'sure are a brave lady."

"Thank you, Timmy, but I believe that the bravest person in the room is you."

"I gotta be brave," he said, trying to sit up straight with pride despite the pain in his body, "'cause I'm a boy. But you're the bravest lady I know."

"Oh but you're wrong about that, Master Poole. The bravest lady you know is your ma."

Mag said nothing, but the nod and smallest of smiles she gave Dev contained more *thank you*'s than any torrent of words could offer.

Fin said, "Timmy boy, y'feel up to talkin'?"

"'Bout what?"

"'Bout what happened to you. Can y'tell us what the lady an' the copper said when they took you?"

It was like the air went out of him, shriveled his body like a leaky balloon.

Dev took Timmy's other hand. "Where's that brave Master Poole who stood up to that big detective on Mulberry Street? That sturdy little fellow wouldn't let that woman and the police officer who took you get away with it, now would he."

He looked up to his mother, his little boy's eyes pleading to hide in her protection.

Maggie kissed the top of his head, brushed his hair with her fingers. "It's okay, Timmy. Y'safe here with us. An' besides, you're my man of the house, right? Y'got the heart of a lion. Even Miss Longstreet knows that."

"Indeed, I do," Dev said. "I've seen that lion's heart, Timmy. I know you're strong enough to help us get justice for you and for all the other children trapped in that horrible place. You can be their hero. You were certainly my hero at Mulberry Street."

That brought the smile back to Timmy's face and the pride back to his soul. "They . . . they didn't say nothin' t'me when they . . . when they hauled me outta here," he said, his words tumbling out slowly. For despite Timmy's renewed pride, the horror of his ordeal nearly strangled his ability to talk about it. "But when we got to . . . to that place . . ."

Fin said, "It's okay, lad. Take your time. We're real proud of you, Timmy boy."

Mag, wiping a tear she didn't want to shed, said, "Sure, Timmy, it's okay t'tell Fin an' Miss Longstreet 'bout those people an' that place. I want those people t'pay for what they did t'you."

With a swallow to stiffen his resolve, he said, "Okay, Ma. Okay."

Fin said, "We know this is hard, Timmy, but it's important. So take your time with the story if y'need to."

He nodded his assent.

"Good," Fin said. "Now, when you got t'the Grace Home, what happened?"

Timmy needed another fortifying swallow, and he had to close his eyes against the horror of his tale. When he opened them again, he said, "Well, the copper helped the lady haul me inside that big place. I was kickin' an' hollerin', b'lieve me!" Relating this disobedient behavior seemed to restore more of his energy, more of his little boy's courage. "I wasn't goin' in there without a fight, right Fin?"

"That's our way, sure," Fin said with a laugh and a light, chummy poke to Timmy's shoulder, which made the boy giggle. "But after they got you inside, did they tell you how they found you an' your ma?"

"Nope, they didn't say nothin' like that. An' besides, I was really carryin' on, hollerin' an' yankin' on them t'let me go. The copper slapped me aroun' some t'try t'quiet me. I didn't wanna get slapped no more, so I shut up. An'. . . an' that's when . . . that's when everything got . . . y'know . . . real bad."

She spoke quietly, carefully. "They took y'downstairs?"

The way he nodded his head yes, his lips tight, his eyes scrunched up, broke the hearts of the three adults in the room.

Fin said, "Listen, little man, y'don't have t'tell us what they did t'you. We know, or we can figure it. But what we want you t'tell us is anything they said. Like why they took you. Your ma said they told her it was t'teach her a lesson. Did they say anythin' like that t'you?"

"No, nothin' 'bout no lesson. But the lady said somethin' about ma talkin' t'the wrong people. An' that maybe she'd watch her tongue after she sees what they could do t'me if she didn't keep t'herself. I tried t'be brave, Fin!" he said, grabbing Fin's arm and holding tight as if it were a life raft in a dark sea he couldn't

186

swim out of. His tears started again. "I really did try!"

"An' you *were* plenty brave, Timmy boy," Fin said. "I know you were. Just lookit you, sittin' here, talkin' about the worst thing that ever happened to you. That's real courage, lad. Your ma an' me an' Miss Longstreet are real proud of you. An' we know y'can be brave jus' a little bit more, 'cause I got one more question, okay?"

With a sigh that seemed to need the breath of the whole world, Timmy nodded his head and said, "Okay, Fin."

"That's the boy," Fin said. "All right now, how were they gonna show your ma what they did t'you? Did they say they were gonna take you home?"

Timmy shook his head no. "Nuh-uh. The lady told the copper who was holdin' me down t'fetch ma and bring her t'that place, but not for a day or two until she told him to. I . . . hollered for her t'leave my ma alone, but that made her mad an' she . . . she . . ."

Maggie cradled him, his tears soaking her robe and seeping between her breasts. She looked at Fin and Devorah through tears of her own. "That's plenty enough for now. The boy needs his rest."

Fin said, "But you're not safe here, Mag. How much you wanna bet that somehow somebody connected with that place knew you been talkin' t'me an' Miss Longstreet, and they're not happy about it. Even though we got Timmy outta that place an' brought him home, they could send someone here again. Y'got someplace safe t'go?"

For the first time in all the years Fin had known her, Maggie Poole, the savvy survivor Black Haired Mag, was scared.

CHAPTER TWENTY-SEVEN

I t was well past six o'clock in the evening by the time Fin and Devorah arrived home after securing Maggie and Timmy at Five Cent Frankie Swann's rented rooms near Silkie's gym. Frankie wasn't too happy about using his small, manly quarters, crammed with sports periodicals and littered with whiskey bottles and cigar butts, as a hideout for a mother and child— though the sight of the battered and bandaged Timmy Poole did touch the one sentimental nerve in his being. Another five cents wrapped in a twenty-dollar bill made the job palatable.

Dev was at first doubtful about Fin's choice of Mr. Swann as a protector, a fellow she considered of dubious character, until Fin pointed out the possibility that the people who had found Maggie, or knew that Maggie had come to see Fin, might still be tracking her. The danger to Maggie and Timmy was real, and in the end Dev saw the wisdom of temporarily housing mother and child with someone who wouldn't hesitate to use violence in the form of a knife or a gun to keep predators out of his residence.

But Dev was angry. She'd been angry since the beaten and bloodied Timmy struggled across the floor and into her arms at the Grace Home for Wayward Children. Even the present safety of Maggie and Timmy at Mr. Swann's did little to quell Dev's anger, nor did a warm bath and a change into clean clothes soothe it.

Fin, too, had bathed and changed from her bloodstained clothes into fresh trousers and a clean white shirt. Thus refreshed, Fin was ready for a relaxing dinner with Dev. "How 'bout we order somethin' brought aroun' from Delmonico's? Nice thick steaks or maybe a coupla lobsters?"

Dev, closing the buttons on the jacket of a trim blue suit, said, "I'm too angry to dine. Every morsel would get stuck in my throat. Fetch my cloak, would you, Lovey? And put on your suit jacket and overcoat as well."

"We're goin' somewhere? Now? Where we goin'?"

"To slay a monster."

Martha Flugg, at first merely surprised if perhaps secretly pleased to have Rogers inform her that her old friend Devorah Longstreet was once again at her door, became stern and thin lipped at seeing the person accompanying Dev, a woman perversely attired in men's clothing. Such an abnormal presence led Martha to assume this could only be Devorah's scandalous lover. The sight of such a person in such inappropriate attire set Martha on edge, causing her to fidget with the high, ruffled collar of her brown dress.

Dev said, "Good evening, Martha. We've come to see Alistair. It's urgent we speak with him."

To Martha's unhappy countenance was added the pursed lips of annoyance at having her hospitality tested by Devorah bringing her socially outcast paramour to the Fluggs' door. Martha looked quickly along the street, hoping no neighbors saw the couple standing at her doorstep. Satisfied no neighbors were about, she said, "I—I don't believe meeting with Alistair is wise, Devorah. And in any event, I can't allow your ... *companion* into our home."

Though Fin's first instinct was to give Martha Flugg a good shove, she remained polite, in part for Dev's sake, and in part because Martha Flugg was not what Fin expected her to be. Fin had assumed the wife of the straightlaced gospel grinder Alistair Flugg would be a drab, Stiff-Necked Sarah, not the handsome, fashionably dressed woman with the intelligent blue eyes and a crown of softly graying blonde hair. Fin's chivalrous nature could not be rude to such a woman. "The name's Fin Donner, Mrs. Flugg. An' as Miss Longstreet told you, our business with your husband is urgent. Lives depend on it. Young lives."

"What do you mean, young lives? Whose young lives?"

"Just that, Martha," Dev said. "Young lives are indeed at stake. If you wish to understand, feel free to join us when we speak with Alistair. You'll find the discussion informative, perhaps even shocking. Now do let us in."

"If you are referring to my husband's activities regarding his campaign against low morals, I won't have you badgering him about it. Considering the life you now lead, I'm sure you don't approve of his crusade. But I beg of you, Devorah, if our past friendship has meant anything, I must ask you not to trouble my household any further and to leave my husband alone." Closing the door, Martha added, "Now I bid you good evening."

That was the end of Fin's chivalrous goodwill for Martha Flugg. Throwing all pretense to social ceremony aside, Fin quickly put her hand to the door to stop it from closing. She pushed it open again, to the shock and even fear of Martha Flugg.

Without seeking Martha Flugg's permission, or even expressing so much as a *Pardon me*, Fin escorted Dev into the vestibule, past a dismayed Martha. "Maybe you didn't understan' us, Mrs. Flugg. Miss Longstreet an' I are here t'talk to your husband, an' we *are* gonna talk t'him. Now, you can join us or you can get outta the way."

"Please, Martha," Dev said, falling back on any remaining fondness from her old friend, "young lives really do depend on us talking to Alistair. He may have the power to save them." Dev's emphatic tone, together with Fin's steady stare, made it clear that the couple would not budge.

Dismayed or not, outraged or not, Martha realized she could not keep these unwanted guests from her home, and she at last nodded a reluctant assent. "Alistair is in the dining room. We were just sitting down to dinner," she said. "Please wait in the library while I tell him you're here."

Once again, while Martha Flugg went off to inform her husband, Dev, now with Fin, entered Alistair Flugg's bastion against the onslaught of all things and attitudes modern.

Following Dev into the library, Fin's first impression was the aroma of the room: the leatherbound books, the lingering sweetness of pipe tobacco. She looked around, acknowledged the first-rate quality of the furniture and accoutrements. Fin also noticed how primly arranged everything was. Everything was too much *just so*, as if a pen or an ashtray might face punishment for being even slightly left or right of its appointed spot. She even laughed about it, a quiet, grim laugh for a room which clearly reflected the rigid disposition of the man who owned it. It further amused her to think that if the room could talk it would ask her to leave.

Alistair Flugg walked into his library. Dressed in a gray suit and black waistcoat, he added his personal primness to the room. Martha followed.

Flugg glared at Fin with something close to hatred, though it wasn't quite that. Fin thought she saw something else in Flugg's examining eyes: unease.

She shrugged it off. She'd been the recipient of more threatening looks. Flugg's unease was his own problem. There was nothing she could do—or would even bother—to alleviate it.

Flugg said, "I must object, Devorah, to your persistence in bringing your disreputable life into my home. And with your upbringing, you certainly know not to arrive uninvited at the dinner hour. And yet, here you are. But now that you are here, what's this about young lives and my ability to save them? I am always interested in saving our youth."

Dev said, "Is that what you call what goes on at the Grace Home for Wayward Children? Saving our youth?"

Flugg walked calmly to his desk. He sat down with the smug smile of a man who deems himself too important for this conversation but courtesy demands he address it. "Devorah, the Grace Home provides impoverished children with food, clothing and—most important—an education. As a matter of fact, I am proud to say that I was instrumental in devising the curriculum. The lessons not only provide basic instruction in reading, writing, and arithmetic, but moral instruction as well."

Fin said, "An' what about how those lessons are taught?"

"I beg your pardon?"

"You heard me, Mr. Flugg. How are those lessons taught?"

Flugg leaned back in his chair, suppressing an annoyance he wished he did not feel in response to this challenge he was certain he did not deserve. "The lessons are taught in the traditional way," he said. "A teacher leads the boys and girls in their exercises. Isn't that how you were educated?"

Fin didn't mind Flugg's barely disguised mocking of her wrong-side-of-town breeding. She didn't care. She was about to rip the man's snottiness to shreds. "As a matter of fact, Mr. Flugg, my education was sorta different, but would you believe it was in that very same buildin'? Talk about your coincidences. But we didn't have a lotta classrooms back then. We learned what you call our moral lessons in those rooms downstairs. You know the ones I'm talkin' about, don't you, Mr. Flugg."

Flugg placed his elbows on the desk and tented his fingers, pressing his fingertips together until they were white. But the expression on his face remained calm, a forced calm which even his wife noticed. She said, "What is she talking about, Alistair? What rooms downstairs? I've toured the building on several occasions on behalf of the Ladies' Auxiliary and never once was I taken to any rooms downstairs or even told of them."

Fin said, "It was down in them cells, Mrs. Flugg, where I learned that people like your husband think the bodies of slum children are made t'be beaten into obedience, even broken if they resist."

Horror was Martha Flugg's first reaction, a horror she was unable to handle regarding alleged cruelties about her husband. She would not, could not believe such things about him and thus banished the horror as one slaps aside a floating balloon. "Well, that was many years ago," she said. "Surely such methods are no longer in practice."

Dev said, "Tell that to the little boy Fin and I rescued today, Martha, a little boy whose bloody legs and feet nearly robbed him of his ability to walk. His name is Timmy Poole."

The horror that Martha did not want to accept threatened to attack her yet again. She pushed against it as much as she could, but still she felt its sharp fingertips scratch at her soul. She said, "Is this true, Alistair? Do such rooms and practices exist at the Grace Home?"

"I shall look into it," Flugg said with irritating nonchalance. "And now, if you don't mind, Devorah, my wife and I would like to have our dinner."

Dev said, "But we do mind, Alistair. You see, there's more to Timmy's story than just the torture he survived. It seems he was targeted for removal from the home of his mother. Granted, the conditions of the home are less than ideal, but I can tell you that his mother loves him dearly and does everything she can to raise him and protect him. His mother is Miss Maggie Poole." A thought suddenly entered Dev's mind, a wisp of something remembered, something said. "Do you know that name, Alistair? Maggie Poole?"

"Certainly not. Why would I know such a low person?"

"I'm sure you come in contact with many such people during your incursions into the city's less respectable establishments. Perhaps Maggie Poole was one of them."

"I do not make a habit of befriending the lowlifes I chase from their lairs, Devorah. Why would you even suggest I'd single out this—this Maggie Poole?"

"Because someone was not happy about Miss Poole's conversations with Fin and me. Someone sent a police officer and a woman from the Grace Home to Miss Poole's tenement to literally steal her son. They said it was to teach Miss Poole a lesson. That lesson was apparently to stop Miss Poole from talking to me and Fin. So, the question is, Alistair, what did this person worry Miss Poole was talking to us about? Was it perhaps about our current investigation? The one involving John Jones, a conversation you so cavalierly dismissed when I spoke to you earlier today?"

Flugg rose slowly from his chair, his face an expressionless mask. "You have delayed our dinner long enough, Devorah, upsetting me, my wife, and certainly our cook. I must now ask you to leave so that my wife and I may dine undisturbed. What's more, I demand that you and your *companion*"—he said it with more of a sneer than his wife did when she'd uttered the word— "never darken our door again." He strode across his library with the huffy dignity of a man convinced of his importance to the world. Passing his wife, he said, "Please see these people out."

Martha laid her hand on her husband's arm. "Just a moment, Alistair. I believe I know that name, John Jones."

"It's a common name," Flugg said. "You could have heard it anywhere. Now come along, Martha. Our dinner waits."

"No, no," Martha said, tilting her head as if trying to retrieve something from her thoughts. "I know I've heard the name. Yes, that's it. I heard you mention it here, in your library, as if you were speaking of him to someone, perhaps on the telephone? Yes, Alistair, I heard you mention Mr. Jones today."

Through a mirthless chuckle, Flugg said, "My dear wife, if I didn't have the deepest affection for you I would scold you for listening at the door. Don't you remember what Devorah said moments ago? That she and I discussed Mr. Jones this morning? I'm sure that's what you are referring to. Now, let's end this unpleasant discussion and proceed to our dinner. But first, you will see our guests out. They have overstayed their welcome."

Fin and Dev were mostly silent in the hansom as they rode through the nighttime city, the streets dark except for the occasional glow of a streetlamp, the sidewalks nonetheless crowded with people on their way to theaters and restaurants, or to partake of the city's less honorable nighttime business. The two members of Donner & Longstreet Inquiries were deep in their own thoughts, picking through all the threads of this baffling case, trying to tie those threads together: Pauline Godfrey was connected to John Jones who was connected to five actresses, at least two of whom may have had the murderous motive of jealousy; Jones tried to peddle Pauline Godfrey to Maggie Poole, who, through her son, was connected to Alistair Flugg through the Grace Home for Wayward Children.

Dev also thought about Alistair and Martha Flugg, about how cold their marriage seemed to be, a state she'd been unaware of while she was still part of the social circle which embraced them.

Fin's thoughts further circled around her conversation with the Hudson Stompers' leader Ned Hennessey, and Ned's hint that some big boy might be pulling all those threads. In a city where street gangs, coppers, and politicians all scratched each other's backs and lined each other's pockets, Fin knew there were plenty of big boys pulling plenty of strings. Could be it's those big boys Detective Coyle is scared of.

As the hansom neared their Irving Place residence, and the clip-clop of the horse's hooves slowed their rhythm, the couple's thoughts slowed, too, each arriving at one particular thread.

"Do y' think—?" "Do you think—?" they said in unison, a not uncommon occurrence in the intertwining of their lives.

Dev said, "You first, Lovey."

"Okay. Y'think maybe Flugg killed Jones?"

"I'm trying not to," Dev said through the last vestige of familiarity she had with her once family friend. "But if he did, then maybe he killed Pauline Godfrey, too. But why? Prior to my mention of her this morning, it appeared Alistair didn't know Pauline, or was even aware of her."

"He could be lyin'. I wouldn't put it past him."

"Yes, I suppose so. He was rather evasive about everything, wasn't he. But . . . I don't know. I feel like something's missing, Lovey."

Fin thought again of Ned Hennessey's remark. "Or maybe someone," she said.

CHAPTER TWENTY-EIGHT

The killer ate dinner calmly.

CHAPTER TWENTY-NINE

t breakfast the next morning, the firm tap of Dev's coffee cup against the saucer roused Fin's attention from an article in the Police Gazette. "We must find out what Detective Coyle is afraid of," Dev said.

"You mean that hornet's nest he said we bumped into?"

"The very one. One of those hornets might be the missing person you spoke of last night. That person might be the one connecting all the threads of this case. It's time to have another discussion with Coyle."

"Yeah, I agree. But this time I'll go over t'Mulberry Street an' do the talkin'."

"Don't you think that's rather risky, my love? As you pointed out at the start of this investigation, your relationship with the police is not the most congenial."

"True, but Coyle tried t'change the rules when he came by an' tried t'warn us off. Well, it's time we made our own rules. By showin' up on his turf, he'll know I ain't afraid of him an' his badge. He'll have t'deal with me."

Dev saw the logic in Fin's assessment, and though she was not entirely convinced of Fin's safety, she reached across the breakfast table for her lover's hand. "Just do be careful."

With a playful if not very reassuring wink, Fin said, "I'll do my best. And while I'm at Mulberry Street, how about y'have another talk with the Godfreys? Maybe there's a thread we're missin' there, a thread they're holdin' but don't even know it."

Fin didn't like being in the Mulberry Street police headquarters any more than the police liked her being there. As she walked toward the desk sergeant's station, the sneers and stares of bell-helmeted coppers milling around or on their way in or out of the building felt like snakes slithering along her skin. As for the wretched down-and-outs who huddled on the floor or waited around for justice that never came, they stared at her well-cut suit, fancy waistcoat, and straw boater pitched at a racy angle but didn't know what to make of her.

The same red-haired, mutton-chopped desk sergeant who'd given Devorah a hard time a few nights ago was on duty again today. If anything, he was even less welcoming to Fin than he'd been to Dev. Dev, at least, had been good to look at, and a lady, too. As far as the sergeant was concerned, Finola Donner, alias Fin Donner, alias Fine Fingers Donner, was a lowlife, a criminal who'd gotten away with far too many sins. Add to that, her indecency to go parading around in men's clothes, she was a pervert to boot.

Despite the sergeant's clear feelings about Fin, she gave him her most effective smile, the cheery one, the friendly smile of an invader who won't back down. It went along with the raggedly courteous lilt in her voice. "Good mornin', sergeant. It's important that I talk t'Detective Coyle. You mind tellin' him I'm here?"

The sergeant sniffed. His heavy mustache twitched. "What if he don't want to speak to you?"

"But what if he does, an' he finds out you didn't let me in?

You know, you could find yourself on traffic duty in the Five Points, directin' carts an' wagons an' tryin' not t'step in horse apples instead of workin' at this nice cozy desk duty, outta the cold an' rain." Fin punctuated it with more of her cheery smile.

The sergeant, searching for a way out of such a bleak future, stared back at Fin while he fingered the brass buttons on his uniform. "I tell you what," he said, thinking he did indeed find an escape route, "why don't you just go on back to the Detective's Room y'self? That way Detective Coyle can have the pleasure of tossin' you out all on his own." The sergeant's smile was less cheerful than Fin's but so much more satisfied.

Fin steeled herself for another round of belligerence from whoever answered her knock on the Detectives Room door. If anything, detectives were even more resentful of Fin than the bell-helmets. Through all her years doing lightfinger work, among the other little felonies here and there, these boys with the so-called brains could never make a case that would send her up the river. And now it was too late.

She smiled about that while she waited for someone to open the door, which is how she found herself smiling in Detective Coyle's face.

He was not smiling. His dark eyes opened wide in surprise and annoyance at the sight of the last person he wanted to see.

Fin said, "I'll save you the trouble of askin' what I'm doin' here, and I'll tell you straight out. Who are you scared of, Coyle?"

Coyle's face paled, but his eyes were defiant. "What the—? Who gave you the cockamamie idea that I'm scared?"

"Aww, c'mon, Detective. You an' I been in the game a long time. Okay, sure, we play on different sides of the board; or at least we used to. But we both know the jitters when we see 'em, an' you had 'em plenty when you came by our place the other night. So why don't you save us both a lotta time an' come clean. I might be able t'get you out from under, an' you might be able t'help me get to the bottom of the Pauline Godfrey an' John Jones business."

Coyle, famous for binding his emotions tight as a corset, simply stared at his interlocutor. "You don't know what you're talking about."

"Maybe, but Ned Hennessey does."

Fin knew well the signs of an animal cornered: a furtive look in the eye, a bristling of the skin. She saw these now in Coyle. "You keep lousy company, Donner," Coyle said, letting a sneer escape.

"Not as lousy as the big boys who are scarin' the pants off the police department. That hornet's nest you mentioned? It ain't just any ol' buncha stingers, are they, Coyle. They're the fellas who run the nest an' boss the other hornets aroun'. The question is, what's got 'em so riled up?"

Coyle, his anger held in tight control, said nothing. But his hand went up as if to push Fin from the door.

Fin grabbed the detective's hand and held it aside. "I ain't goin' away, Coyle. Not until I get the story about John Jones. He was a nobody, a nothin'-much actor, a loser who lived in a rattrap. But a buncha silk suits an' top hats had some sorta connection to Jones, an' they don't want anyone nosin' aroun' his business or his death. Might embarrass 'em. Might certainly upset their wives. An' there ain't nothin' more dangerous than an angry wife. Ah, I see you're gettin' the picture, detective. You look like you could use a physic to settle your stomach. How 'bout I spot you to a cuppa coffee, maybe throw a little somethin' in it t'settle the nerves so we can talk."

A woman was just leaving with her purchase of two yards of blue moiré silk fabric and a yard of white lace when Dev walked into the Godfreys' shop.

Mrs. Godfrey, yet again attired in her ruffled yellow blouse and brown skirt covered by her navy blue apron, put her long-bladed fabric scissors back into the large pocket of her apron and gave Dev a nod of acknowledgment. She then busied herself putting spools of lace back on their shelves before she joined her husband at the center counter.

Mr. Godfrey, once more the very picture of the prosperous if hardworking merchant, his white sleeves held in place with black garters, appeared pleased to see Dev. "Ah, Miss Longstreet, I tried telephoning you but there was no answer at your exchange. I wanted to let you know that we received the results of the private autopsy you arranged. Thank you for having it sent directly to us. I must say, though, I was surprised the doctor was a woman. I would not have thought women have the stomach for such gruesome work."

"You'd be surprised at what we women have the stomach to do," Dev said. "But as to the autopsy, what did it report?"

Mr. Godfrey's manner changed from efficient to mournful, his jowly cheeks sagging with the weight of his grief. "To no one's surprise, Pauline had fallen victim to narcotics, but one with which I'm not familiar. Something called heroin."

Dev acknowledged this information with a nod and a sigh of sympathy. "Indeed, to no one's surprise. I think we may safely assume Mr. Jones is responsible for that unfortunate state of affairs. Regarding the heroin, it's a more insidious refinement of morphine. Its recent development was supposed to relieve patients of pain more effectively than plain morphine. Unfortunately, its addictive properties are deadly."

Mr. Godfrey, a businessman to the respectable classes and completely unfamiliar with the inverted moral codes of criminal life, blurted, "Why would he do such a thing?"

The look on the man's face, a look of utter bewilderment

filtered through crushing sadness, his tears barely held in check, broke Dev's heart. The Godfreys, hardworking, straightforward people, suffered a loss no parent should have to endure, and thus Dev spoke gently. "Mr. and Mrs. Godfrey, I am going to tell you something awful, something which answers that very question. Perhaps you both should sit down."

"Miss Longstreet," Mr. Godfrey said, putting his arm around his wife's shoulder, "our daughter was murdered in the worst possible way, her throat ripped open. Nothing you tell us could be worse than that."

"Of course," Dev said. "All right then, it seems Mr. Jones likely romanced young attractive women for the purpose of making them pliant by making them dope fiends."

"But to what end?" Mr. Godfrey said.

"To no good end, I'm afraid." The grim story Dev was about to tell required a steeling of her nerves, and a reminder to herself that as an investigator grim stories came along with the grim lives she investigated. Taking a breath, Dev began, "It appears that Mr. Jones was perhaps a conduit for placing these girls into prostitution. This is an unfortunate practice by handsome but unsavory men who are part of the criminal sex trade. First they lure young women with romantic promises, then introduce them to addictive drugs like opium or heroin. This makes the women completely dependent on the man. They'll do anything he asks, any sordid act including prostitution, so as not to be cut off from the supply of dope. Now, exactly where Mr. Jones placed the women he seduced we don't know. We do know he tried unsuccessfully to sell three girls, one of which was likely Pauline, to a prostitute downtown. It was she who alerted me and Fin."

Mr. Godfrey held his wife close, perhaps to keep her from collapsing at such devastating news, perhaps to hold himself up as well. He conspicuously cleared his throat to keep from crying, while his wife, her birdlike face lowered against her husband's chest, muttered, "Filth, filth."

Mr. Godfrey, gathering himself as best as he could, said, "I take it this opens another line of inquiry into Pauline's murder? I must say, Miss Longstreet, I am impressed with your efforts thus far."

"Thank you, but we are not near enough to our goal quite yet. Yes, that is one line of inquiry, but Fin and I are pursuing others. If I place them before you, perhaps you might recall a detail that Pauline may have mentioned, no matter how inadvertent or seemingly unimportant at the time."

Mrs. Godfrey snapped from her husband's embrace. "Do you mean to impugn our Pauline's reputation yet again? Haven't you maligned us as parents quite enough?"

Dev found Mrs. Godfrey's outburst rather unsettling, its vehemence, Dev believed, out of line with what must certainly be the woman's desire to bring her daughter's killer to justice. But the heat and pain emanating from Mrs. Godfrey reminded Dev of her own mother, of the vehemence with which she banished her daughter from the family's door. It was, Dev now understood more deeply than she had previously allowed, a vehemence born of maternal pain, the pain of disappointment in Dev and disillusion about her daughter's life.

This understanding brought its own pain to Dev, but it tempered her tone with the grieving mother standing before her. "Mrs. Godfrey," Dev said, "I believe you and your husband have been exemplary parents. I am sorry if my inquiries have suggested otherwise. That was not my intent. Please understand that investigations often turn up secrets, things hidden by the innocent as well as the guilty. Only by uncovering these secrets can we hope to arrive at the truth. Now, I will be as delicate as possible, but if you wish to get justice for Pauline, you must be prepared for what will certainly be difficult conversations."

Mr. Godfrey, drawing his wife close once again, said, "Miss Longstreet is right, my dear. I know this is difficult for you. I know how hard you've tried to be a good mother to Pauline. No one here is faulting you." To Dev, he said, "Please, Miss Longstreet, proceed with your questions."

"I can't be seen with you," Coyle said, pulling Fin away from entering a tavern popular with the police officers stationed at the nearby Mulberry Street headquarters.

If Coyle's fear was almost palpable when he visited Fin and Devorah's residence, his fear was all over him now, no matter how hard he tried to disguise it with a stony face and averted eyes, his derby hat pulled low on his brow.

"All right," Fin said, squelching a smile. She tried as hard to hide her amusement at Coyle's queasiness as Coyle tried to hide his fear. "I know a nearby spot where they won't know who the hell you are," she said, "so they won't hold it against me to be seen with you either." This time, she let a smile sneak through.

With barely a curt nod, Coyle followed Fin south along Mulberry Street, across East Houston to Jersey Street, an alley grimy with industrial refuse, rodent droppings, and discarded whiskey bottles. Even now at late morning, the alley was dark, the sunlight blocked by hulking, sooty brick warehouses on either side. Tucked between two warehouses was a nameless, bare bones saloon catering to the warehousemen and the women who kept them company either for love or for pay.

The place was quiet, nearly empty with just two obviously out-of-work fellas nursing cigar stubs and beer at the bar, the hour being too late for a beer-and-sausage breakfast, too early for a beer-and-sandwich lunch. Fin and Coyle took a back corner table far from the front windows and as far from the bar as the narrow space allowed.

Coyle said, "I suppose they ain't got coffee in this joint."

"They got nickel beer an' cheap whiskey. What'll y'have, Detective?"

"You're buying. You decide."

The barkeep gave Fin the usual once-over when she went up to the bar to order two beers, but unlike the specialized clientele at the Curtain Call Bar and Grill, this tiny saloon with its plank bar and dirty spittoons was the kind of spot where the barkeep just didn't care who drank his nickel beer. His place wasn't so in-the-chips that he could turn away any nickels. And the two at the bar didn't much care about Fin either. After a cursory glance and a slight wince, they returned their attention to their beer and cigar butts. They had their own problems, which Fin didn't figure into in the least.

Fin carried the two foaming mugs of beer to the table, took a seat opposite Coyle, put her hat on the table and said, "Okay, Coyle, it's time to open up an' tell me why you're scared of gettin' stung. As coppers go, you ain't the worst. Somethin' tells me maybe you even got a bit of honor; otherwise you wouldn't've sent Mr. an' Mrs. Godfrey t'me an' Devorah t'look into their daughter's killin'. So it's time t'polish up y'badge, wipe the dirt off it, detective. Think about it while you drink your beer. I got time."

Coyle pushed his hat back, swallowed a slug of beer, his eyes firmly fixed on Fin. When he put his mug down he licked the foam from his lips. "First tell me what Ned Hennessey said."

Fin took her own swallow of beer, then shrugged and said, "Okay, sure. Here's the part you maybe already know: that Jones was romancing young women t'lure 'em into gettin' on the dope."

Coyle took another swallow, then gave Fin a reluctant nod.

Fin continued, "Uh-huh. But here's maybe somethin' you don't know, an' it's probably the somethin' that's annoyin' the hornets who you're scared will sting you: Hennessey heard tell that Jones was gettin' outta hand, tryin' to sell his doped-up dollies to brothels aroun' town for his own profit. For some reason, whoever was controllin' Jones maybe didn't like that."

"So you're thinking the hornets stung Jones to death?"

"Could be," Fin said. "But there might be another angle in Jones's death. The oldest angle in the book: jealousy. You know, the woman scorned stuff."

This elicited the first look of surprise Fin saw on the detective's face since she started telling her story.

She said, "Oh yeah. It seems our boy Jones was quite a Romeo, an' as an actor with a pretty face he had his pick of a lotta showgirls. Devorah an' I talked t'some actresses who ran aroun' with Jones. A coupla them were mighty upset about his runnin' aroun' with other women, an' one's even got the strength an' the talent t'do the dirty deed."

"Okay, but how do you know?" Coyle said. "Does this actress have a criminal history like yours?" Thinking this funny, Coyle smirked under the new beer-foam mustache on his lip.

"I don't know her history, detective," Fin said. "I know she's got the strength because when she ain't actin' on the stage, she's a butcher, real handy with a knife. I saw her carve up slabs of meat like they was butter."

"You think this butcher dame might've sliced Pauline Godfrey, too?"

"I ain't sayin' she did, but you gotta admit, it's a possibility."

Shaking his head, Coyle said, "But Jones wasn't knifed, he was shot. You were there," he added with sly zest.

"But you forgot about the talent end, Detective Coyle. This theater girl played circus acts, a bit of a contortionist or somethin' like that, athletic, anyway. So, yeah, she's got the talent to get herself in an' outta the window in Jones's upstairs room without anyone seein'. Okay, that's what I got; Hennessey's stuff an' the stuff Devorah an' I learned by askin' aroun'. Now, a deal's a deal, so now it's your turn. What the hell is settin' your pants on fire?"

Coyle took a deep swallow of beer, wiped his foam mustache with the back of his hand, pursed his lips and looked at Fin as if he'd rather be in a torture chamber than here in this saloon. When he finally brought himself to speak, he gave Fin a name and a story that should've shocked Fin but didn't. It made her sick to her stomach, and it made her angry.

A woman in a gray cloak and gray veiled hat walked into the Godfreys' shop just as Devorah was about to ask a question. Seeing the threesome of Dev and the Godfreys at the cash register counter, the woman said, "Oh, I'm sorry, I'll wait my turn, but might I look at some widths of red ribbon while I wait?"

Mrs. Godfrey said, "No need to wait, Mrs. Hilsen. My husband can assist you while I chat with this lady."

Mr. Godfrey, loath to challenge his wife—who usually handled the ribbons and notions trade—in front of Mrs. Hilsen, a treasured, longtime customer, managed to stammer, "Well, I . . ."

"Oh, go on, William, dear," Mrs. Godfrey said. "I can speak to Miss Longstreet."

Mrs. Hilsen smiled a hopeful smile at Mr. Godfrey. Giving in, and resuming his role as the proprietor of the establishment, he said, "Yes, of course. Won't you come this way, Mrs. Hilsen?" and led her to the side counter where the spools of ribbon were displayed.

Mrs. Godfrey, alone with Devorah, said through a sad smile, "Now, what would you like to know, Miss Longstreet?"

Mrs. Godfrey's abrupt dismissal of her husband at a crucial moment of questioning put Dev a little off balance. After a glance at Mr. Godfrey at the ribbons counter, she reestablished her control of the conversation and returned her attention to Mrs. Godfrey. "Well, there are certain facts which could prove useful," she said, "perhaps by recalling Pauline's general habits before she met John Jones. For example, when you and Mr.

Godfrey first met with us, you and he agreed that Pauline had been an exemplary daughter but that she could also be, well, too modern in your opinion. Just what did you mean by that?"

The question evidently weighed heavily on Mrs. Godfrey. Her deep sigh came across to Dev as perhaps a reluctance to speak about a painful issue regarding her now dead daughter.

Putting a hand gently on Mrs. Godfrey's arm, Dev said, "I understand this is difficult for you, but the more I know about Pauline and her life, the better chance of tracking a path to her killer."

Mrs. Godfrey took a handkerchief from a pocket of her apron, and with a shaking hand she dabbed her eyes. "Yes, of course. I'm sorry. Well, what I meant was that the girl was becoming too quick to follow certain unbecoming trends."

"Indeed? Such as what?"

"Such as wanting to go away to college, study something useless like literature or music when she should have been content to continue to work with us here in our shop."

"I see. So you and Mr. Godfrey didn't approve of Pauline's desire for higher education?"

"I had my doubts, yes, but in her father's eyes Pauline could do no wrong. Never mind that sending her away to college would cost us a lot of money. I mean, I'm not getting any younger, Miss Longstreet; I was looking forward to Pauline taking over for me here in the shop so I could retire to a life as the respectable wife of a prosperous businessman. But . . ." She finished with a shrug and another dab of her eyes.

Dev said, "So Mr. Godfrey agreed to allow Pauline to attend college?"

Mrs. Godfrey nodded assent. "Funny thing about men, Miss Longstreet," she said through a smile which struck Dev as oddly petulant, "for all their posturing about being strong and unsentimental like us women, they crumble when their little girls so much as smile. Daughters can wind their fathers around their little fingers with their sugary giggles or little tears. When I married Mr. Godfrey, Pauline was just a tot, but she could already win her way with Mr. Godfrey."

Mrs. Godfrey's words threw Dev into memories of her own father, and how she, too, had been the light in her father's eyes, until that light went out when she told the family she was in love with Fin Donner.

But there was another element in Mrs. Godfrey's statement which jolted Dev back to the here and now. "Oh, then you are Mr. Godfrey's second marriage?"

Mrs. Godfrey dabbed her eyes again. "Yes. The poor man was a widower when I married him. His first wife was a lovely woman who worked here in the shop. I was working down the street at the time, in a small and dreary millinery shop," she said in a rather pinch-penny way, "so I knew the first Mrs. Godfrey briefly. She died in childbirth, you see. Very sad. Very sad, indeed. Pauline never knew or remembered the first Mrs. Godfrey. So you see, Miss Longstreet, I am the only mother Pauline had ever known. And I did my best. I assure you, I did my best for the girl."

"I have no doubt, Mrs. Godfrey. Taking on another woman's child can be quite difficult, I'm sure. And since you raised Pauline from a tot, you saw her grow and develop into an attractive young woman. So perhaps you can shed light on her social life. Did Pauline ever bring home friends you and Mr. Godfrey disapproved of? Friends who may have led her into trouble?"

This brought another heavy sigh from Mrs. Godfrey, though Dev thought she saw a hint of anger buried inside the woman's despair. "Well, there were a few of those modern girls Pauline took up with. You know the type: girls who like to stay out late and think it's old-fashioned to obey their parents."

It was all Dev could do not to laugh. Mrs. Godfrey's definition of disobeying one's parents didn't come close to the disobedience Dev brought to *her* parents. Staying out late simply didn't compare to choosing one's disapproved-of lover over one's family.

Dev's discipline as an investigator kept the laugh in check, and she was able to continue her questioning. "These modern girls, did any of them have any reason to be angry with Pauline? Perhaps feel jealousy toward her?"

Mrs. Godfrey considered the question, crinkling her eyes as if deep in thought. "Well, it could be. I mean, Pauline didn't say anything directly, but then again, once she began acting on her own, who knows what she kept from us? Why do you ask? Has your investigation found any such persons?"

"If you recall," Dev said, "we mentioned a group of actresses who were involved with Mr. Jones and who may have known Pauline as a result."

"Ah yes, I do remember. Neither Mr. Godfrey nor I recognized the names; at least, Pauline never mentioned them to my knowledge. Are you saying one or more of them may have been jealous of Pauline? Jealous enough to—?"

"It's a line of inquiry at this stage, Mrs. Godfrey."

"But a promising one, yes?"

"Perhaps. But let's get back to Mr. Jones for a moment."

"That despicable man," Mrs. Godfrey said, nearly hissing it. "I'm glad he's dead, Miss Longstreet. A dope peddler and a seller of young women. He was filth. People like him should be rounded up, just like that fellow in the newspapers is doing. You know, that Mr. Flugg."

Chapter Thirty

F in's nerves were stretched to breaking by the time Devorah arrived home.

Dev, for her part, was thoughtful when she walked in the door, even contemplative, ruminating on her conversation with Mrs. Godfrey.

Before Dev had a chance to share her thoughts, Fin spoke up first as she followed Dev into the parlor. "You ain't gonna believe this, my girl. Or maybe you will, but Coyle opened up plenty."

"Indeed? That's excellent," Dev said and sat down in one of the leather armchairs. "I'm all ears. And then I'll tell you what transpired at my meeting with the Godfreys. It was most—" She was interrupted by the ringing of the telephone on the little table beside her. Dev picked up the contraption, put the receiver to her ear and said "Hello?" into the mouthpiece.

"Devorah? It's Martha Flugg."

"Well hello, Martha. I must say, I certainly didn't expect—"

"Please, let me speak. I can't stay on the telephone long, lest Alistair returns home from his meeting at City Hall and finds me in his office. If he knew I'd telephoned you . . . he'd well . . ."

"What is it, Martha? Are you all right?"

"Yes, I'm fine. But I have something to tell you, something that's difficult for me to say behind my husband's back, but I find that I must. So please listen carefully."

"Yes, of course, Martha."

"Devorah, I remember when I heard Alistair speak of Mr. Jones. It wasn't during his morning conversation with you. It was after you left and he was alone in his office. He must've been speaking on the telephone. I don't know who he spoke to, but I heard him mention Mr. Jones. And Devorah, he sounded upset, annoyed, speaking loud enough for me to hear in the hall—oh! I hear Alistair. I must go, Devorah. I must hang—" There was a click at Martha Flugg's end of the line.

No one answered the Fluggs' doorbell. No one answered Dev's knock on the door, nor the pounding of Fin's fist.

"It's no use," Dev said. "No one's home, not even Rogers, their butler."

"They left in an awful hurry," Fin said. "It's only been fifteen minutes since we left our place." Fin gave the door one final heavy, frustrated pounding.

With a last, lingering shred of warm feeling for her old family friends, Dev did her best to give the Fluggs the benefit of the doubt. "Well, it is lunchtime," she said. "Perhaps they went to a café?"

"You don't believe that any more than I do," Fin said. "You said Martha Flugg's telephone suddenly went dead. Not even a goodbye, nothin'—" Fin stopped talking when the door was finally opened by a heavyset woman in an apron over a simple brown dress, a white net cap covering her hair.

She said, "They're not at home."

Dev, examining the woman's get-up, said, "You are presumably the Fluggs' cook, yes? But where is Rogers?"

"It's his afternoon off. And sure, I'm the cook," the woman said. "I ain't supposed to open the door when Rogers ain't here, but I couldn't stand that pounding anymore. But like I said, they ain't home. So, good day to you."

"Just a moment," Dev said. "I assume they're not lunching at home, so perhaps they went out to dine?"

The cook's discomfort was evident in the stiffening of her posture and the hesitancy of her speech. "I doubt they'll be eating any lunch. Mr. Flugg said that Mrs. Flugg wasn't feeling well, that he was taking her to have her looked at."

"Taking her where?" Dev said. "Why didn't they call for their family doctor to come by?"

"That were none of my business, or yours either. All I'll say is that the missus isn't the type to go against Mr. Flugg, so if he wants to take her to be looked at, she goes. Now, good day to you." She quickly shut the door.

Alarm registered equally on Fin and Devorah's faces. Fin said, "Are you thinkin' what I'm thinkin'?"

"I'm afraid so, Lovey."

Once again, Fin's revolver gained them entrance to the Grace Home for Wayward Children. And once again, the aghast gatekeeper at the point of Fin's gun was the slender gent with the bony face who'd been forced to admit them when Fin and Dev were here last.

When all three were inside the reception area, Fin took the man's arm and pulled him aside before he could take refuge behind the desk and use the telephone to alert any guards. Giving the man a forceful stare, Fin said, "Where'd he take her? Downstairs? Did he take her downstairs?"

"Take who downstairs?"

"Listen fella, don't play games with me. Miss Longstreet

here is the respectable one. Me? I got all the respectability of a rough saloon in a dangerous neighborhood, meanin' I ain't afraid to get brutal. So let's try this again: where did Flugg take his wife? It better not be downstairs."

Dev, though rather appalled at Fin's strong-arm bravado, nonetheless recognized its effectiveness. And if truth be told, Dev, with some mild embarrassment, found herself a little titillated by it.

She noticed though, with satisfaction, that the bony-faced man was not at all titillated, but was pale and terrified, so terrified it was difficult for him to speak.

Dev said in her most civilized tone, "Do stay calm, Mister Whatever-Your-Name is. No harm will come to you if you simply tell us where Mr. Flugg took his wife."

Raising his eyes before opening his mouth, the man finally said, "Upstairs, to the infirmary. He . . . he said Mrs. Flugg was not feeling well."

Fin said, "Give me the telephone."

The frightened man obeyed, handing the machine to Fin over the reception desk.

Fin grabbed the telephone, lifted the receiver from its cradle and ripped it from its wiring.

Fin's recollections of the infirmary were of a grim place almost as frightening as the punishment cells downstairs. What she found when she and Dev arrived there was a tidy medical room with bright white walls, an antiseptic odor of pine soap and alcohol, a sleeping Martha Flugg stretched out on an examining table, an angry Alistair Flugg, and a surprised, white-haired and whiskered gentleman in a white coat.

Flugg, his face pinched, his eyes hooded, said, "There is just no getting rid of you, is there, Devorah, you and this

215

obscene companion of yours. It's not enough that you've twice interrupted my mealtime, now you have the nerve to barge in on a private medical examination of my wife. That she is not well is no surprise, considering the disharmony you've caused our household."

Dev said, "Martha is not well because of whatever it is you and this gentleman have given her. I presume he is the physician here at the Grace Home, and thus subject to your will?"

The doctor, his face flushed, said, "I strenuously object! I am a respected member of the medical—"

Fin said, "Shut your trap," to the doctor. To Flugg, she said, "It ain't your wife who's the sick one, Mr. Flugg. It's you."

"I beg your pardon?"

"It ain't my pardon you should be beggin' for, Flugg. It's all those people you hurt, all those women you tormented."

"Those women," Flugg hissed, his hands balled at his sides, "those painted Jezebels and the vile, money-grabbing madams who profit from them and who live in corruption, they deserve—"

Fin, disgusted, cut him off. "I'm not talkin' about the women in the places you raid, Mr. Flugg. They know your game; they got a game of their own an' can take care of themselves." Still looking at Flugg, Fin addressed Dev, "Did you know, my girl, that our moral crusader here, our Mr. Alistair P. Flugg, has some very deep, dark secrets? I was itchin' t'tell you all about it when you came home this afternoon, but after Mrs. Flugg's telephone call, you rushed me outta the house, an', well, here we are."

The doctor said, "You two seem to have personal business with Mr. Flugg. Perhaps I'd better go."

Fin's quick, "I don't think so, doc," stopped any movement by the frightened doctor. "You see, if you're part of Mr. Flugg's nasty doin's, then you'll be beggin' for pardon, too. An' if you ain't part of it, then maybe you should know who you been dealin' with, in which case, maybe you oughta sit down."

The doctor, a sheepish fellow, sat down.

Dev said, "I'll see to Martha."

Flugg stepped in front of the sedated Mrs. Flugg to block Dev, his face contorted into sneering contempt. "You'll do no such thing, Devorah. I'd advise you to leave here at once, and take your . . . your *friend* with you."

"Or what, Alistair? I, for one, wish to hear what Fin has to say. Perhaps it will help me decide if you are a murderer."

"*Murder?* You think me a murderer? I will not stand for such an insidious accusation."

Fin, sick and tired of Flugg's arrogance, pulled out her revolver and pointed it at Flugg. "Shut up, Flugg. Get out of Miss Longstreet's way, an' don't interrupt me while I spill your dirty secrets."

The color of Flugg's face changed from irate red to terrified gray. He not only stepped out of Dev's way, he, like the doctor, sat down, folding his frame onto a small wooden chair like a collapsing set of pleats.

Dev, now at Martha Flugg's side, noticed with alarm the dot of blood caused by the puncture wound to her neck. "Just what did you give her, doctor?"

"Only something to relax her, help her sleep. I promise you it's nothing stronger than that. She was hysterical, you see."

"I shouldn't doubt it," Dev said.

Fin said, "An' when Mrs. Flugg wakes up, will she crave more of whatever you gave her?"

Fin's statement made the doctor so nervous even his whiskers trembled. He said, "What are you implying? I administered a simple sedative, that is all. Just a dose of chloral hydrate. It's in common use in any hospital."

Dev said, "Yes, I've read of its use to calm patients or induce sleep before surgery. But Lovey, what has this to do with Alistair?"

Fin said, "It seems, my girl, that Mr. Alistair P. Flugg, upright crusader against sin is the man behind John Jones."

Dev's initial surprise bordered on disbelief, a knee-jerk refusal to accept that despite his appalling flaws, the man she'd known since girlhood, a man who'd been to her family home, could be associated with a scoundrel like John Jones. Her surprise registered in her quickly raised eyebrows, which soon lowered slowly as something within her finally fully acknowledged the degraded soul of Alistair P. Flugg.

Fin, sensing her lover's quandary, said, "Oh yes, Dev, Jones was in Flugg's employ, at least accordin' to a police detective we both know but who I won't name just in case any of Flugg's big shot pals want to destroy the fella's career on the force. You do know what I'm talkin' about, don't you, Mr. Flugg?"

Flugg, a man unaccustomed to being challenged, stared at Fin as if desirous to leap from the chair and rip her to shreds. But Flugg remained seated, held fast by the aim of Fin's revolver.

"Y'see, Dev," Fin said, enjoying Flugg's discomfort, "while Mr. Flugg's been busy raidin' brothels an' gambling dens an' paradin' aroun' as an upright citizen tryin' t'clean up the city of what he thinks is filth, he's been sorta leadin' a double life. Accordin' to our detective pal, Flugg an' some of his big shot friends—"

"That hornet's nest he mentioned?" Dev said.

"The very one. Anyway, these big shots have some special needs, the sorta needs they weren't findin' at home, if you know what I mean," Fin said with a wink, which Dev answered with a mischievous smile. Fin continued, "But unlike some of our town's more colorful politicians, these big shots couldn't be seen at regular brothels, where they'd more'n likely run into those very politicians. No, these boys are the cream of New York's crop, with reputations so fancy they was born with their names already engraved on plaques. These are the big shots whose money owns the politicians. Well, these fancy fellas had to get their jollies on the sly. I 'spose they coulda hired professional ladies of the evenin', the type that meet you in a hotel room. But even that was too dangerous for these gentlemen. What if one of them ladies or a hotel clerk threatened to talk? Made threats t'pay up or else? No, these fellas needed ladies who'd not only keep their mouths shut, but would do whatever these fellas wanted them t'do no matter how degradin'. These gentlemen wanted ladies whose tongues wouldn't wag and whose young bodies could be controlled. So that's where you came in, ain't it, Mr. Flugg?"

Lest the angry Alistair P. Flugg entertain any ideas of attacking his tormentor, Fin kept her revolver trained on the seated Flugg and even raised it higher, her gun arm outstretched further to press the point.

"I gotta admit, the plan was pretty slick," Fin said. "These fancy fellas needed a front, the sorta fella no one would ever suspect of dirty business. They found that person in the great moral crusader, Alistair P. Flugg, a man whose hatred of women allowed him to run a scheme which he figured sent certain women to the fate they deserved anyway. But whaddya know, he'd make a pile of money at the same time. Fancy houses on Washington Square don't come cheap, you know."

Dev said, "Alistair, you married into one of the oldest families in New York. Martha's dowry, invested wisely, could have sustained you both for the rest of your days. Did you squander Martha's money? Is that why you became embroiled with Mr. Jones?"

Flugg's arrogant anger could take no more battering. The revelations from Fin, and now this scolding from Devorah, a woman of good breeding he'd had high hopes for but in the end proved no better than the trollops he'd condemned, broke Flugg's spirit. His shoulders sagged in humiliation, his face grew pale and his cheeks pinched. He couldn't even look at Devorah.

Fin said, "Oh, that hangdog expression don't cut no ice with me, Mr. Flugg. Not after what you and Jones did to those girls. You see, Lovey," Fin said to Dev but kept her eyes and her gun on Flugg, "through his pals at City Hall an' some coppers who were part of Flugg's raids, Flugg found John Jones, a down-an'-out actor but a good-lookin' swain who wasn't above doin' the shady for a few bucks. Mr. Jones was hired to seduce young girls, naive girls like Pauline Godfrey, get 'em hooked on dope so they was dependent on Jones an' would do what he told 'em t'do. An' you know what happened to them girls? They was passed aroun' t'those big shots who couldn't be seen at the regular brothels, an' who couldn't just go out an' find willin' women on their own. The risk to their reputations, not t'mention their marriages, was too great. But a doped-up dolly? Perfect. Sooner or later she'd die of the dope, which would keep her mouth shut for good. And there'd always be new girls to replace her. So you see, my love, all Mr. Flugg's protestin' to us that he didn't know John Jones was just a lotta hot air. Now you know why Flugg hadda keep his own wife quiet. It was because of that phone call she made, tellin' you that she heard her husband talkin' on the phone about Jones."

Dev, sick at heart at what her family friend had become, was nonetheless torn between anger and sadness. "And you murdered him, Alistair, when things got out of hand," she said, the words like sand in her mouth. "Did you kill Pauline Godfrey, too? Did she do something to complicate things for you?"

Flugg roared, "NO!" and bolted up from his chair. "Kill Jones? Are you mad? He was an excellent provider! What my wife heard, what my darling, sweet Martha heard," Flugg said without even a whisper of tenderness for his still prostrate wife, "was a telephone call not *from* me but *to* me informing me that Jones had done the stupid thing of falling for that Godfrey trollop. Evidently he'd been disconsolate and guilt-ridden about introducing her to the dope, and the miserable idiot committed suicide. Call me whatever you like, Devorah. Call me a hypocrite, a scoundrel, but I'm no murderer."

Fin said, "Fancy words, Flugg, but can you back them up with an alibi?"

"Yes! I was conducting a raid at Madame Lou's brothel the night that Jones died. That is easily verified. Ask her yourself."

Fin didn't have to. Madame Lou said as much when Fin shared a jail cell with her. She wasn't about to let Flugg completely off the hook, though. "And what about Pauline Godfrey?"

"When was she killed?"

"Monday afternoon."

Flugg sat down again, relief all over his face. "I was in a meeting with the Mayor at City Hall. But don't just take my word for it. Ask him. Oh, but I'm sure you wouldn't believe him. Your kind doesn't believe anything from respectable people."

"With good reason," Fin said.

Flugg shrugged that off. "Well, never mind. There will be a record of it, and a photograph for the press files and the city archive."

Dev said, "Just a moment, Alistair. There is something missing from your story."

"Missing? There's nothing missing."

"Whoever you spoke to on the telephone, didn't they tell you that Mr. Jones had tried to peddle some of the women to local brothels? Surely that would anger you if Jones made a profit behind your back."

Flugg's toothy sneer reminded Dev of a raptor she'd seen pictured in a zoology book: vicious, predatory, soulless. "And you think I would murder him for such a low transgression?" he said. "Anyway, as I said, I was elsewhere the night Mr. Jones died."

"You could have hired someone to have him killed," Dev pressed.

Flugg waved that away. "Frankly, I didn't care what Jones did with those women after their usefulness was spent. There were always more where they came from."

There rose in Dev a rage she'd never before experienced, not even through the horror of the dismissal by her family, not even through the taunts she and Fin sometimes heard in the street. Alistair Flugg's icy, offhand dismissal of women's lives dug deep into Dev, producing a physical pain as real as if she'd been attacked by claws. In retaliation she would have slapped the man then and there had not Martha Flugg stirred on the examining table.

After a weak moan, Martha said, barely above a whisper, "Alistair? Where . . . what . . .?"

Dev held Martha's hand, stroked her cheek. "You're all right now, Martha. Fin and I are here. No one will hurt you."

Martha struggled to sit up, finally managing with Dev's help. She stared through drugged, misted eyes at her husband. "Why, Alistair?"

"Because, dearest, you got in the way. My lucrative arrangement would have been destroyed. Well, it looks like it's destroyed anyway, so congratulations, my dear. Without my little business we'll have to fire the servants and sell the house. Your sweet and easy life is over, Mrs. Flugg. Perhaps you could take up selling hats." Flugg's chuckle tempted Dev once again to slap the man's face so hard his teeth would lodge in his cheek.

She kept this violent impulse in check, and said instead, "You're a fiend, Alistair. All those lives you ruined, all those women destroyed. All that moralizing, those self-righteous raids, just a front to cover your dope peddling schemes."

"I didn't ruin anyone's life, Devorah," Flugg said with a scornful wave of his hand. "Those women were already ruined. Trash, the lot of them."

Martha, her head clearing, her thoughts sharpening, her despair deepening, said, "How bitter you are, Alistair. You are not the cheerful man I married, nor the loving father to our precious daughter, Eliza. When did the bitterness set in, Alistair? Was it when Eliza married a man you disapproved of? Eliza's husband is a fine man, Alistair. He—"

"He's trash! And he turned our daughter into trash, consorting with all manner of people so beneath her station."

The words, at first caught in Flugg's angry throat, blurted out in a stormy torrent, so that when he finally said, "As far as I'm concerned, our daughter is dead," Alistair Flugg was crying.

Martha placed what began as a tender touch on her husband's shoulder, but her fingers quickly curled into a pitiless claw.

Dev went to the telephone on the infirmary's wall and instructed the operator to connect her with police headquarters on Mulberry Street.

The doctor sat with his head in his hands.

Fin kept her revolver aimed at Flugg.

CHAPTER THIRTY-ONE

listair P. Flugg, who'd previously courted the attentions of the press when conducting his very public raids, covered his face against the illuminating bursts of the news photographers' flash powder. This same Alistair P. Flugg, who'd only recently been the voluble crusader for moral righteousness, kept bitterly quiet when pelted with reporters' questions. Only his entry into a paddy wagon offered humiliating relief.

Once Flugg had been taken away by the police, a police matron escorted Martha Flugg, still weak from her ordeal and hazy from the drug, to Bellevue Hospital for rest and recuperation.

The terrified doctor of the Grace Home for Wayward Children, his reputation likely in ruins, was allowed to go his own way with a warning from Detective Coyle not to leave the city.

Alone now in the infirmary with Fin and Devorah, Coyle at last felt at liberty to speak freely. "He'll face no punishment, you know," Coyle said, referring to Flugg. "Unless his associates come forward and corroborate your accusations, which of course they won't do, the case will be thrown out. Flugg's got powerful friends. They'll protect him."

Fin said, "Sure they will, to save their own necks. But even after he's free an' clear of the charges, his once good name will be smeared an' those powerful friends will drop him like a lost wallet in a sewer."

"Very likely," Coyle agreed.

"Count on it," Fin said. "It'll be business as usual. You're gonna have to watch yourself, Detective. Those hornets can still sting you."

Coyle, never one to let his emotions show, nonetheless couldn't hide the roil of emotions in his dark eyes: disappointment, anger, fear.

Dev, sensing the detective's disquiet, sought to reinstate purpose into his policeman's sense of himself. "Now that we know that Alistair didn't kill John Jones or Pauline Godfrey, and Jones evidently had no hand in the Godfrey killing either, that leaves Miss Godfrey's murder still unsolved. Are you now willing to become involved in the investigation, Detective Coyle?"

This was a challenge to Coyle's honor and he knew it, which made his hesitancy to answer all the more searing to his policeman's soul.

"He can't," Fin said. "The coppers are gonna close ranks. Remember about those hornets, Dev. They'll want peace and quiet in the nest again. They'll sting whoever gets close to their secrets, and Pauline Godfrey was among their secrets."

Coyle said, "You two can get stung just as bad if you keep asking questions about Miss Godfrey."

Dev said, "We have two grieving parents who are depending on us, Detective. And we have very thick skins."

With their options narrowing, their prime suspect dismissed as Pauline Godfrey's killer, Fin and Devorah availed themselves of much needed sustenance at Dockerty's 21st Street Oyster House, a popular spot famous for its broiled Saddle Rock oysters, wide assortment of condiments, extensive selection of ciders and beers, and its tall arched windows throwing light into the intimate, whitewashed-walled room. The lunch crowd had thinned when Fin and Dev walked in shortly after two-thirty. They found a cozy table in a corner where they could review their missteps in the Godfrey case in the hopes that nourishment and conversation could clear their thinking.

But the discussion did not go well, even with the broadening of thought induced by a second pint of ale for Fin and hearty draughts of cider for Dev. The solution to the murder of Pauline Godfrey remained elusive, hidden deep within the thus far unanswerable question: why? With Alistair Flugg's motive for retribution now discredited, Fin and Devorah raked through every detail, every conversation, probing to get to the root of *why* Pauline Godfrey was killed.

The cool slide of each oyster down Dev's throat was the only pleasure she enjoyed in this otherwise desultory lunch. "Well, we still have one motive," she said.

"You mean the jealousy angle," Fin said. "Those actresses."

"Indeed. Two in particular, I think, stand out as possibilities. Miss Silver—"

"I still think of her as sassy Suzanne Sawdy from 50th Street," Fin mused.

"And Katherine Hazelton. Frankly, my money's on Hazelton."

"Yeah, mine, too," Fin said. "The way she handled those knives at the butcher shop, I bet she could slice a throat as easy as a juicy sirloin."

"You've just killed my taste for steak," Dev said.

It was shortly after 4 p.m. when Fin and Devorah stepped out of a hansom cab in front of Brennan's Butcher Shop. The weak late afternoon sun rendered the scene of hurrying housewives in shabby shawls, children by their sides in patched dresses or knee pants, laboring men carrying barrels or wooden crates across their shoulders, and the usual complement of local street toughs, in a near painterly softness contrary to their harsh lives. Looming over everything were the tracks of the elevated train and the huge gas tanks which any minute would throw their shadows over the neighborhood as the sun lowered in the sooty sky.

Dev put her handkerchief to her nose against the pervasive odor of gas as she and Fin made their way across the sidewalk and into the butcher shop.

Katherine Hazelton, a hind quarter of beef slung over her shoulder, her apron smeared with blood, was just coming through the swinging door from the back of the shop when Fin and Devorah walked in. That Miss Hazelton was not happy to see the pair was evident in the way she slammed the beef onto the butcher block behind the display case.

Dev said, "Hello again, Miss Hazelton. My, but you're strong. That hunk of beef looks like it weighs, what, about thirty pounds?"

"Hello and goodbye, Miss Longstreet. I nearly lost my job on account of your friend here," Hazelton said with a nod toward Fin, then took a cleaver from the row of butchering knives hanging on the white tile wall behind her. "My boss wasn't too happy that I was getting questioned about a murder."

"But clearly he didn't fire you," Dev said.

"Only after I did a lot of fast talking. Look, Mr. Brennan is out on a delivery. He'll be back any minute, and if he finds you here pelting me again with questions about that dead girl I'll lose my job for sure."

Fin said, "Nothing lined up in the theatrical trade, I take it?"

"No, not that it's any of your business."

"True," Fin said. "Our business is findin' out who killed Pauline Godfrey so that her parents can grieve properly. Miss Longstreet an' I think maybe you can help us out. Maybe you've even been keepin' somethin' from us. Like where you were this past Monday afternoon."

With a chop of the cleaver that made Dev jump, Katherine Hazelton said, "Like I already explained, I work days in this butcher shop. Where else would I be?"

Dev said, "That is precisely what we're trying to discern, Miss Hazelton. You are being quite cagey about your whereabouts. You know, we have reason to believe you were jealous of Mr. Jones's relationship with Miss Godfrey."

"I didn't give a fig for that girl."

"So you say."

"And that's all I'm going to say. You can't prove I wasn't here on Monday."

"Of course we can, Miss Hazelton," Dev said. "We can ask your employer."

The change in Katherine Hazelton, from belligerent to frightened, seemed to Dev to reduce her from a grown woman to a scared, petulant child. It gave Dev the chills. "No, don't do that," Hazelton said. "He'll think I—if he sees you here asking more questions, he might think I—well, he could think—"

"That you were out doin' murder?" Fin said. "Could be you sure had reason to, Miss Hazelton. An' it's startin' t'look like you ain't got no alibi for your whereabouts at the time of Miss Godfrey's killin'."

"I know my rights," Hazelton said, still petulant, taking a carving knife from the wall and expertly, ferociously, slicing the beef with precision. "I don't have to speak to you. I don't have to tell you where I was. Only the police can ask those questions, and they haven't been around, so I'm guessing that they don't care and that you two are just fishing. Well, I'm not biting.

Now, get lost." The knife came up and then down again, slicing smoothly around the bone.

"Touchy, ain't she," Fin said when she and Dev were outside the butcher shop and walking toward Third Avenue in search of a hansom.

"Indeed," Dev said. "But unless we can prove where Miss Hazelton was or wasn't at the time of Pauline's death, we can't determine for sure if she's the one who cut Pauline's throat." She added with a shudder, "The woman certainly has the talent. The way she handled that cleaver and that carving knife . . ." A short groan finished her sentence.

"Yeah," Fin said. "But it's a dead end until we can figure where she was. Meantime, we can have another chat with Suzanne. Seems to me she fits the jealousy angle, too."

"She does," Dev said. "But, well, I don't know, I have this unnerving feeling that something is missing, something we're overlooking."

"Like maybe someone else in the woodwork?"

"Maybe."

"Then I think we'd better have a chat with our clients again."

"The Godfreys?" Dev said. "I don't know, Lovey. I think I may have gotten as much from them today as we're going to get. They said they don't know Miss Hazelton or Miss Silver or any of the other actresses, and I believe them."

"I do, too. But if anythin' is missin' from this case, it could only be tied up with somethin' or someone involved with Pauline Godfrey. An' the only people who can tell us any of that is Mr. an' Mrs. William R. Godfrey. Their shop closes at six o'clock, right? It's only a little after five now. If we find a cab, we can make it."

CHAPTER THIRTY-TWO

ixth Avenue was clogged with end-of-workday commuters hurrying along the streets or up the stairs to the elevated trains, or riding in cable cars, hansoms, or other horse-drawn conveyances pressing through the snarl for the right-of-way. Here and there, an automobile added to the clog, its driver honking the horn. Horses brayed, drivers shouted and cracked their whips, the elevated train clattered loud above the avenue, all the noise creating the boisterous music of modernizing New York—a music loved by some New Yorkers, loathed by others.

Fin and Dev were among the former, though this evening the excitement they usually felt for the rambunctious grandeur of their city was muted by their tangled thoughts and the disappointment that they had yet to solve the case of Pauline Godfrey and thus provide the girl's grieving parents the solace of justice.

As Fin and Devorah arrived at the Godfreys' shop along the Ladies Mile, the last of the day's customers came through the door clutching their bundles of fabric and ribbons, then joined the rest of the throng along the avenue.

Inside, Mr. Godfrey tallied the cash register while Mrs.

Godfrey tidied the sales counters, putting spools of ribbon and lace and bolts of fabric back in place on shelves.

Fin, ever chivalrous, offered to assist Mrs. Godfrey. "Them big bolts of fabric look heavy, Missus. Lemme give you a hand."

"Thank you, but no need. I'm nearly done," Mrs. Godfrey said, and lifted a bolt of rose petal chintz into place on a shelf just above her shoulders.

Mr. Godfrey said, "Pauline used to do a lot of the lifting, but I must say Mrs. Godfrey has risen to the task beautifully. My lovely wife has proven to be quite strong. I remember when Pauline was a tot how Mrs. Godfrey would carry her all over the house to comfort the child's crying." Mr. Godfrey smiled with the sentimental memory, his eyes crinkling as his smile broadened into one of good humor. "Whoever says that females are the weaker sex clearly has not met my wife."

"Indeed," Dev said with admiration. "Stepping into your late wife's shoes and assuming the task of motherhood could not have been easy."

Fin, a bit at sea, said, "I beg y'pardon?"

"Oh, of course you didn't know," Dev said. "In all the activity of the past few hours, we didn't have a chance to talk about it. It was during my discussion with Mrs. Godfrey earlier today when I learned that Mr. Godfrey is a widower. The present Mrs. Godfrey is Mr. Godfrey's second wife."

"I see," Fin said with a respectful nod to the current Mrs. Godfrey. "Well then, my high regard for you, Missus. Yours ain't been an easy road, I'm sure."

Mrs. Godfrey, never comfortable around Fin, gave her a tight smile.

Mr. Godfrey once more puffed with pride, his jowly face near blushing, which gave him yet again the appearance of a russet pear. "A better helpmeet and mother I could not have asked for," he said. "I am a fortunate man indeed." He held out his arms and addressed his wife, who was still busying herself with tidying the shop. "Come here, my dear. You've worked hard enough for one day. Miss Longstreet and her companion clearly want to talk to us again. Let's hear what's on their mind."

Mrs. Godfrey removed the contents of her apron pockets—a tape measure, scissors, assorted fabric chalks—and placed them on the counter before putting each away in their assigned drawers. Her efficiency was quick, her movements sharp, which, Dev thought with amusement, was in keeping with the woman's birdlike facial features. "What is there left to talk about? You hired these people to find Pauline's killer," Mrs. Godfrey said, putting away the chalk, followed by the tape measure in another drawer, and opening a third drawer for the scissors. "So far all they've come up with are unanswered questions." Mrs. Godfrey suddenly dropped the scissors, her hand snapping aside.

Alarmed, Mr. Godfrey said, "What is it, my dear?"

"In my haste, I'm afraid I nicked my finger on my scissors."

"Shall I make you a bandage?"

Mrs. Godfrey sucked at the little wound. "No, it's nothing, William. Just a trifle. You needn't worry."

"Maybe I should think about hiring a young woman to assist you. You've worked so hard and doubled your tasks since . . . since Pauline . . ." But he couldn't finish. Grief for his murdered daughter once again descended on the poor man with the weight of a boulder.

Mrs. Godfrey, now at her husband's side, her arm around his waist, said to Dev and Fin, "Perhaps we've had quite enough about Pauline for one day. Your presence is upsetting Mr. Godfrey."

Rallying from his grief, Mr. Godfrey wiped away tears he was clearly embarrassed to shed in front of Fin and Devorah. "No, no, my dear," he said, forcing an attitude of manliness. "If there's been any development in the case, I think we must hear about it and see things through. After all, the police have been no help, and Donner & Longstreet are our only hope. Surely you want to find Pauline's killer as much as I do."

"Of course, William," Mrs. Godfrey said, nodding as if the question needn't even have been asked. "But how much longer is this investigation going to go on? It's taking a terrible toll on us. You haven't had a decent night's sleep since this whole business began."

"But my dear, we must—"

"We must think of ourselves, William. And as your wife, I must think of you, comfort you." A dutiful stroke of her husband's brow underscored her concern. "It was difficult enough to live with Pauline's disobedient association with that vile John Jones and then witness the misery he made her suffer. It was a terrible agony for you, William, don't you remember? It broke my heart. Oh yes, it truly broke my heart."

Once again, Mr. Godfrey nearly slipped into tears. "And mine, too, my dearest," he said.

Mrs. Godfrey stroked her husband's cheek. Looking up at him, she took his face between her hands, her slender fingers strong from years of work. "Well, do you want to live through it all over again? Because that's what will happen if we keep having to listen to all these questions. I don't know if I have the strength, William. I . . . I just don't know." She took a handkerchief from the sleeve of her ruffled yellow blouse and dabbed her eyes. Her husband put his arm around her. With a sharp but piteous whimper, Mrs. Godfrey said, "Perhaps it's time to call a halt to all these questions, William, so we can just heal."

"Mrs. Godfrey," Dev said with tenderness, "Fin and I know how painful this must be for you. But if you want justice—"

"What I want is peace, Miss Longstreet," Mrs. Godfrey snapped. "My husband and I need peace if we are to rebuild our lives without Pauline. We have only each other now, and I must tend to my husband and to this shop where we earn our living." She put her handkerchief to her eyes again.

Mr. Godfrey said, "Perhaps my wife is right. We do need

a little peace, at least for today. We can resume our discussion another time, perhaps tomorrow, after Mrs. Godfrey and I have had some rest."

"I see," Dev said. "Well, until tomorrow then." Taking Fin's arm, the investigating team of Donner & Longstreet walked through the Godfreys' shop to the door. As Fin opened it, it seemed to Dev as if the door opened so slowly as to barely move at all. She had a feeling of time slowing down, nearly stopping, giving her mind an expanse of time to deal with the sudden rush of thoughts, recollections, horrors revived, secrets hinted at. Pieces of an ugly puzzle seemed to float into place before her eyes. She felt her body stiffen at what it presented, a scenario of something unthinkably abhorrent, a hostility she understood all too well.

She said to Fin, "No. We are not leaving."

Dev turned around. Fin, puzzled but trusting her treasured Dev's instincts, walked beside her as they returned to Mr. and Mrs. Godfrey.

Addressing Mrs. Godfrey, Dev said, "This ordeal must've been hell for you."

The tilt of Mrs. Godfrey's head gave her face even more of an avian appearance, as when a bird is alert, perched on a telephone wire and feeling the buzz of electricity beneath its talons. "Well of course it has," she said. "No family should have to endure what Mr. Godfrey and I have endured."

"Quite," Dev said. "Mr. Godfrey should not have had to endure the vicious murder of his beloved daughter. And perhaps, Mrs. Godfrey, you feel you've endured more than your share of family burden. You raised Pauline as your own, and yet she did not grow to become the obedient, dare I say old-fashioned young woman you expected her to be. Instead, she was not only too modern for your taste, her worse sin was to remain the apple of Mr. Godfrey's eye, a privilege you wanted only for yourself. Believe me, Mrs. Godfrey, you are not the first mother to resent or disapprove of her daughter." It took all of Dev's discipline to say this last and not cringe or cry at the memory of being turned away by her family. Remembering her mother's face, stony and cruel and lacking all maternal love as she sent her only daughter out the door, threatened to crush Dev's spirit. But the presence of her loving and sturdy Fin beside her, and her own unshakeable insistence on maintaining the demeanor of a professional investigator gave Devorah strength.

Mr. Godfrey, flustered, frightened, said, "I . . . I am not quite sure what you are getting at, Miss Longstreet."

Relying on that professional demeanor now, Dev said, "Mr. Godfrey, I believe your wife is a murderer."

Mr. William R. Godfrey, respectable businessman, a pillar of the mercantile community, looked at Devorah as if she suddenly spoke in an indecipherable alien tongue.

Fin looked at her beloved Devorah with shock, and then curiosity, and finally a discreet but adoring smile.

Mrs. Godfrey looked at Devorah with no expression on her face at all.

Chapter Thirty-Three

Mrs. Godfrey's sudden laugh, a burst that stretched her thin lips across her teeth, made Dev's skin prickle, caused Fin's fingers to curl, and Mr. Godfrey to stare at his wife as if she was no longer a human woman but something strange and feral.

The woman's cackle grew more shrill, slicing through the air in the fabric shop and the nerves of everyone hearing it, until Dev decided to put an end to it with a slap across Mrs. Godfrey's face.

Mr. Godfrey, already horrified by Dev's accusation, snapped, "Miss Longstreet!" horrified again by this physical attack on his wife. He took his umbrage no further, though, either exhausted by what must've felt like the unceasing assaults over these last days to his comfortable, predictable life, or he simply gave in to the effectiveness of Dev's slap, for it stopped Mrs. Godfrey's laugh in her throat.

Mrs. Godfrey's next sound was a hard cough, and then a sniffle which preceded a crooked smile. When she spoke through that smile, Dev's skin prickled again. "If you think my husband is going to pay you for such nonsense," Mrs. Godfrey said, her voice as brittle as the look in her eyes, "you are sorely mistaken, Miss Longstreet. You are only trying to cheat us out of our money with your ridiculous accusation."

Mr. Godfrey, his normally ruddy jowls paled to gray, looked at Dev with confusion and pleading. "Why would you say such a . . . such a monstrous thing about my wife?"

"Because I believe it to be true," Dev said.

Bewilderment paralyzed Mr. Godfrey, leaving him unable to either caress or comfort the wife he would not or could not believe could commit murder. Stiff with incomprehension, he could not even step away in horror. He simply stood beside his wife, rigid and gray as a headstone. "On what grounds, may I ask?" he said with desperation. "What evidence do you have?"

The question might've unsettled Dev because in point of fact she had no solid evidence at all. What she had was that puzzle that fell into place, the pieces connecting with perfection.

One piece, though, was missing. This last piece, if Dev was correct, might satisfy Mr. Godfrey's questions and even force a confession from Mrs. Godfrey.

But if she was not correct, then the whole puzzle could fall apart, the pieces having formed the wrong picture in the first place. Her accusation of murder against Mrs. Godfrey would be a heinous mistake, one which would be ruinous to the reputation of Donner & Longstreet Inquiries.

Dev needed to find that missing piece. "Mrs. Godfrey, you can prove me horribly wrong with the answer to this one simple question: where were you on Monday afternoon around three o'clock?"

There was something clownish if also macabre in the way Mrs. Godfrey pointed a finger at Devorah. "There, you see, William?" she said through a smile which Dev wasn't sure was a smile of relief or just smug. "She has no evidence, and this is all a sham. Well, snoopy Miss Longstreet, I was right here, of course, on Monday afternoon. Where else would I be? With Pauline still galivanting around with that Jones villain and not here in this shop where she belonged, I couldn't just wander off and go hat shopping, now could I."

Mr. Godfrey's already paled cheeks went chalky white. His jowls seemed to harden, making it difficult for him to open his mouth to speak. In a voice sounding more like a croak than the melody of human speech, he said, "No . . . no, you were not here. You said you were going out to pick up our shipment of a new supply of threads. When you returned I remarked that you were gone longer than expected, and you . . . you said there was an unusually long line at the post office."

"Well, there was," Mrs. Godfrey insisted. "William, you can't actually believe—?"

"Missus," Fin cut in, "if I were to go to the post office an' ask if they was unusually busy on Monday afternoon, what would they say?"

Without even a glance at Fin or acknowledging her question, Mrs. Godfrey placed her hands on her husband's chest and slid her fingers up to his shoulders. "William," she said, her tone eerily calm, "are you going to let these two . . . these two *unnatural* women badger us like this?"

"Please, my dear, just answer the question. Please."

But Mrs. Godfrey did not answer the question. She just looked at her husband, her eyes now glassy, her lips pursed tight until they broke into a sneer so cold both Fin and Dev shivered. "I've tried to be a good wife, William," she said through the sneer which shifted slowly into a pucker and finally into a pout. "All these years I've tried, ever since the day you married me, your little brat in tow. That's why I went along when you insisted on hiring these people. After all, who would ever believe that a devoted wife would kill her husband's oh-so-charming daughter?"

Mr. Godfrey, his skin now an unnatural shade of pale green, tried to speak, but could only babble, "What . . . what are you saying? What are you—"

"But don't you see, I had to do it, William," Mrs. Godfrey cut him off. "I had to do it because she had more of your love than I did. That uppity girl who I bathed, whose dirty diapers I changed, whose tears I wiped away even as her childish whining got on my nerves—well, I put up with it because I looked forward to the day when she'd take over here in the shop and I could finally live the easy life of the wife of a successful businessman. But then she wanted to go off to that college, and you were going to allow it. Really, William! What does a shopgirl need with college? And then . . . and then . . ." came out in a tight stutter, Mrs. Godfrey's lips barely moving while her fingers tightened on her husband's shoulders. "And then that Jones fellow came along and made things worse for me by worrying you. Your suffering for your daughter took more of you away from me, William."

The weirdly stretched smile now on Mrs. Godfrey's face sent a sensation of icy pinpricks down Devorah's spine, and brought to Fin recollections of the dangerous vagrants made mad by hate and hardship.

Mrs. Godfrey spoke through that smile. "But you know, then I thought maybe Mr. Jones did me a favor. I didn't know he'd made Pauline a dope fiend, but anyone could see he was making her sick, sick to the point of dying. But the little fool wouldn't die," Mrs. Godfrey sneered. "The damn tramp just wouldn't hurry up and die, and I couldn't stand for it anymore. Do you understand, William? Do you understand what it's like to swallow one's rage day after day until it feels like it could eat you up chunk by chunk from the inside? So I followed her because it was time to get rid of her. I knew she was going to meet Jones that day. I followed her and let my rage and my good scissors do their job, slit her throat fast, so fast I was gone before anyone noticed. I didn't even see her fall, though I would've enjoyed seeing the brat die. You're all mine now, William. You understand, don't you? I do love you."

Mr. Godfrey, his body shriveling inside his clothes, slid his wife's hands from his shoulders and dropped them in horror. He leaned against the counter to keep from falling, his knees weak, his body nearly folding. Fin quickly went to his side to assist the suffering man.

When he'd steadied, Fin asked him, "Is your telephone in the back office?"

Without fully understanding, Mr. Godfrey nodded as if by automation.

But Devorah understood and nodded her acknowledgment as Fin took Mrs. Godfrey's arm. "I ain't lettin' you outta my sight, lady," Fin said. At first, Mrs. Godfrey resisted, and attempted to pull her arm away. But despite the woman's strength, Fin, hardened by the life of the streets, proved the stronger, and Mrs. Godfrey had no choice but to submit to Fin's grip. She walked beside Fin to the back office with the timid steps one takes when forced to an uninviting destination, escorted by an undesired companion.

Alone now with Devorah, Mr. Godfrey, looking like he'd misplaced his own life, said, "How did you know?"

Her heart aching for the anguished man, Dev said, "Pieces which had been dangling in front of us from the beginning eventually coalesced today. At first, I couldn't see them because I didn't want to see them. In that respect, Mrs. Godfrey is correct: who would believe a mother would kill her daughter? But looking back, I realized there were wrong notes right from the start, when you and Mrs. Godfrey came to us for help in finding Pauline's killer."

"Wrong notes?"

"Well, yes," Dev said. "On the night you sought our help, your wife's attitude was, shall we say, less than generous toward Pauline. I dismissed it then and continued to dismiss it as the pain of a grieving mother and her anger at the man who ruined Pauline. Even as the investigation continued and ran into dead ends regarding other suspects, I still could not entertain the idea that a mother might murder her own child. But I finally came to see it because, unbeknownst to you, Mr. Godfrey, I am painfully aware that mothers can do cruel things if they harbor resentment, even jealousy."

There must have been something in Dev's voice, or perhaps her demeanor, which caused Mr. Godfrey, even through his own suffering, to look at Devorah with what could only be described as sympathy.

With a simple, efficient nod of acknowledgment, Devorah resumed her professional deportment. "Fin and I of course examined the jealousy angle, but we were looking in the wrong direction. Pauline's murder was not jealousy over a lover; it was jealousy over your doting on your daughter, perhaps even fear that Pauline would likely be the beneficiary of the bulk of your estate when the time came. This financial motive suggested itself when Mrs. Godfrey told me today of her employment in the shabby millinery shop down the street. After she'd married you, her life rose from threadbare to prosperous."

"A gold digger," Mr. Godfrey said with unexpected resentment. It was as if something inside him snapped, some floodgate opened and whatever love he'd had for his wife was suddenly and forcefully flushed from his being, replaced by a bitterness which seemed to emanate from him like a vapor.

The man's resentment of his wife's possible financial considerations reminded Dev of Mr. Godfrey's repeated mentions of money since this investigation had began. She even recalled the way he'd handled his derby hat the night he and his wife showed up at their door, as if its loss or damage would mean more to him as lost cash than the loss of something personally enjoyed or loved. "I wouldn't say your wife was a gold digger, Mr. Godfrey," Dev said, surprising herself to be even minimally defending a murderess. "Women's economic opportunities are limited. Marriage is often a woman's only route to financial stability."

This explanation didn't soften Mr. Godfrey's attitude. If anything, his face hardened, and even his jowls became unnaturally stiff. The bitter vapor which flowed from him now appeared to extend to Devorah and indeed to all womanhood. Only his eyes moved to Dev, demanding she continue her explanation of Pauline's murder and his wife's guilt.

This sudden change in Mr. William R. Godfrey, from a somewhat drab man of mild personality to a man consumed by acrimony, nearly caused Devorah to cringe under his stare. She would've liked nothing more than to escape his company, but she understood that as the father of a murdered daughter he was due the explanation he demanded, and so she soldiered on. "Yes, well, another problem Fin and I had to grapple with was who among the suspects might be strong enough, quick enough, and angry enough to accost Pauline and slit her throat right there in the street. Our other suspects could certainly fill the bill, and to my mind Mrs. Godfrey, a middle-aged woman, might not have had the capacity to overtake the young Pauline, perhaps still somewhat vital despite the deterioration of her health. But as Fin and I have seen, and as you proudly attested to, your wife is quite strong, capable of working with heavy bolts of fabric and lifting them on and off shelves throughout the workday. Moreover, Mrs. Godfrey is quite expert with scissors. I am aware that fabric scissors are exquisitely sharp, and the scissors I've seen Mrs. Godfrey use are long-bladed, perfect for cutting long lengths or widths of fabric and for efficiently slicing a throat."

A bell-helmeted officer led Mrs. Godfrey out of the shop and into a paddy wagon at the curb.

Mr. Godfrey, a sad and angry man but dutifully adhering to the responsibilities of the matrimonial state, used the office telephone to arrange for an attorney for his wife.

Outside the shop, where streetlamps glowed in a misty dusk, a crowd had gathered as crowds always do to ogle the drama of crime. In the center of it all were Fin, Devorah, and Detective Charles Coyle.

Fin said to Coyle, "So it turns out there were no hornets in this nest after all, detective. Just your ol'-fashioned rage killin'."

Coyle, typical of his tight rein on his feelings, didn't smile or frown. Without a scintilla of emotion for the resolution of Pauline Godfrey's murder, Coyle said in his usual soft voice, "It's lucky you two cornered the woman into a confession, Donner, because you really had nothing. No proof of guilt, no evidence that the scissors were the murder weapon, nothing."

"Luck had nothing to do with it, Coyle," Fin said with a wink at her beloved Dev, her partner in life and crime. "You can thank the brilliance of Miss Devorah Longstreet. She put all them puzzle pieces together an' put Mrs. Godfrey into the picture. Anyway, now that you got your own confession from Mrs. Godfrey, you can tidy up the Pauline Godfrey case."

"Sure," Coyle said without enthusiasm.

"Why so dreary?" Fin asked.

But it was Devorah who answered. "Because at Mrs. Godfrey's trial, the minute Pauline's association with John Jones is mentioned in the proceedings, those hornets everyone is so afraid of will buzz through the police department, their stingers out."

CHAPTER THIRTY-FOUR

Arriving home in a somber mood despite the resolution of the case, Fin and Devorah fortified their spirits with snifters of brandy and the satisfying news accounts in the *New York Evening World* about the arrest of Alistair Flugg, the police closure of the Grace Home for Wayward Children, and the return of the children to their families; or, if that was no longer possible or advisable, those remaining children placed in humane care at more enlightened charitable institutions.

Fin telephoned Silkie's gym, where Five Cent Frankie was sure to be, and where Timmy Poole, seated between his mother and Frankie on a bench, his feet still bandaged and painful, was nevertheless having the time of his life despite his mother's worry about Frankie taking mother and son away from the safety of his rooms. Frankie was delighted with Fin's news that it was safe for Mag to take Timmy home. Though Frankie had taken a liking to the boy, and wouldn't mind a tumble with Timmy's tantalizing mother, getting his quarters back for his solitary sporting life was welcome.

After a light dinner of cold cubed lamb with mint sauce, accompanied by a salad of asparagus and tomatoes on a bed of Boston lettuce, Fin and Devorah retired to the parlor and the comfort of their big leather armchairs where they enjoyed an after-dinner coffee and looked forward to another night of rapture in their bed. In fact, Fin did not even wait to finish her coffee. The glow of lamplight on Dev's face was so lovely, the sight lured Fin from her chair and led her to her lover, where she bent to kiss her.

As ever, Fin's kiss, the touch of her hand as it slid from Dev's cheek to her breast, aroused in Devorah a passion intense and urgent, as if every pore of her skin, every vein of her blood, became swollen with desire beneath Fin's fingers.

Fin, always sensitive to Devorah's pleasure, slid her arms around her and drew Dev up from her chair. Their arms around each other's waists, Dev's head resting on Fin's strong shoulder, the lovers drifted toward their bedroom.

But their desires were thwarted—and in the same intrusive fashion as when the Godfreys arrived just days ago—by a knock on their door.

Dev said, "Shall we ignore it?"

After a moment's thought and temptation, Fin said, "What if somebody needs our help?"

Dev reluctantly nodded her agreement, and gave a frustrated sigh as she slipped her arm from her lover's waist.

It was with equal reluctance that Fin left Devorah's side and went to the door. Hoping against hope that the caller was not a prospective client requiring the services of Donner & Longstreet Inquiries, thus someone she could not turn away, Fin opened the door and faced a smiling Maggie Poole.

"Where's Timmy?" Fin said with concern. "You didn't leave him alone, did you, Mag? He ain't healed yet."

"Are y'really askin' me that, Fin Donner?" Mag said, her voice, always whiskey-and-tobacco raw, now noticeably tired. "Of course I didn't leave my boy alone. He's still with Frankie, havin' a swell time. I'll fetch him on my way home. So, y'gonna let me in or not? Kinda drafty out here in the hall." Mag pointedly pulled her cloak more tightly around her.

Stepping aside in the doorway, Fin nodded to Maggie to come in. As they walked through the hallway to the parlor, Fin said, "So what brings you around, Mag?"

"I need t'talk t'you and Miss Longstreet."

"You in trouble?"

"Nothin' like that. Why so suspicious, Fin?"

"I ain't suspicious, Mag. I just worry about you."

In a manner sly and seductive, Mag said, "Y'always was the chivalrous kind, Fin Donner. Too bad y'already spoke for."

A small, lopsided grin was as close to blushing as Fin would ever come. She gently took Mag's cloak from her shoulders, giving her the gift of momentary courtliness before hanging the tattered garment in the armoire. "You'll find your own knight some day, Mag," Fin said.

"I ain't waitin'."

In the parlor, Mag greeted Dev with a smile and a humble, "Hello, Miss Longstreet."

"Good evening, Maggie. All is well with you and Timmy?"

"Thanks t'you an' Fin, me and Timmy are gonna be jus' fine. Matter of fact, that's why I'm here. I have plans I wanna talk t'you about."

"Please sit down then, and do tell us all about it. Would you like something to drink?"

"Well, that brandy y'gave me last time would be nice, thanks."

As Mag seated herself in one of the leather armchairs, Dev was aware that despite Mag's wild black hair, her shabby green dress and cracked high-button shoes, despite the lines of a hard life etched into the remnants of her beauty and revealed by the lamplight, the woman had an allure which could not be denied. With Dev's unwarranted jealousy now banished, she was finally able to really see Maggie Poole, the notorious Black Haired Mag, and realized for the first time that the woman's allure came from within: Maggie Poole had an inner heat. She possessed a comfort with that heat and an acceptance of herself that overrode the struggles and deprivations of her life. Together with that voice of hers, ragged but sultry, a voice ripe with lust and life, Dev was finally able to admit that Maggie Poole had charm.

Fin poured brandies for Mag, Dev, and herself while Dev sat down in the other armchair.

Mag started to drink the liquor down in one swallow, then remembered how Fin and Devorah took polite sips. Though the little sips didn't provide the kick she usually liked in her imbibing, Mag took pleasure in the brandy's slide of warmth down her throat. After a satisfying few sips, she wiped her mouth with the back of her hand and smiled a wistful smile at Fin and Devorah. "First of all," she said, "I gotta thank you two for gettin' Timmy outta that horrible place an' bringin' him back t'me, an' then keepin' us safe with Five Cent Frankie. I owe you an' I know it. If I can ever do anythin' for either of you, anythin', y'hear me? Just name it."

Dev said, "You don't owe us a thing, Miss Maggie Poole. Just keep on being the loving mother you already are to your brave little boy. That's all the thanks we need."

Relaxed by the brandy and Devorah's kindness, Mag sank more deeply into the big chair, then sat up again, looking first at Fin, then at Devorah. "Well, now, y'see, that's why I'm here." She spoke slowly, quietly, nearly a whisper, as if not to abuse the kindness already shown her. "I wanna get Timmy an' me outta that rotten hellhole we live in. I wanna send him t'school an' such. An' I want a better life for us. I want my boy t'be proud of me."

"Oh Maggie," Dev said, nearly moved to tears, "Timmy is already proud of you. He made that very clear the night first I met him at the Mulberry Street police station."

Fin choked back a tear of her own, burying it in a swallow

247

of brandy, then said, "Devorah an' I are proud of you, too, Mag. You been plenty strong for Timmy, an' for yourself." She lifted her glass in honor.

Dev said, "And yes, the two of you deserve a better life. How can we help?"

"Well,"—there was a twinkle in Mag's eye, a naughty twinkle but with a dash of pride— "I've been puttin' some money aside for a while now. I wanna open a proper whorehouse. It'll be a classy place, classier even than that Madame Lou's joint. It'll have only clean girls that I'll treat real good. I know what it's like t'be tossed aroun'. I want my girls t'feel safe."

Dev, her lips parting, ready to express her shock and disapproval of profiting by the commerce in women's bodies, clamped her lips shut again. It hit her with the force of truth in her soul that she hadn't the right. Nor could she object to the smile on Fin's face upon hearing Mag's plans, because Mag's hopes and Fin's evident approval once again brought Dev face to face with an alternate world with an alternate morality survived through hard courage. And Devorah had to admit, after the experience of recent days, Maggie Poole had an abundance of courage.

Buoyed by Fin's smile, Mag went on. "I ain't got enough money yet but I'll get there. Meantime, I gotta prepare. If I want classy clientele I gotta be classy myself. So if it's okay with you, Miss Longstreet," Mag said with hope in her voice and something close to pleading in her eyes, "will y'teach me how t'talk?"

EPILOGUE

On June 1st, 1899, Mrs. William R. Godfrey was found guilty of the murder of her stepdaughter, Pauline. The judge, one Ephraim Bing, upon sentencing Mrs. Godfrey to death, lamented that stoning was no longer in fashion. "For surely," he said, "only a woman possessed of the devil and who betrayed all natural motherly instincts could commit such a heinous crime. The quick death offered by that newfangled electric chair is too humane for the likes of you."

On June 30th of that same year, the day of her scheduled execution at Sing Sing prison, when asked if she had any last words, Mrs. Godfrey, seated in her stone cell, was reported to have merely lifted her head in an attitude of annoyance. It was further reported that she kept this attitude during her walk to the death house.

During his wife's trial, Mr. William R. Godfrey did not attend the trial proceedings, but instead closed his fabric shop and moved across the country to Portland, Oregon, to escape the misery and memories of his ordeal. He opened another fabric and notions establishment in Portland, which thrived under his expert management and tight-fisted accounting. Soon a successful merchant once again, William R. Godfrey was pursued by a number of local women, though his recent marital experience left him with a deep suspicion of the female sex. The intertwined social and business requirements of the community being what they were, however, Mr. Godfrey eventually married one Miss Charlotte Ridgewood, an attractive enough woman from good family. Unfortunately, after a year of marriage, Charlotte Ridgewood Godfrey died under inexplicable circumstances. The townsfolk of Portland rallied around Mr. Godfrey in sympathy. After a suitable period of mourning, Mr. Godfrey eventually married Miss Miriam Massengill. Mrs. Miriam Massengill Godfrey, like her predecessor, enjoyed household and fashionable luxuries paid for with her husband's money, and she, too, expired a year after the wedding. By then, the science of forensics had advanced sufficiently to detect what had heretofore been an undetectable poisonous substance in Mrs. Miriam Massengill Godfrey's trachea and the lining of her stomach. William R. Godfrey was arrested, tried, convicted, and hanged in the Oregon State Penitentiary.

As Detective Charles Coyle predicted, Alistair P. Flugg after only a week of incarceration was indeed released from jail at the behest of assorted politicians and city officials who thereafter had nothing further to do with him. Moreover, his wife Martha, now living with her daughter and son-in-law in Philadelphia, instituted proceedings to divorce him, a circumstance Mr. Flugg was in no position to contest. His fortunes socially and financially depleted, humiliation trailing him like an odor, Alistair P. Flugg spent Christmas Eve alone in his fine library where he took a photograph of his daughter from a desk drawer, put a gun to his head and pulled the trigger.

Maggie Poole, the once infamous Black Haired Mag, spent three months under Devorah's tutelage in elocution and deportment. As for Devorah, though she was still ill at ease with Maggie's choice of profession, she nonetheless delighted in her student's transformation from slovenly to sophisticated.

Fin was particularly pleased with her old friend's metamorphosis, and with Devorah's part in it. For like Fin's own story, it took Dev's guiding hand, and her faith in the outcome, to give Maggie Poole the tools and confidence to take her place in the world.

Maggie soon opened an elegant brothel on West 12th Street, months perhaps even years sooner than she'd hoped, the result of an envelope of cash slipped anonymously under her tenement door.

Acknowledgments

A Crime of Secrets represents a new direction for me as a writer. All of my previous books and short stories have been set in more recent history or even in our own time, and they've all featured a single main character, the protagonist who moves the story forward and takes the secondary characters along. Here in *A Crime of Secrets*, not only have I set the story over a century ago, thus requiring scrupulous research for facts, atmosphere, social mores, and manners of speech of different classes of people, I've also explored the thinking, feelings, actions and motives of two main characters, two protagonists equal in stature and narrative importance: Fin Donner and Devorah Longstreet. It's been a thrilling experience, if at times a schizophrenic one.

I'm certainly not the first author to feature two main characters. Writing multiple voices is one of the techniques of storytelling. And while I can't speak for authors who handle multiple protagonists as a matter of routine, for me it induced a state of literary terror.

For which I am grateful.

I am grateful because I could use that terror to inform the tone and atmosphere of this crime novel, and I could use my terror to demolish my previous comfort zone and grow as a writer.

Thus, my primary acknowledgement is given to The Terror: the experience of taking a frightening leap of faith from a very great height, finding that the fear actually kept me buoyed in the air, letting me fly over doubt and finally make it across the valley of literary death to land on the far cliff.

Understand, though, there was nothing particularly heroic about this. Though writing is a solitary experience, life isn't. There were plenty of friends who gave support; literarily and in more fundamental ways, ways which directly impacted my well-being. Without that cushion of well-being I might not have been able to write this book at all, nor the other stories I wrote during this time. So thank you from my heart and still surviving soul to Barry Katz and Mitchell Karp, Ramekon O'Arwisters and Carlo Abruzzese, Dana DeKalb and Peter Goldstein, Cheryl Pletcher and Lynn Ames, Seth Ruggles Hiler, Andrea Marshall, Stan Copland, Jan Schleiger, Claude Pollack, Claudine Dumoulin, Joe and Michelle Marinelli, Richard Eagan and Liz Ostrow, and, as always, my big city anchor and best pal Allan Neuwirth, and to the magnificent team at Bywater Books.

ABOUT THE AUTHOR

Native New Yorker Ann Aptaker's Cantor Gold crime/mystery series has won Lambda Literary and Goldie Awards. Her short stories have appeared in two editions of the *Fedora* crime anthology, *Switchblade Magazine's Stiletto Heeled* issue, the *Mickey Finn: Twenty-First Century Noir* anthology Volume 1 and the upcoming Volume 3, and in *Black Cat Mystery Magazine*. Her novella, *A Taco, A T-Bird, A Beretta and One Furious Night*, was published by Down & Out Books for their *Guns and Tacos* crime series. Her flash fiction, *A Night In Town*, appeared in the online zine *Punk Soul Poet*, and another flash fiction, *Rock 'N Dyke Roll*, is featured in the Goldie Award-winning anthology *Happy Hours: Our Lives in Gay Bars*. Ann has been an art curator, exhibition design specialist, art writer, and a professor of Art History at the New York Institute of Technology. She now writes full time.

At Bywater Books, we love good books just like you do, and we're committed to bringing the best of contemporary writing to our growing community of avid readers. Our editorial team is dedicated to finding and developing outstanding writers who create books you won't want to put down.

For more information about Bywater Books, our authors and our titles, please visit our website.

www.bywaterbooks.com

CPSIA information can be obtained
at www.ICGtesting.com
Printed in the USA
JSHW020924270623
43842JS00001B/3